Praise for the novels of Laura Caldwell

The Year of Living Famously

"Sharply observed, fresh and compelling,
The Year of Living Famously is a captivating look
into the cult of celebrity."
—Leslie Stella, author of *The Easy Hour* and
Fat Bald Jeff

"A stylish, sassy novel that shows the dark side that
haunts the world of glamour and glitz. Laura Caldwell
paints a sensitive picture of two ordinary lives thrown
into turmoil by the pressures of fame."
—*USA TODAY* bestselling author Carole Matthews

"Hollywood power players, paparazzi and overzealous
fans—Laura Caldwell takes readers inside the precarious
world of celebrity with a captivating story about the cost
of following your dreams and the high price of fame."
—Jennifer O'Connell, author of *Bachelorette #1*

A Clean Slate

"Told with great energy and charm, *A Clean Slate* is for
anyone who has ever fantasized about starting over—
in other words, this book is for everyone!"
—Jill A. Davis, author of *Girls' Poker Night*

"Weightier than the usual fare, Caldwell's winning second
novel puts an appealing heroine in a tough situation and
relays her struggles with empathy."
—*Booklist* (starred review)

"*A Clean Slate* is Laura Caldwell's page-turner about a
woman with a chance to reinvent herself, something most
of us have imagined from time to time...."
—*Chicago Tribune*

"*A Clean Slate*...told with a little mystery, a little humor,
and more than a few twists and surprises."
—*News-Dispatch*

Burning the Map

"This debut novel won us over with its exotic locales (Rome and Greece); strong portrayal of the bonds between girlfriends; cast of sexy foreign guys; and, most of all, its touching story of a young woman at a crossroads in her life."
— *Barnes & Noble.com*
(Selected as one of "The Best of 2002")

"Caldwell's debut is a fun, snappy read."
— *Booklist*

"The author produces excellent settings and characters. It is easy to identify with her protagonist, Casey. We learn that maybe the rat race isn't all it's cracked up to be. This is a very thought provoking book."
— *Heartland Reviews*

Laura
Caldwell

the Year of Living
Famously

RED
DRESS
INK
™

First edition November 2004

THE YEAR OF LIVING FAMOUSLY

A Red Dress Ink novel

ISBN 0-373-25075-4

www.RedDressInk.com

Printed in U.S.A.

ACKNOWLEDGMENTS

Thank you, thank you, thank you to my wonderful editor, Margaret O'Neill Marbury, my fantastic agent, Maureen Walters, and everyone at Red Dress Ink (especially Tania Charzewski, Laura Morris, Craig Swinwood, Donna Hayes, Isabel Swift, Margie Miller, Tara Kelly, Sarah Rundle, Don Lucey, Belinda Hobbs, Jessica Regante, Liba Berry and Carolyn Flear).

Thanks also to Kelly Harden, Ginger Heyman, Trisha Woodson, Beth Kaveny, Suzanne Burchill, Pam Carroll, Jim Lupo, Hilarie Pozesky, Clare Toohey, Mary Jennings Dean, Jane Hamill, Kris Verdeck, Ted MacNabola, Joan Posch, J. Erik Seastrand, Patrick Meade and Alisa Spiegel.

Once again, most importantly, thanks and my heart to Jason Billups.

LAURA CALDWELL
graduated from University of Iowa, before getting her
law degree from Loyola University Chicago School of Law.
Laura was a trial lawyer for many years, specializing in
medical negligence defense and entertainment law. She is
widely published in the legal field, as well as in numerous
mainstream publications.

Laura is a writer and contributing editor at *Lake Magazine,*
and an adjunct professor of legal writing at Loyola University
Chicago School of Law. Please visit her online at
www.lauracaldwell.com.

I awoke one morning and found myself famous.
—Lord Byron

Part One

chapter 1

Until that night in Vegas, I was the girl in back of the nightclub line, the girl who always had to wait for a cab. I was ordinary. I was just like anyone else.

I was with my friend Bobby that night, and we were staying at Mandalay Bay, where Bobby's talent agency had unknowingly sprung for a two-bedroom suite. Bobby's a film agent, and he was there to watch one of his clients in some high-end cabaret show. Bobby and I met when we were in grad school in Manhattan (me at FIT for fashion design, he at NYU for creative writing). Although he lived in L.A. now, and we hadn't seen each other in a year, we were fabulous purveyors of the witty voice mail and the novel-length e-mail, so we still knew all about each other; we felt as connected as we had back then.

We hit the Strip with a vengeance that Friday night, throwing ourselves headlong into the glitter and the lights, pretending we weren't in our early thirties, that the vodka martinis wouldn't make our heads scream the next morning. We roared with laughter at the stories we knew by heart and updated each other with new ones, our exaggerations and outlandish details showing how much we'd learned about creativity in grad school.

At midnight, we were fairly stumbling through the lobby of the Bellagio, past the jangling slot machines and the occasional shouts of triumph from the craps tables, when Bobby stopped and peered through the crowd, his dark eyes narrowing.

"Is it Trent?" I said, referring to Bobby's friend we were supposed to meet. The guy's full name was Trent Tanning, which sounded made up and Hollywood. I wondered whether I would like him at all.

Bobby shook his head, and his tight, black curly hair gleamed under the lights.

A pack of about ten people were moving through the tables and slots. Muscle-bound guys flanked the group, swiveling their heads menacingly, like they'd pummel you if you got too close. In the center was a woman who looked familiar—tall and model-thin with hair the color of oatmeal. The others gravitated toward her, glancing at her constantly, leaning in to whisper in her ear.

When they were about ten feet away, they turned and began walking in a different direction.

"Lauren!" Bobby yelled, and the entire entourage froze like deer that sense a rifle is near.

The big guys glared in Bobby's direction and held out their arms as if to shield the group. The woman looked vaguely in Bobby's direction, but then her studied expression shifted into a luminous smile.

"Bobby Minter!" she called. "What are you doing here?"

She wafted through her group, past the big men who appeared annoyed at the break in formation. She was wearing a vintage taupe dress with a cowl-neck.

By this time I had figured out that she was Lauren Stapleton, the actress. I'd seen a few of her films—romantic comedies, the type people see when they need one hundred and twenty minutes of escapism. Lauren played the geeky but gorgeous girl, the one you wanted the hero to fall for, which he certainly would in the last few scenes, leaving the audience feeling all was right with the world, that it was okay, in your own life, to be divorced, overweight and in debt.

Bobby hugged her. "I'm mixing business with a little too much pleasure. Lauren, this is my friend, Kyra Felis."

She gave me the wide, toothy grin I'd seen on-screen. She towered over me in her blond greatness, making me feel tiny and dark. Of course, I *am* tiny and dark—about five-one with wide brown eyes and black-brown, shoulder-length hair. None of this has ever been a problem before, but beside Lauren it all felt inadequate.

"You're in the business?" she asked me. Her voice was pleasant but bored, as if to say, *Isn't it all such a pain in the ass?*

"Oh, God no," I said.

Something snapped shut in her face, and she turned to Bobby. Soon, they were engaged in a serious discussion about whether a producer they knew had a heroin addiction or whether it was just cocaine. Bobby always got very dishy when he spoke to movie people, a trait that amused me, since Bobby's real goal in life was to write quiet, literary novels.

As they talked, I noticed one of the men from their group, a tousle-haired brunette in a suede jacket, standing at a nearby blackjack table. He was making one of the normally stoic dealers bite his lip with laughter.

I wandered over to the guy, not even sure what drew me. I wasn't looking for a pillow partner, and although I was bored by Bobby and Lauren, it was something more than that. I keep asking myself why I took those ten steps, because it seems to matter. Everything would be different if I hadn't.

There I was, drawn to that slightly shaggy hair, the dark gold suede of his jacket, the glow that emanated from this guy as every player at the blackjack table gazed at him and laughed.

I heard the last lines of his joke as I neared. "So your man says, 'No, I'll shove it up *your* arse.'" Although I hadn't heard the beginning, I could tell it wasn't my type of humor. In fact, under normal circumstances, even if I had been looking for a little action, I would have turned around right then. But it was his elegant manner despite the crass words. It was his light Irish brogue that sounded, somehow, like warm caramel on the tongue. It was the good-natured, almost childlike, grin that made me chuckle along with the rest of the group.

"Like that one, did you?" he said when he saw me.

"I've heard better."

"Yeah?" He smiled. His teeth were unnaturally white and straight. I should have known then he was an actor.

"Definitely," I said.

"So let's hear one." He faced the blackjack table. "Lads, the lady has a joke to tell."

There were two older men in golf shirts, a Hispanic guy who looked about fifteen and two mafioso types with slicked-back hair and jackets with huge shoulder pads. They all looked at me expectantly.

"Oh, no," I said. "No jokes from me. I can't remember them."

"Bollocks," the Irish guy said. "You can't tell me that you've heard better and not tell one yourself."

"That's true," said one of the mafia dudes. "Ya gotta tell one now."

"Really, I don't have any." I hoped Bobby would call my name.

"We're all waiting," the Hispanic guy said.

I'm not normally a blusher, but I felt my face coloring. The golden Irish boy was grinning, his face bordering on a smirk, the two older men seemed impatient and the mafia guys looked as if they'd fit me with concrete boots if I didn't get on with it.

The Irish guy leaned in. "Do you want me to save you?" he said in that wonderful voice, his breath warm in my ear. I felt like kissing him then. The desire came that quick.

"Um, sure," I said, not clear what he meant. Not caring.

He leaned even closer, so the suede lapel of his jacket brushed against the skin at the scoop-necked opening of my dress. I was wearing one of my own designs, a fifties-inspired number with a high waist, and I wondered if he thought it attractive.

"I'll give you a wee one," he said, "and then you can tell them."

I can no longer remember the beginning of the joke. Something about a priest in a rowboat. I was too aware of the nearness of him, too focused on that warm, smooth voice. Then there was a staccato of sounds like quiet gunfire and everything went white, white, white. It took me a moment to realize it was cameras flashing. In the next moment, the Irish guy was jerked away by one of Lauren's bodyguards.

"Can't you leave me alone?" Lauren said as she licked her lips prettily and shook her hair away from her face.

The photographers got a few more shots before the bodyguards grabbed Lauren, too. Within seconds, the pack of photographers was running after the group, leaving Bobby and me alone.

"Welcome to Hollywood," Bobby said.

I laughed at the commotion. "What was that?"

"Paparazzi," Bobby said. "Par for the course. I bet Lauren leaked where she would be."

"She'd do that?"

"Lauren? Oh, sure. C'mon, let's find Trent." He took my arm and led me toward the bar.

"So, who was that Irish guy?"

I tried to sound only mildly interested. Bobby and I had fooled around once in grad school and since then we didn't often talk about the people we were sleeping with or the ones we *wanted* to sleep with.

"Some actor. Declan something. He's in her new film, so they're dating now." Bobby made air quotes with his fingers as he said the word *dating*. "She had to do something to deflect attention from that rapper business." He named a rapper who Lauren used to be involved with, someone who was now in prison for drug trafficking and murder-for-hire.

By then Bobby's eyes were darting around the room, looking for Trent, bored already with the topic of Lauren and the Irish guy. So I dropped it. I'd never see him again anyway.

I'm a minor celebrity now.

A minor celebrity should be distinguished from a true-blue-can't-shop-for-Tampax-without-a-photo-being-taken celebrity. That's not me, thank God, not anymore. I couldn't stand the constant staring, the feeling that you always have to look presentable when you stop at a gas station. A minor celebrity, in contrast, is someone who gains notoriety for something quite small or, rather, on the coattails of someone else. In my case, I suppose both of these are true.

Only occasionally does anyone recognize the minor celebrity on the street, but once introduced at a party, people respond with, *Oh, I know you. I read about you in* People *magazine.* And suddenly others at the party who've heard the comment turn to catch a look at you, and the buzz slips through the party like smoke. Soon, people are watching how much salmon mousse you put on your cracker, whether you're getting blotto on that red wine.

My celebrity status has been good for the sale of my designs, certainly. All my clothes with my diamond circle logo (some of them with real diamonds now instead of CZs) are moving fast. Still, I was never one of those people who worshipped celebrities, probably because I didn't need it. I've always had at least a vague sense of who I am, where I'm going, what I want to do with the next minute of my life. This trait made me something of a freak when I was younger, one of those girls who was bored by the cliques in school, the sharing of nail polish and the double-dating for dances. I was more interested in reading the novels and short stories my parents left behind or making skirts from old tablecloths.

It's not that I didn't have friends throughout my life. There was Bobby. There was Margaux and the girls here in New York. And of course there was always Emmie, my godmother, who's cared for me since I was a kid.

Anyway, I suppose the point I'm trying to make is that, relatively speaking, I had it together. I knew myself, my life, my place in it. So if you're looking for a story about a poor neurotic girl who finally turned her life around, this isn't it. This is about how I met Declan McKenna, and how my world went spinning.

chapter 2

As it turns out, the next place I saw Declan was in the *National Enquirer.* I knew the paper, of course. I'd seen it in the grocery store, but I'd never bought it, never thought I'd buy it.

The first of many phone calls that day came from Bobby. He was already at his L.A. office at 7:00 a.m., and he was going through the trades and all the papers, looking for mentions of his clients like he did every day.

"Kyr," he said when I answered. "Go get the *Enquirer,* and call me back."

"Why?"

"Just do it."

"Forget it," I said. "I've got a job this morning, and I'm already late." I was working for a few temp agencies at the time, doing meaningless, thankless jobs in places where no one wanted to get to know you, since you'd be gone in a few days anyway. The meager, occasional cash from my designs couldn't sustain me, not in a city like New York, nor could the modest payments from the fund my parents had set up.

"Pick it up on your way," Bobby said. "Trust me."

And because I did trust him, I bought an *Enquirer* at the corner newsstand before I caught the subway to a marketing office in Midtown.

"Okay," I said, calling Bobby from the copy room of the office, where, thankfully, you could call long distance. "What am I supposed to look at?"

"You didn't find it?"

"Jesus, Bobby, I'm *working*," I said, as though an entire corporation of employees waited for the decisions I would make that day.

He sighed. Bobby was a great sigher, a habit that had grown more pronounced since he'd become an agent. "Page twenty-four."

I put the paper on the copy machine and flipped toward the end, ignoring stories about Cher's latest surgical misadventure and a two-headed baby born to an ex-*Baywatch* star.

"Oh my God," I said when I found it.

"You're famous," Bobby said.

There, in grainy black and white, was a photo of me and the caramel-voiced Irishman. Our heads were close together, the blackjack table in the background. My fifties-style dress gave the photo a timeless quality. The Irishman and I were making what looked like secret smiles. In fact, from the angle the picture was taken, it appeared as if we were about to kiss.

Above the photo, the caption read, *Is Lauren Losing Her Touch?* and to the right was a tiny inset photo of Lauren Stapleton wearing an extremely annoyed expression. I could tell by the mandarin collar of her shirt that the photo hadn't even been taken on that night in Vegas.

"Bobby, what is this?" I said.

He chuckled. "Isn't it great? They call you 'the mystery woman.'"

I scanned the article and caught the name of the rapper Lauren used to date, a handy list of her other ex-boyfriends and some speculation about how she'd lost her latest beau, the Irish actor, whose name was Declan McKenna.

When I got home that day, there were seven messages from people who'd seen the picture or heard about it. Who knew so many people read this stuff?

I called Margaux back immediately. "Isn't it a riot?" I said to her.

"Your fifteen minutes of fame," she said.

I never wanted to be famous. I had hoped to be a successful fashion designer someday, but I never desired celebrity.

Before all this started with Declan, I used to think about Michael Jordan, about how he couldn't go anywhere in the world, not even the far reaches of Africa, without his iconic face being recognized, without someone, many people usually, scrambling for his autograph or snapshot. Michael Jordan, I thought, can't do the things that make *me* happy— having a quiet glass of wine (or three or four) at a café, taking a stroll through my neighborhood in a pair of old jeans and no makeup. Of course, now I have some trouble with those things, too—people occasionally do double takes as I walk by, others sometimes come up and interrupt my glass of wine to ask for an autograph. But let's face it, I could still go to Africa without a problem.

For weeks, I've done nothing but write this book, this story about Declan and me, but today, I put it away and went to lunch with Margaux and some girlfriends from my early days in Manhattan. We went to Gramercy Tavern, one of those places that feels so New York—old hardwood floors, worn Oriental carpets, a mahogany bar stacked high with spirits. It was precisely these places I missed desperately when I lived in L.A.

We were all dressed in slim pants and high shoes, perfect makeup adorning everyone's faces. I noticed two of my friends were wearing structured blouses I had designed, the ones with the circle pin on the collar. It's always exhilarating yet strange to see someone wearing my designs and even stranger to see that circle pin, exactly like the one my mother always wore. I *wanted* other people to wear these clothes with the circle pins, and yet still it was odd. I thanked them, but I wondered why they'd never worn any of my clothes before. I suppose it's easier now that you can get them at Barney's.

I had seen some of these girls individually since I moved back from L.A., but we hadn't all been together like this. I was jumpy and jittery, for a reason I couldn't ascertain, except maybe that I had been jumpy and jittery for so long now. I thought I would shake that anxiety when I came back to New York, but it lingers, the wonder of whether someone is waiting around the corner.

In the days of yore, we used to talk about the men we slept with, the parties we'd gone to, the handbags and shoes we'd bought. For the last few years, though, the primary topics of conversation have been babies, babies, babies, redecorating the apartment, babies, the house in East Hampton, and more babies.

Of the six of us, only Margaux and I aren't on the mommy track. And as happy as Margaux and I are for the mommies, and they for us, there's often a weird envy/disdain thing going on. It works both ways, as far as I can tell. I suspect the mommies pity us ignorant girls who don't know the heart-soaring joy of seeing your baby fall asleep on your belly. But they envy us, too, for our unadulterated sleep, our still-intact sex lives and our ability to fly to Paris at the last minute just because we feel like it. Margaux and I, on the other hand, feel sorry for these women with their red-rimmed eyes and their talk of breast pumps, but we worry that we're missing out on something big.

I had been opting out of these lunches since I got back to New York, because I wasn't sure what to expect, and to be truthful, I have a low threshold for intense discourse about the jog-stroller market. Today, though, Margaux had talked me into it. Margaux is an intellectual-property attorney, and she called from work, even though it was a Saturday.

"You've got to come to lunch," she said. "I need some support. I'm outnumbered by the mommies."

I had nothing else planned, and once I got to the restaurant, despite my jitters, I was glad I'd joined them. It seemed my friends had come out of their maternal fog and were becoming interested in other things again. Lydia, a real estate agent turned full-time mom, told a story about a bat mitzvah where the guest of honor, a thirteen-year-old girl, wore five-inch Jimmy Choo stilettos.

"Honestly, she was gorgeous," Lydia said, playing with the cigarette she was no longer allowed to smoke there. "But it was sick. I heard her talking about condoms."

We shook our heads in wonder. Across the table, Margaux smiled at me big and deliberately, as if to say, *See, this isn't so bad*. She took out a clip and pulled back her unruly blond-brown hair that she's always struggling with.

After that, Darcy, a statuesque redhead, who's an ex-model and rarely lets you forget it, talked about sitting courtside at a recent Knicks game after smoking pot in the bathroom. "I got so paranoid." she said. "It was the first time I'd smoked since I had the baby, and every time some player came near me I thought they were going to attack me. I finally made Jake take me home at halftime."

We laughed and called for more wine; it felt good to be with everyone again.

But eventually I noticed that the questions directed at me had begun to increase in number, and soon I felt as if I was being grilled by a pack of reporters. I knew my friends were simply interested in me—the new me who had seemingly emerged over the last year—but the attention made me uncomfortable. It's one of the reasons why I left L.A. And yet this is my life now—for better or for worse—because of Declan. Everything lately has happened because of Declan.

But where am I in all this? This is the question I'm mining by writing this book. It's not meant to capitalize monetarily on our relationship, although I'm sure many will accuse me of that, because it certainly will sell. Already, I've received calls from six literary agents who've heard from Emmie that I'm writing a book. They know that even with an unpublished writer like me, this book should skip off the shelves.

What I'm trying to figure out, I suppose, is if the me that I used to be—the one these women used to know—is still there, somewhere inside my shell, not a leaf in the wind, but a still-green bud on a tree somewhere in Manhattan.

chapter 3

If there was a Nobel Prize for dating, the inventor of e-mail would surely win. An e-mail is worlds better than that first phone call, one filled with odd starts and stops and shots of silence. E-mail allows you to be the witty person you wish you were. You can spend five hours on the perfect little quip, and yet once you type it and send it zinging across the country, it appears to the reader that it just flew from your fingers with complete ease.

To: Kyra Felis
From: Declan McKenna

Kyra, I hope you don't mind that I got your e-mail address from Bobby Minter. What I'm supposed to say now is that I'm hugely sorry for the photo in the *Enquirer*, which made it look like you and I were about to snog, but truthfully it gives me the excuse I've been waiting for. We were never properly introduced. I'm Declan, and I'm the eejit who was telling the terrible jokes at the blackjack table. I had a jar or five too many, but I should let you know I'm like that a lot anyway. I hope the photo didn't cause any problems for you. By the way, did you not want to hear the end of the joke I started telling you?

To: Declan McKenna
From: Kyra Felis
Hey, Declan, great to hear from you, but please, please, please don't ever tell me the end of that joke. The beginning was painful enough. Speaking of pain, I assume the photo caused you many more problems than it did me. How are things with Lauren?

To: Kyra Felis
From: Declan McKenna
Ah, a crafty girl you are, getting in that question about Lauren. No, no, as I'm sure Bobby has told you, Lauren and I were business partners more than anything else, and now, as CEO and president of that business, she has summarily fired me. Can you provide comfort?

To: Declan McKenna
From: Kyra Felis
If by "comfort" you mean the pharmaceutical kind, alas, I am, unfortunately, not your girl, but let me know what else you had in mind. (Also, if you do find a pharmaceutical-comfort connection, let me know that, too.)

To: Kyra Felis
From: Declan McKenna
My mind reels at the potential comfort you might provide. You have created a monster.

To: Declan McKenna
From: Kyra Felis
I assume now that you mean comfort in only the most banal sense—the handing of slippers to place on the feet, the stoking of the fire.

To: Kyra Felis
From: Declan McKenna
Care to elaborate on your fire-stoking process?
By the way, can you provide any comfort in the real estate sense? I'll be in New York this summer to shoot a picture (another earth-shattering part for me, where I shall probably be on-screen for two entire minutes). The production company wants to know what neighborhood I'd prefer, although they've warned me that my flat will be the size of a toothbrush, no matter the neighborhood. I suppose a more pointed question is this—what neighborhood do you live in?

And so it went. Soon, I had news that Declan was getting an apartment for the summer near mine in Carnegie Hill, and within weeks we had gotten enough banter out of our systems to actually chat on the phone, although *chat* seems a paltry word compared to what really occurred. We spent hours talking, like a couple of teenagers, about everything and nothing. We traded stories about growing up in the city (me in Manhattan, he in Dublin). He told me about his parents who had waited patiently for the Irish divorce laws to change, got the divorce decree and then promptly remarried each other seven months later. When Declan spoke about Dublin and his family, particularly his mother, it was in a tone so adoring that it made me adore him. He told me how he'd been in L.A. for three years, working at coffee shops and clothing stores in between the occasional commercial and bit film part. He had wanted to be an actor since a girlfriend brought him to an audition for the Gaiety School of Acting in Dublin. He was nineteen then, and he was hooked. Aside from being a great actor, he wanted nothing else, he said, except maybe a woman who would listen to his jokes.

That warm brogue of his did me in every time I heard

it. Even the sound of it coming through my answering machine seemed to tinge my apartment with happiness.

Declan came into my world at exactly the same time I began wanting someone in my life, some *man*. Before that, I'd been alone for quite some time. By "alone" I mean that I didn't have a boyfriend and hardly any dates. Part of the reason was that I had wasted a year and a half of my late twenties with a bar owner named Steven. I'd met him at his bar, of course, and let's face it, a bar owner is a god in his own establishment. The place was called Red (it has since gone under and is now a rug store), and it was on one of the tight little streets that branch out from Times Square.

When I do get involved with someone, it happens fast, and Steven was no exception. Within a few months, I was spending most of my time at Red or his apartment in the West Village. But the glamour of hanging around the same club every night wears away quickly. I told Steven over and over that we had to spend time away from Red, away from the regulars who were always hitting him up for free drinks, the money pushers who shoved tens in his hand to get in the VIP room, the women who were always ready to sleep with him. He tried, but he always felt that no one could run the place like him. I've heard raising horses provides the same dilemma—no one can take care of them the same as you—but at least horses can spirit you away from a disaster.

I, on the other hand, couldn't seem to leave Steven, because despite his countless hours at the club and his drinking (which was starting to scare me) he was usually the sweetest person I'd ever met. He brought me flowers at four in the morning on his way home from Red. He would get up after only a few hours of sleep and drive me to some temp job so I didn't have to take the subway. But Steven was one of those guys who doesn't age well, cannot grasp the thought of getting old. As I started to tire of the bar scene, he seemed to cling to it, even though he was almost forty and his face was starting to look as leathered as a saddle.

We fought about it constantly until one night when, while he was drunk and I sober, he raised a hand to me. I mean just that. He raised his hand and drew it back, his face contorted with fury. I hate to say it, but my immediate re-action was to cower. I shrunk away from him; I held up an arm to cover my face.

Into my mind rushed a flurry of thoughts—*Isn't there a shelter for abused women down the street? No, that's just for some-one who's abused all the time. I'll call the cops. I'll sue him. I'll kill him.* He must have seen my expression change from cowardice to anger then, because he dropped his hand and started to cry. I left that night.

After that ugliness, and until Declan, I spent most of my time by myself—I wanted it that way—but suddenly it changed, *I* changed, and I found myself wanting someone to fill the empty seat in my life. Maybe it had to do with the fact that I turned thirty-three a few weeks before I met Declan. I couldn't get it out of my head that I was almost halfway to seventy.

Whatever the reason, I hated myself for having that need. Yet it wouldn't go away. I, Kyra Felis, who for the last few years had been so proud to be on my own, was beginning to have pangs of jealousy toward the couple picking over mangoes at the sidewalk market and the two men sharing a cup of coffee, their hands entwined on the table. When it came to couples, I was an equal-opportunity envier. Gay, straight, old, young, I wanted to be part of all of them. I wanted that witness to my day-to-day motion. I had begun to feel that without it, I might slide into obscurity, noticed by few, clothes worn by only one or two. What would remain of me but a couple of scribbled designs? I'm making it sound too dramatic, I see that, because I did have wonderful people in my life. Emmie, for example, was someone who told me to get it together when I was feeling sorry for myself, someone who would buy me a Pucci scarf at Bergdorf's when my line of poet's blouses was once again rejected by that boutique on Lex. But Emmie was a juggernaut, and so even in her early eighties, she was busy. She still worked occasionally for the literary agency, and she had her cronies, and her house in Nantucket for weekend getaways.

So I wanted that witness to my everyday life. And that's exactly what I got. Times ten.

chapter 4

The phone rang on a Wednesday morning.

"Hey, gorgeous," Declan said. "It's me."

"Where are you?" I wasn't expecting to hear from him until the end of the day.

"I'm at the airport. I just got in and wanted to let you know. I'll call you when I'm unpacked."

"Okay," I said warily.

Why was *I* the first one he was calling? Didn't he have other friends to contact? People from the production company? But at the same time, my ego preened that it was me he couldn't wait to see.

Four hours later he called again. "Christ," he said, "I only brought two duffels with me, but there's still no room for it all. The landlord is mad, and my roommate is an eejit."

"You have a roommate?"

"Didn't I tell you?"

"No." Despite the fact that he'd warned me about how small his part in the movie was and the equally tiny size of his place, I'd envisioned a lovely, clean modern apartment, where I might spend a chunk of my summer. I'd been swayed by the fact that he was "shooting a movie." It sounded so official, so important, so…magical.

"I want to see you," he said in a low, undeniably sexy voice. He probably said it like that because his "eejit" roommate was near, but he snared me with those words, that voice.

I told him I'd meet him at a diner near 95th and Madison. I tripped around my apartment, changing my outfit three times, and finally settled on the first one, a flouncy, black A-line skirt I'd designed back in school and a light lavender sweater with a pair of black-and-white-checkered sandals. I applied lipstick and gloss, then wiped it off. What if he kissed me right away? I put my hair up in a ponytail, then dragged it out and fluffed my hair with my hands. I looked at my watch. The diner was only blocks from my place, but I had waited too long to leave. What if he was already there? What if he left because I was late?

That thought shot me out of the apartment. I hurried down the street as fast as my sandals would allow. Without the blind effortlessness of a phone conversation, without the unhurried ease of e-mail, I wasn't sure how we'd get along. I dreaded seeing him again as much as I craved it. The end of dreams and assumptions is never pretty, and I feared that end.

It was a beautiful April day, the sky an aqua blue. Carnegie Hill is the neighborhood where Emmie had always lived, and therefore, the area where I grew up. Upper upper East Side, wonderfully close to the park, brick walk-ups, charming cafés.

After college, I lived in the Village. In retrospect, I see that I was trying to distance myself from Emmie, not for any scandalous reasons like child prostitution or wire hangers, but rather a need to establish myself in my own little world.

But what I quickly realized was that I missed Carnegie Hill. I missed being close to Emmie. I missed the sense of space the park lent the neighborhood. My sporadic income from the occasional sale of my clothing lines, freelance-design gigs and temp jobs wouldn't normally support a decent apartment here, but I had the very modest trust fund from my parents, which I used only for rent. I arranged for the bank to cut a check directly to my landlord every month, so I couldn't screw it up, and I'd lived here ever since.

As I turned the corner onto Madison, I saw him. He was standing outside the diner, looking both ways, back and forth. He had on dark jeans, black leather shoes and a short-sleeve, untucked gray shirt. I thought he looked adorable, although fairly panicked, with his hands at his sides, clenching and unclenching. This somehow calmed me.

His perplexed face broke into a smile when he saw me. "I thought maybe I had the wrong one," he said as I neared. "There are a million diners on this street."

"Sorry," I said.

I'd reached him by then, and we both seemed unsure of what to do. Kiss? Shake hands? Throw ourselves on the sidewalk and have at it?

Declan solved the problem. In a moment that was years long, but entirely too short, he put his arms around my waist and pulled me to him. I squeezed my eyes shut and hugged him back, letting him lift me off the sidewalk. His hair was wet at the back—he must have just taken a shower—and he smelled like shampoo and minty shaving cream. I hoped he would never put me down.

But he did. We stared at each other, both a little taken aback, I think.

"How are you?" I said, apropos of absolutely nothing.

"Shaggered. But happy to see you."

"Me, too."

"You look gorgeous." He glanced at my outfit. "I love women in skirts."

I smiled like the shy girl in a fifties movie who has just met the football star.

"What now?" Declan said.

Our e-mails had been so suggestive, our phone calls so flirty, and the hug so intense, that sitting in a diner making benign talk seemed so very wrong. I wanted to bring him back to my apartment and into my bed, but that seemed a tad quick. So I took him to meet Emmie.

Everyone adores Emmie, especially men. If she'd been younger, I might not have loved her as much because she would have constantly stolen my dates.

Declan and I walked down Madison. When a crowd of high-school students poured out of a shop, nearly charging into us, he put his hand on the small of my back and drew me close. A few steps later, he slipped his hand in mine. I stopped breathing for a moment. I placed my sandaled feet one after another, and acted as if nothing were new, as if this was all very commonplace. But I couldn't stop smiling. I felt the grin spread across my face and stay there. I squeezed his warm hand a little more. When I glanced at him, he was grinning, too.

"All right, so you've mentioned Emmie before," Declan said. "Is she your best pal?"

"Well, sort of."

I hadn't given him many details about Emmie or my family situation—it seemed too grave a story to drop on someone too quickly—but now I explained that Emmie had raised me after my parents died in a train wreck going from Manhattan to Philadelphia.

Both of my parents were writers, my father an author of historical memoirs, usually on presidents or war heroes, my mother a fiction writer of short stories and young-adult stuff. On that day, when I was eight years old, my mother had a reading at the main library in Philadelphia for her new story collection. She and my father always tried to accompany each other to author events. They were the most supportive couple, Emmie said. The Philadelphia trip was also intended to be their twelfth-anniversary celebration. They'd been married ten years, but they always celebrated the day they met, rather than the day they tied the knot.

They'd reserved seats in the first-class section. I imagine they went immediately to the dining car and ordered champagne, toasting each other as the concrete landscape gave way to the green hills of eastern Pennsylvania.

A half hour before reaching Philadelphia, the train encountered a semi stalled on the tracks. *Encountered.* Probably too tame a word, because the train slammed into it, killing the truck driver instantly, and crushing the first six train cars, including the dining car, like flattened beer cans.

"Jesus fecking Christ," Declan said. He squeezed my hand tighter. "I'm so sorry. Is it still tough for you?"

"No. I wish I could say it was, but it was a long time ago. It gets harder to remember them all the time."

I told Declan that Emmie was my godmother, as well as the literary agent for both my parents. I'm sure Emmie never thought that anything would happen to them. I mean, who ever truly envisions a married couple will die together? Emmie was single by choice. It must have been a great shock to her when she had to take delivery of a tiny eight-year-old too smart for her own good.

I didn't tell Declan right then, but I found out years after my parents died that there was a custody battle for me. A few, actually. My mother's sister, Donna, who lived in my mother's hometown of Plano, Texas, lobbied the courts with her husband to take me into their home with their four boys. My father's parents made a plea, too. They lived in New Jersey. But my parents' wills had stipulated that Emmie be my guardian, and Emmie spent about a year's salary making sure she got to keep me. As I said, I never knew this at the time, but I wish I had. It would have been nice to know, in that weird, confusing time after my parents died, that I was wanted so desperately.

My father's parents died within a few years of his death, so it's a good thing I didn't live with them. I've visited my aunt Donna and her family a number of times. She is an unnaturally thin woman who grinds her teeth whenever her husband, a bearish man who owns a chain of gas stations, speaks in his loud drawl. Her sons seem to scare her. I can see now that she probably didn't want me for the sake of taking care of her sister's child, for my well-being. I think she just wanted a friend, some kind of buffer in that house full of testosterone.

Whenever I visit Aunt Donna, I take her old Ford Escort (her husband drives a Mercedes) and drive around her town, wondering what I would be like if I had been raised by her. Would I still be a designer? Would I be living in Manhattan? Or would I be working in the home office of my uncle Larry's gas stations? Would I still be creative and sarcastic and melancholy at times, or would I have adopted a nonstop sunny, albeit fake, personality to offset Aunt Donna?

Anyway, by the end of my explanation about Emmie, Declan and I had reached her building, a place called Hortense Court on East 92nd, right by the park. Through the glass pane of the front door, you could see the lobby. The marble was chipping, and the paint on the ceiling peeled in thin strips, giving nothing away about what the apartments inside were really like.

"She's like your mum, then?" Declan said. He had one

foot on the stoop, but it seemed as if the other might be ready to run.

I almost laughed at his wary face. I could see him thinking that he'd only just got here and already he was forced to meet my de facto parent.

"Not exactly," I said. "She fed and clothed me. She got me into school and signed me up for ballet classes. You know what I mean?"

"I understand food," Declan said, "but not the ballet."

"Well, she's not really the mothering type, and believe me, she's someone you should meet. She is the grande dame of New York."

"I thought that was you."

"I'm the second one."

"Ah," Declan said. "So I might fall for Emmie."

I stood above him on the stoop so that I was a little taller than he. "I'll fight her for you."

His eyes widened in mock delight. "It's what I've always dreamed of," he said.

"C'mon." I used my key and opened the lobby door.

He still didn't move. "A little kiss for strength?"

I looked him up and down. "Why do I get the feeling you'll want a grope next for good luck?"

"That'll work."

"I better just hold your hand for now," I said coyly. I took his hand and pulled him inside.

"Emmie, it's me!" I yelled as I stepped into her place.

"Kyra, sweetie!" I heard her call from the bedroom. "I'll be there in a minute." I hadn't phoned Emmie to let her know we were coming, but I knew it wouldn't matter. She was used to people stopping by all the time. She thrived on it.

"Come in," I said to Declan.

He took a step in, glancing around the place.

Emmie has owned her apartment since the sixties. Sometime before I came along, she bought the apartment next to hers, knocked out the center wall and created a large, eclectic space where nothing matched, but everything had its place. One half of her living room, her original living room before she bought the other side, was lined with dark wood bookshelves from floor to ceiling. But even with all those shelves, books were stacked everywhere—under end tables, at the sides of the maroon velvet couches, on the wide round coffee table. This was Emmie's side of the apartment. Her bedroom and kitchen lay behind the living-room wall.

On the other side of the living room, the books continued their dominance, but there the decor was more functional. Groupings of chairs and coffee tables took up most of the space, and the kitchen had been decked out with restaurant appliances for entertaining purposes. This side was where Emmie had her "salons," as she called them, the gatherings of the crème de la crème of the New York publishing world. Famous authors, editors and fellow agents from work—they all came here to talk books, to gossip.

When I moved in as a child, Emmie gave me the tiny bedroom on the salon side of the apartment. That room was my own, papered with clippings from *Vogue* and my own childish sketches, but the rest of the place was decidedly Emmie's. I knew how quickly people could be wrenched from your life, and I didn't want to lose Emmie, too. So I learned fast to tiptoe around the Dresden figures on the end table and to always make sure there was scotch in the crystal decanters, ice in the silver bucket. There was no official bedtime at Emmie's. If one of her salons was in full swing, I could slip through the apartment and stay up as late as I wanted. I liked it better when there was no one there with us, but that wasn't often.

"Kyra, Kyra." Emmie's voice trilled from the hallway.

She stepped into the living room, wearing gray wool slacks pressed to a fine point and a black cashmere turtleneck. At that time, Emmie only worked two days a week, acting more as a figurehead at the literary agency than anything else, but she always dressed for the day like a professional. No bathrobes or sweats for Emmie. She has very short auburn-red hair ("I dye it, sweetie, so that I'll *die* a redhead" is what she's always said), and her eyes are still the most striking teal blue.

"Oh, and you've brought a friend! Delightful!" She wafted into the room and kissed me on the cheek, then Declan. "Welcome," she said. "I'll get tea." And then she was gone just as quickly, puttering away in her service kitchen.

"Nice to meet…" Declan said to her retreating back. He turned to me quizzically.

"She has a lot of visitors," I said.

Soon Emmie was back, carrying a tea tray. Declan jumped off the couch to take it from her.

"Gallantry," she said. "It's so rare these days."

She sat on a maroon velvet chair, "the queen's chair" I used to call it as a kid, and began pouring tea. Her signature ring, a sapphire set in a gold braided band, glinted in the afternoon light that streamed in the windows. "I detected an accent," she said to Declan. "Tell, tell."

"Oh," Declan said. He looked at me, then back at her. I nodded in encouragement. Emmie always just jumped right into conversations like this—she abhorred pleasantries—and I was used to her running the conversation from the get-go.

"All right," Declan said. "Well, I'm Declan McKenna, and—"

"Declan McKenna? Oh!" Emmie interrupted. She looked at me and smiled. I had told her only a little about our Internet and phone flirtations, but Emmie could read me well enough to know I'd been delighted.

I shot Declan an embarrassed smile. "We're just stopping by to say hello, Emmie."

"Of course." She handed Declan a cup. "Are you a writer?"

"No," Declan said.

"Pity. You have the perfect name."

"I'm an actor."

"Ah." Emmie sounded disappointed, and Declan, as all men do, rushed in to appease her, telling her how he'd moved to the States from Ireland and how he was in town shooting a film.

"Mmm," Emmie said, sounding more impressed now. "And remind me how you two know each other." Emmie would cut off an arm before she would read the *National Enquirer,* and I hadn't told her about my photo.

"We met in Vegas," I said.

"When you were with darling Bobby?" she said.

I nodded.

"Interesting." She patted the chair next to her. "Declan, move over here, won't you?"

I groaned a little, but God love him, he crossed the room without hesitation and sat next to her. I remember thinking they looked lovely together: Emmie with her cap of ginger hair and her lined, pale face; Declan with his amused grin, his white teeth, his golden-brown eyes.

"Do you mind if I smoke?" Emmie said.

"Christ, no. I'll have one with you." Out of his pocket, Declan pulled a red book of matches.

I left them alone for a moment. When I returned, Emmie was in her prime entertainer mode, telling the story of a dinner she'd had with Prince Charles when he was a teenager. Declan's quirky, rolling laugh filled the room. He cracked a joke about the royal family "splitting heirs."

Emmie laughed and clapped her hands. Then she gave me a little bow of her head. Declan had been accepted.

When cocktail hour arrived (5:30 p.m., sharp, for Emmie), she whisked the tea tray away and brought out a bottle of champagne in a silver bucket.

"To Declan," she said, raising her glass, "and the success of his film."

Declan beamed. We all touched glasses.

Two hours and another bottle of champagne later, Declan and I left Emmie's apartment. It was dark already, in that strange, sudden way that darkness falls when you've been drinking in the late afternoon.

"She's fantastic," Declan said. His hand was in mine again, and we were walking up Madison. We were moving in the direction of my apartment, although we hadn't planned anything yet.

"I'm glad you like her," I said.

"Now don't get me wrong, here. She doesn't hold a candle to you."

I sneaked a sideways glance at him. "Is that right?"

There was a second's pause, during which we kept walking, both of us looking straight ahead. "I don't mean to give you a fright saying that," Declan said. "I'm not usually like this, you see?"

Have I already said that I was smiling so much that afternoon? It seemed I couldn't drag that grin off my lips, and right then it became wider. "Sure, I see," I said.

Another pause. Declan held my hand tighter. "Where are we going?"

We'd reached my apartment by then. Without a word, I tugged him toward the door.

"Yeah?" he said, looking up at my brick building.

"Yeah," I said.

★ ★ ★

Afterward, when we were lying in bed, he stared at my face. How strange to be studied like that, when there hadn't been a man in my bed for so long, but how amazing to be there next to him. It was simply right.

"What kind of name is Felis?" he said, surprising me. I thought he was working up to something sexier.

"It's Puerto Rican. My father was from there. My mother was Irish." I said this proudly, though I'd never been to Ireland or even Puerto Rico, and I knew so little about my heritage.

"Thank God you're half-Irish! Now I can marry you," he said in a jokey tone.

His words sent a zing up my spine—terror and thrill in equal parts.

The next morning, Declan slept later than me, and when he came into the kitchen, he found me standing naked at the counter, eating my normal breakfast—pickles and peanuts.

"Nude breakfast?" he said.

I nodded. He growled in return.

"Christ, what's this?" he said, walking to the counter. He glanced down at the two jars side by side. I had a small serving of peanuts poured into a cap. The pickles I pulled out one by one.

"Breakfast, just like you said."

"What happened to oatmeal and runny eggs and slabs of bacon?"

"You must be thinking of breakfast in Dublin. But what you're seeing here is the perfect start to a morning." I picked up the jar of pickles and waved my hand under it like a game-show hostess. "Vegetables," I proclaimed. Then I lifted the peanuts, and with the same underwave, said, "Protein."

"You can get vegetables and protein by having tomatoes and eggs."

"Ah," I said, popping a peanut in my mouth, "but those foods only keep for a week or two. Meanwhile, my breakfast foods last for months."

"You mean you eat this every day?"

"Pretty much." I offered him a pickle.

It snapped as he took a bite. "You're fecking weird," he said between chews. "And I like it."

chapter 5

To: Kyra Felis
From: Margaux Hutters
Hey, girl, what's up with no return phone calls? Don't you love me anymore? Wait, don't tell me—you're still running around with that actor. I thought he was leaving after a month or two. Hmm. Well, do tell, because I'm so bored. Peter is away again on a trial in Delaware, and he doesn't even know when it will end. Work is painfully dull. Meanwhile, Manuel, my massage therapist, still wants to help me "relieve more tension," if you know what I mean. And I'm starting to consider taking him up on that offer.

To: Margaux Hutters
From: Kyra Felis
Don't you dare sleep with your massage therapist! You are married, for Pete's sake (pun definitely intended). And, yes, Declan is still in town. I'm sorry I haven't been calling you back. He's consumed me. You liked him when you met him, right?

To: Kyra Felis
From: Margaux Hutters
Of course I liked him! What's not to like about that sexy accent and that cute butt of his? It must be so glamorous, hanging out on a movie set. Maybe you'll be discovered. Speaking of which, did you hear from the catalog that was considering buying your trumpet skirts?

To: Margaux Hutters
From: Kyra Felis
Rejected by the catalog. Again. But I won't let it get me down. I'm too happy in other areas right now. I have to tell you, though, the movie set is anything but glamorous. Declan got me credentials to hang out for a few days, but it was like waiting at an airport. Declan shares a trailer with a bunch of other actors, and they sit in there all day playing Scrabble. Every once in a great, great while, someone knocks and tells them they're on. They do one short scene about fifty million times, then go back to the trailer. It was as painful as listening to someone tell you about their dream. You just keep wondering when it might end. But Declan is happy, so that's all that matters.

To: Kyra Felis
From: Margaux Hutters
Declan is happy, you're happy. My God, would you listen to yourself? What happens when the movie is over?

To: Margaux Hutters
From: Kyra Felis
I know, I know. Other people's glee can be so tedious, right? As for the movie, they're done shooting this week, but Declan's agent got him a bunch of auditions. In fact, he already landed one commercial, which shoots next week. So…drumroll, please…he's staying until September!

It was the everlasting summer. I've never felt that a summer was long, that it stretched on and on, that it was nearly all beautiful—sun and blue and street-side cafés—but that's what it was like for those first few months with Dec, as I'd begun calling him, and me.

It was a perfect time to wear my most feminine clothes. I broke out all my fifties-style dresses with the flounced skirts, and I wore them with polka-dot sandals. I've never been the girl who could get away with wearing cargo pants and a ripped T-shirt. At my size, I look too much like a boy with boobs. And so I carried my pink alligator clutch bag, and I wore my yellow twin set, my hair in a high, bouncy ponytail. Oftentimes it's hard to find occasions to dress so girlie, but falling in love gives you a built-in excuse.

Declan didn't look like a typical movie star, if there is such a thing. Tall and broad, yes. Wavy, longish, coppery-brown hair that women wanted to rake their fingers through, yes. Honey-brown eyes, sharp and knowing, yes. But his complexion was somewhat ruddy, and his waist became a little soft when he drank too much beer.

His coloring was all off, at least for me. I'd always preferred men who were dark. Bobby was just my type, in fact, with his inky-black curls, his olive skin and almost black eyes. I'd had a mad crush on Bobby after we met, when we were both in graduate school. The crush dissipated, mostly, and we became tight buddies. Years later, we had sex one night, something we needed to get out of our system. It had been lingering there, after all. But it was odd. He was too familiar and yet the intimate parts of him so male, so foreign. Luckily we were both stoned, and the whole experience is rather hazy.

Anyway, even though Declan wasn't necessarily my type, I adored the way he looked, even from the start. He was taller than me by at least ten inches, yet he was always ducking down when we hugged, trying to place his head on my collarbone, as if sensing a warmth there and burrowing for that heat. But since he wasn't the Latin-lover type, the blond-surfer type or the tousled bad boy, I never really thought he'd be all that famous. That sounds terrible. It sounds as if I didn't have faith in him. That wasn't it. I just couldn't imagine someone like him, with the lilting brogue and the goofy laugh, being an international superstar. I don't think he could have imagined it, either.

That summer we talked about how much he simply wanted to make a living as an actor. I knew what he meant. I just wanted to make a living as a designer. I didn't want to be a famous designer; I wasn't bold enough to think it, I didn't need that. But when people asked, "What do you do for a living?" I wanted to be able to say, "I'm a designer" and I wanted that to be all. I didn't want to go into a lengthy explanation about how I was trained to be a fashion designer, how I was *trying,* but how I had a small trust fund and was doing freelance design jobs and temp work in the meantime.

I had started working at temp agencies in my early twenties, in order to fill out the periods when I couldn't sell a line of clothing or couldn't get a freelance design gig. At the time, many of the others who were sent on the same jobs were my age, at my stage in life—people I could run around with. We would go out for drinks at the end of the day and make fun of the stiffs in the office where we'd just worked, self-satisfied because we didn't have to make our livings there. But by the time I met Dec, I was often the elder. I was the one who was pitied. I saw it in the faces of the twenty-one-year-olds who had just migrated to the city, smug in the fact that they would move on shortly, that the temp jobs were just stopping grounds for their eventual greatness. I knew them. I knew their misplaced arrogance, and I didn't blame them for their pity. I didn't even fight it, because I'd begun to look at myself the same way.

Declan understood all this. He'd folded jeans all day while working at the Gap; he'd suffered the humiliation of waiting on Al Pacino at a coffee shop and accidentally spilling steamed milk on him. He felt he might be on the verge of making a steady living, since he'd landed three roles over the last fourteen months, including the movie in Manhattan, but his family was still suggesting that maybe he should come home to Dublin and work with his dad as a courthouse clerk.

Luckily, I didn't have family pressure. Emmie would no sooner pressure me than she would move to Nebraska. To Emmie, each person is her own master. The only people she bossed around were her authors, and even then she trusted their judgment about the course of their careers and life. How lovely it was to have someone like Emmie who thought that you, and only you, could decide your fate. Occasionally, though, I thought about how nice it would be to have someone question me, give me a little push.

One night, Declan came to my apartment with a clumsily wrapped present, roughly the size of a softball.

"Open it," he said, handing it to me. "Fast."

The wrapping paper was green foil, obnoxious and yet seemingly perfect from him. "It's cold," I said, feeling it.

"Hurry, gorgeous," he said.

I tore off the paper. I could tell he'd wrapped it himself because of the long, tangled strips of tape that wound around the thing.

I saw what was inside and I giggled. "A pint of ice cream?"

"Not just any ice cream," he said, sounding indignant. "This is Ben & Jerry's! There's more crap in here than you

chapter 6

I knew that I was in love with him for certain when Emmie got hit by that car.

She was on Astor Place by her office, coming out of the little wine bar that used to be a speakeasy. She liked to tell people that she could remember drinking there during Prohibition, which was a complete fabrication. Emmie was barely out of the womb when Prohibition began, but she was one of those people who took pride in her age, rather than hiding it. She expected complete respect for living as long as she had.

Right before the SUV struck her, she was on the arm of Gerald Tillingham, another literary agent who was a few years older than she, but who had retired over a decade ago. She and Gerald had been an item back in the sixties after his first wife died, but now they were just buddies, old cronies who saw each other once a month to drink Pimm's and gossip about their friends. Sadly, the fact was that many of their friends had passed away.

Gerald had too much to drink, Emmie would tell me later when she was conscious and able to speak in coherent sentences. He had offered his arm to her like a gentleman, but it was he who needed support. They were crossing the street when Gerald faltered, one of his knees giving way. As Emmie struggled to catch him, the SUV turned the corner too fast. Startled by the car, Emmie lost her grip on Gerald and he fell again, and it was she who got hit. The SUV stopped immediately, but her leg was already broken, her lung punctured.

By the time I arrived at the hospital, Emmie was out of surgery, her leg pinned, her lung repaired. They said the lung would always trouble her and that I should get her to quit smoking. I said I would try, though I knew she would never do it. Despite the irony, Emmie would sooner die than give up cigarettes.

I pushed open the door quietly because the nurses said she was sleeping, and also because I was afraid of what I might see. And there she was, propped high on the bed to allow her lungs to drain, her leg huge and lumpen with plaster, metal prods piercing it. She was indeed asleep, the makeup on her papery cheeks faded, her dyed reddish hair fuzzy and misshapen by the pillow. Emmie would have hated how she looked. She took pride in her expensive cosmetics and the clothes she selected with care. The sapphire ring wasn't on her right hand, and that absence was the most shocking of all. I'd never seen her without it.

I sat on the edge of her bed, half hoping the movement would wake her. It didn't, and I couldn't bear to sit there very long without helping her somehow, without doing *something*. To watch her sleep like that was an invasion of privacy, like spying on someone on the toilet.

I left the room and went in the stairwell to call Declan. I had a cell phone by then, which he'd bought me. I had been one of the lone holdouts in all of Manhattan, one of the few people who weren't connected by the head to their cellular. But Declan said it made him "absolutely mad" when he couldn't find me. So I let him buy it. Later in L.A., I became a master at the thing. I grew attached to it like other people to their pets. But in New York, it was still a novelty, and I felt a rush of gratitude that I had it, that I had Declan to call.

He came to see us in the hospital that night. I told him it wasn't necessary, but he wanted to come. Emmie was groggy but awake by then, and he chatted with her as if she hadn't nearly died; he brought her magazines and told her his awful jokes. But it wasn't only that which made me say "I love you" in front of the hospital later that night. It was what happened when I left for ten minutes to go for coffee. I came back and found him feeding Emmie ice chips with a white plastic spoon. He was bent at the waist, his hair falling over his eyes, his arm outstretched. Emmie's lips were pink and cracked; they were pursed and straining for that white spoon. His sweetness, his ability to do that, along with Emmie's almost childlike response, undid me.

September came too fast, but Declan was back in L.A. for only three days before I was on a plane to spend a week with him. Those few days apart had been agonizing. The things that used to make me content—getting a coffee on the corner, seeing a movie at Bryant Park—seemed empty and flat without him there.

I arrived in L.A. for our visit on a Tuesday afternoon. Outside, I was buffeted with warmth and sunshine. I'd never been to Los Angeles, and I couldn't have been more thrilled.

Declan pulled up in a rusty white hatchback. He leaped out of the car and ran around to the sidewalk. He picked me up and twirled me around, and I imagined we looked like the ending of an old movie.

"Kyr." He nuzzled his face in my collarbone. "I've missed you."

The car smelled strongly of mildew, and there were wrappers from bags of potato chips (crisps, Declan would call them) on the back seat. But it didn't bother me. I was in love and it was sunny, and nothing else mattered. Until we got to the apartment.

Why is it that men will spend money on expensive dinners, work out for hours a day, and even wax the hair on their backs in order to attract and keep women, but they won't do a thing to their home?

Declan's apartment was in Venice Beach. It had a balcony with a plastic table and two mismatched chairs, and if you looked to the left, you could see the silvery blue of the ocean. But inside was chaos. Not a quirky, lovable chaos, the likes of Emmie's place. No, this was a teenage-boy type of chaos that would have made any self-respecting woman flinch.

I knew about Declan's first love, a girl from Dublin named Finnuala, and I knew he'd dated an ad exec in L.A. a few years ago. But maybe this was why he'd been single for a while. In New York, I'd assumed the mess was due to two men living in a small space. Apparently it was just Declan.

The carpet, a worn, dingy gray, was littered with gym shorts and T-shirts and old copies of *Variety*. The walls were contractor white and marked with greasy fingerprints. In the kitchen, crusted-over dishes and forks commandeered the sink. The bedroom had cardboard boxes instead of a dresser, and, worst of all, a futon.

My first sexual experience, an exchange of oral pleasantries, was held on a futon my freshman year at Vassar with a boy whose name was Thadeus Howler. Thadeus was from the South, had a slow rolling drawl and went by the nickname of Dixie. Dixie Howler, you might not be surprised to hear, came out of the closet a few years after our night together and is now one of New Orleans's most celebrated cross-dressers.

Both Dixie and I, I believe, were on that futon that night because we were both late bloomers in the sexual arena. We both needed to get some experience, and you didn't want to practice lingual technique on someone you actually *liked*. So there we were, fumbling and slobbering in the dark on his lumpy, cheap-cologne-smelling futon. I have never since been able to look at a futon without cringing.

And I did cringe in Declan's bedroom that day. He could barely get me to take a step inside the doorway.

Next on the house "tour" was the bathroom.

"Sorry, love," he said, flicking on the lights. The counter appeared encrusted in old, calcified dollops of toothpaste and shaving cream. The tub boasted a gray ring and little patches of black clinging to the grout.

"I was going to spend yesterday cleaning," Declan said, "but I got a callback for this Denny's commercial, and I had to see my acting coach, and… What? Is it that bad?"

"No," I said. "It's so much worse than that bad."

I turned the lights off—too painful—and went back in the bedroom to stare at the futon.

"I've been meaning to hire a cleaning crew. You know, one of those all-day jobs," Declan said.

"Okay."

"And I'll do…What else will I do?" He seemed to be talking to himself, walking through his apartment, like he was seeing it for the first time. "Christ, it's horrible, I know. But I don't know where to start."

He came in the bedroom and put a hand on my shoulder. His eyes said, *Help me.*

"That's got to go," I said, pointing at the futon, buried under jeans and wet, crumpled towels.

"Right. Right. Good." Declan nodded, his eyes excited, a man with a mission. "I'll call the cleaning people, and there's a bed store up the street. You'll pick one out, okay? And we'll stay at a hotel for a day or two."

"You'd do that?" I knew his agent had received a check from the movie this summer but hadn't paid Declan his part yet. I knew he didn't have money for cleaning crews and new beds and hotels. But Declan was always going out of his way to make me happy.

"Of course, Kyra," he said. "It's worth the interest on my Visa, and this is your home, too."

I didn't know what he meant—I was only visiting for six days, after all—but I liked the sound of his words, the sound of his brogue when he said my name. So I put my arm around his waist, and we headed downstairs to the mildewy hatchback.

A few days later, after the place had been scrubbed and organized by women from a company aptly named Angel Maids, Declan and I lay in his new bed. *Our* new bed, he kept saying. It was almost eleven in the morning, and we were meeting Bobby for lunch in an hour, but we were languid in each other's presence. The ocean air puffed in the window (finally opened for the first time after one of the Angel Maids chipped off the dried paint that had sealed it). The air was like a balm, making us even more lazy.

Declan rolled over and ran his hand over my bare belly. "Let's go to the beach today after lunch, shall we?"

"Yes, please!" I said. It was a joke between us. We'd overheard a mother the day before telling her little boy that if he was going to say the word *yes,* he should instead say, "Yes, please," but if he was going to say *no,* he should say, "No, thank you."

Declan chuckled and snuggled his face into the crook of my shoulder.

"I'm having such a good week because of you," I said.

Dec pulled his face back and studied me. "I'm having a good life because of you."

He put his face back on my shoulder, nuzzling me there.

I knew then that I would do almost anything, go almost anywhere, even sleep on a futon or keep my clothes in cardboard boxes to be with him.

On the plane ride on the way home, I sat across the aisle from an older woman. She was probably around Emmie's age, but she didn't carry her years as well. She wore brown perma-press pants and a cheap pink sweater that had pilled from too much wear. Her bifocals were affixed to a green cord that hung around her neck. Her shoes were ugly, tan orthopedic ones with a rubbery ivory sole. She had on nylons, too, a deceptively invisible garment of torture, in my opinion.

At one point, she crossed her legs, and that's when I saw the most striking thing. She wore a thin gold chain around her right ankle, under those beige nylons. A clandestine piece of jewelry. She had a secret, it seemed to me, and I felt the same way. But my secret was Declan. I was in love. In the very grip of it. No one on the plane could see it, at least not at first glance. But if they looked closer, they might have seen my too-wide eyes, my frequent glances at the card he'd given me at the airport, my secret anklet of a smile.

When I got back to New York, it was fall. I'd left in eighty-degree weather only seven days earlier. My cab to LaGuardia had been hot and stinky, the driver wearing a sweat-stained white shirt. And yet when I returned, there was an unmistakable crispness in the air. Women wore camel boots and thin leather jackets; the men were in cable-knit sweaters. Everything felt different, too—the fall always ushers in a sense of purpose to New York—and so everyone bustled by me on that first morning back as I strolled to my coffee shop, debating whether to call the temp agency today or wait until tomorrow. The sudden introduction of fall, like the drop of a heavy red curtain onto a Broadway stage, seemed a betrayal to me. It was as if the city already knew what I didn't—that I would soon be leaving for the sunny, synthetic shores of la-la land.

Emmie used to keep a collection of telegrams in old candy tins. These tins were stacked in the corner of one of her bedroom closets, and when I had the apartment to myself, which was often, I sometimes liked to extract them from her closet, feeling the swish and rustle of her clothes brush by my face as I dug for them. I would sit on her bed with its purple velvety spread, the apartment large and silent around me. With great anticipation, I took the telegrams out one at a time, making sure not to disturb the order. I was enamored with the precise folds, the thick, yellowing paper, the Western Union banner across the top.

Emmie. Have reached Paris but the books are not ready for my reading. Can you call Scribner?
MacKenzie Bresner

Dearest Emmie. The *QE2* is not all they say. Am bored already with two more weeks until we reach land. Will you send me a telegram? Say anything. I simply need entertainment of your sort.
Britton Matthews

MacKenzie Bresner and Britton Matthews were Emmie's star authors, and those telegrams from Britton were my favorites. He was famous, of course; even at age nine I knew that, even with him being dead for at least five years. But more than being a famous writer, he was Emmie's true love, the reason she'd never married. They had had an affair that went on for a decade, well before I came along. It was the old story, Emmie told me (although at the age I was at, no story was old). He had refused to leave his wife, and Emmie refused to stop loving him. And so those telegrams from him were illicit and old-fashioned and fascinating.

I had told Declan about Emmie's telegrams when I was

in L.A. We were sitting on his balcony in the rickety plastic chairs, reading the Sunday paper.

"I think people should still send telegrams," I said. I was reading a piece about the telegrams Harry Truman had sent around the world on a regular basis.

"I'm serious," I said when he made a goofy face at me. "They're so much more romantic, and they're more permanent than e-mails. They have substance." I explained about Emmie's tin of telegrams then.

"Well, love," Dec said, "I don't think it's possible to send telegrams anymore. They're extinct."

His comment put me in a momentary funk. The death of telegrams. Could it be true? But I quickly forgot about it, because soon Dec was pulling me back into his apartment, into our new bed.

Back in New York, back in the fall season that had taken me by such surprise, I only remembered that conversation when someone buzzed my apartment one day.

"Who is it?"

"Western Union," said a man's voice through the crackling intercom.

I stood up straight and looked around my apartment, as if I might find that I'd been transported back in time to the forties.

I pressed the intercom again. "I'll be right down."

I raced down the three flights of stairs, forgoing the elevator. Outside, I expected to see a man in a pressed Western Union uniform with a jaunty khaki hat, but he was a bike messenger with a large silver nose ring and a blue helmet.

"Kyra Felis?" He handed me a large yellow envelope. "Have a good one." He trotted back to his bike and was gone.

I sat down on the front steps. A crisp wind whipped my hair. For some reason, my heart was pounding. I pulled the tab to open the envelope. Inside was a sheet of thick paper.

Petal-soft yellow instead of age-old like those in Emmie's candy tins.

```
Kyra. The telegram is not dead. I thought you
should have your own, just like Emmie.
   This is not a one-off. If you like, I will send
you a telegram every week for the rest of time.
But instead, why not come to L.A.? Our bed misses
you and I am not the same anymore without you
around. I'm not talking about a visit. Will you
move in with me? I love you.
Declan
```

Margaux and I played phone tag for days. I couldn't bear to break the news on voice mail.

I did reach my model friend, Darcy. "You're leaving the city?" she said incredulously, as if I were moving to one of the outer rings of Jupiter.

I called Bobby, who whooped and yelled. "Finally!" he said. "You're coming to the right coast. God, it's going to be amazing!"

When I did get ahold of Margaux, she had a coughing fit on the phone.

"Are you smoking again?" I said.

"As if that's important!" She choked some more. "L.A.? Are you fucking kidding me?"

"You know, I could use a little support here."

"*I'm* the one who needs support. You're leaving me alone with the mommies!"

"You'll come visit me," I said.

I prayed she would. I prayed *anyone* would visit me. Emmie rarely left Manhattan anymore, except to go to her house in Nantucket, and so the possibility of getting her to travel to the West Coast was slim. It had been twenty-four hours since I'd called Declan and sang, "Yes, yes, yes!" in a gleeful voice, but since that time, I'd been plagued by nagging thoughts—I would have no girlfriends, I would have no job, I didn't even know how to drive.

I reminded myself that most of the time I communicated with my friends by phone or e-mail, and that wouldn't change. I had no real job in Manhattan that would make it hard to leave. I could continue working on my designs in L.A., and I could always look for freelance or temp jobs there. And Dec promised to teach me how to drive, although this thought irrationally terrified me. I was fine in the back of a cab, but operating an enormous vehicle (they all seemed enormous to me) was conceptually like manning an F-16 fighter jet.

"I guess I do like L.A.," Margaux said, "and I'm supposed to take a deposition there in six months or so. But hey, you'll probably be back by then anyway."

"Excuse me?" I said. "Could you be less helpful?"

"I'm sorry, Kyr, but you know…"

"No, I don't know."

"It's just that you barely know the guy, and you're moving across the country. It's like when you had only known Steven for so long and then you were with him every second of the day."

"Declan is not like Steven."

"Of course not." She coughed again. "I'm sorry. I'm just being a bitch because I don't want you to go. I can't believe you're leaving New York."

I looked out my window, at the cabs rumbling down 95th. I thought of Central Park and Emmie's salons. I thought of my spot in the Bryant Park Library where I liked to sketch. I thought of lunches with the girls in Gramercy Park and bottles of wine at 92, my favorite neighborhood place. I could barely believe I was leaving, either. But I knew Declan was different than my ex, Steven. I knew, somewhere deep inside, that Declan was the man. He was it. And so, if I had to spend my life in L.A. to be with him, if I had to leave New York, I would do it.

I took Emmie out to dinner to tell her I was moving. In the past, she'd always had a sprightly walk, a lively air about her, even as her back became slightly stooped and the wrinkles set into her face with more determination. Now, she walked slowly and cautiously, leaning hard on her cane, and it took us forever to walk the few blocks to the restaurant. Each plodding step seemed a trial for her, but she refused a cab.

"I'm not going to take a taxi around my own neighborhood," she said proudly.

I asked Emmie about the woman we had hired to help her around the house since the accident.

"She wears *ponchos,*" Emmie said derisively.

Other than that, she didn't talk much on the way to dinner. It was too hard for her to concentrate on her footing and to converse at the same time. The silence was torturous. I became increasingly nervous about delivering my news. With each slow, painful step, I felt more and more like I was abandoning her, although she would probably hate that thought. Emmie hated pity.

Finally we reached the restaurant and tucked ourselves into a booth, Emmie's leg raised to the side and propped on a folded towel by the proprietor. We ordered a bottle of champagne, Emmie's perpetual favorite.

In my early adulthood, I used to say I hated champagne, refused to drink it, but really it was just a way of establishing my independence. I needn't have worried. Emmie and I are so very different. She is strong and cheerful to a fault, while I am more moody. Emmie has spent the last few decades free from entanglements with the opposite sex, and yet aside from the few years before Declan, I moved from one man to another.

I wondered, as I sat across from her, watching her re-adjust her leg and take a sip of champagne, what my mother would have thought about me moving to L.A. Would she have been supportive? Maybe disapproving and telling me it was my life to ruin? It was a futile exercise, this trying to imagine my parents in the present. I had no groundwork for envisioning myself as an adult in their world. They were forever frozen in their thirties, and when I thought of me with them, I was still eight years old.

"I'm moving in with Declan," I blurted out.

Emmie raised the champagne flute to her mouth again, as if she'd heard nothing surprising. Her sapphire ring glittered navy blue with the movement.

"Will you have enough room in that place of yours?" she said.

"I'm moving to L.A."

Emmie put her glass down. "Why?"

"He needs to be there for his acting." And then, because that wasn't enough, "I'm in love with him."

She took a deep breath. She put a hand to her chest, as if something had caught there.

"Are you all right?" I started to stand from the table.

"Of course, sit down," she said, irritated. She moved her glass away. She signaled the waiter and asked for another towel to put under her leg. "My, how I hate getting old. It's making me sentimental."

"Oh, come on," I said in a kidding tone, hoping to lighten the mood. "What's that supposed to mean?"

"Everyone is leaving me," she said. Her voice was small. In fact, her whole body had seemed tiny since the accident.

"Emmie." I reached over to touch her hand.

She pulled it away and shook her head. "I don't want sympathy. I'm just stating a fact. I've run around my whole life with too many people to see and too many things to do, and now there's barely anything left. Britton is gone, your parents, most of my writers…now you."

"I'm not gone in that sense, and hey, you still have the agency."

"Kyra, dear, they keep me on because I helped build that place. They can't oust me unceremoniously, and I won't leave. But don't think they aren't hoping I'll die quietly in the middle of the night."

"It's not true."

"It is," she said definitively. She tried not to seem upset by this, but I knew better. The agency had been Emmie's life.

Emmie lifted the bottle out of the bucket, spraying water over the table.

"Let me do it." I took the bottle.

I expected her to protest, to say that she could do it herself, but instead she let me take it from her.

"You know what?" I said. "Maybe I won't go. I don't need to move." I was in agony at that moment. I wanted desperately to be with Declan every day, but how could I leave Emmie?

When she heard my words, she pushed herself up and sat straighter. She threw her shoulders back, as if throwing off her earlier words and thoughts.

She lifted her glass. "Kyra," she said, "you've got to follow love if you can find it. I won't have it any other way. Now, from what I recall, Los Angeles is a cesspool, but if you *must* live there, it might as well be with an Irishman who loves you. I want you to tell him something, though. If he doesn't take care of you, if he wounds you in any way, I will find ways to grievously injure him. Agreed?"

It was Emmie's way. I lifted my glass and touched it to hers.

Part Two

chapter 8

"We should be landing in about twenty minutes," the pilot said over the intercom. "That's about five minutes early." As if he should get a gold statuette.

I looked out the tiny oval window. Dirt-brown mountains. Arid stretches of sand interrupted by white ribbons of road. Soon there were grids of tiny houses, little blue squares of swimming pools. My new home.

The first few weeks were sparkly and wonderful. The ocean, viewed from Declan's strip of balcony, was glittery blue, inviting. We spent the first few days in a sweaty, happy haze, unpacking all that I'd shipped from New York. Most of his "furniture" was tossed, and my eclectic mix of old wood pieces settled into place.

"God, it's loads better now that you're here," Declan would say as he stopped and surveyed the living room. I kissed him when he said things like that. It seemed I kissed him all the time.

Once most of my stuff was in, and most of Dec's in the garbage bin behind his house, the apartment wasn't bad. It didn't have the character of my place in New York, but the kitchen was now a sunny place that we'd painted yellow and white, and the living room was a cozy enclave with plump chairs and the low coffee table that had been my parents'. I'd splurged on new linens for the bed, four-hundred-thread-count sheets in a cool Zen green I felt was very L.A.

We fell into a pattern in those days. The late mornings and early afternoons, we spent at Cow's End Coffee. First, we would read the papers, stopping every few minutes to read an article out loud to one another.

Later, we put away the papers and I worked on my designs, while Declan went over his lines for an audition or an acting class. Often, I raised my gaze from my sketch pad and watched him. His eyes narrowed and focused intently on the page; sometimes his lips moved as he read. I wondered, as I watched him, why he wanted to be an actor. He'd told me how he had fallen in love with acting, but I still puzzled over why anyone would want to spend their life pretending to be someone else. Did this represent a chink in his character? Something deficient? And yet I adored his devotion to his work. I loved how much he wanted to learn, to excel.

Nearly every night those first few weeks, we watched the sunset from the Venice pier, standing next to the Mexican fishermen and the families with strollers, our arms wrapped around each other. In Manhattan, sunset meant that the city turned orange and then navy blue for a few minutes, but here, it lasted forever. The ocean spread out like a vast liquid carpet, and the sun was a mammoth pink globe. Later, we ate somewhere in the neighborhood, laughing with the waiters and the other patrons, anyone who would smile back at us. And how could they not? We glowed.

★ ★ ★

I tried hard to make L.A. my new hometown. One day, when Declan was at an audition, I went to Fred Segal in Santa Monica. To me this outing smacked of something a true Los Angeleno would do. I knew of Fred Segal, the jeans designer, but I had never heard about his L.A. stores, and my ignorance had been met with abject horror by one woman.

"You've never been to Fred Segal?" said Tara, wife of Brandon, one of Declan's acting friends. A week or so after I moved, Declan had invited the couple for dinner at a restaurant called C&O in Venice so that I could get to know some people. But Tara only wanted to lord over me how much I didn't know about Los Angeles. She had already giggled maliciously when I said I didn't have a car and didn't think I would get one. (In retrospect, I can't blame her.)

"They're some kind of shops?" I said.

"Some kind of shops?" Tara sent Brandon a smug look, as if to say, *Isn't she just precious?*

"Sweetie," she said, placing a hand on mine. "Fred Segal is *the* place to shop. And for good reason. It's casual, it's delicious, and you will spend way too much money. Trust me. Just go."

And so a few days later, after Declan left, I went to Fred Segal, and found that Tara was right. It was very L.A.—a glorified mall—but there was no Gap, no Barnes & Noble, just tiny boutiques filled with gauzy pink slip dresses, silver salad tongs in the shape of tree branches, decadent bath products that smelled like lavender.

Most of the boutiques were individually owned, and I tried to talk to the managers or owners about taking a look at my clothing line. The fact was, I had no such line ready at the time, but I figured I'd lure them in, then figure it out. But all I heard was, "No thanks, we only buy from a few reps."

Dejected, I wandered the stores. I bought Declan some English shaving cream in a decorative can that set me back fifty dollars and a leather journal for Emmie, then I had lunch in an Italian café. I drank pinot grigio and ate salad with a crowd of people doing exactly the same thing. Except that all those people had lunch partners or spoke constantly into their cell phones.

I called Bobby from mine.

I'd seen him the previous week for drinks at the Sky Bar on a night when Declan had his acting class. There was a huge line stretching from the bar into the Mondrian Hotel lobby, and every beautiful person in line looked as if they were famous or counting on being famous soon. Bobby walked to the front, said hello to the bouncer with an earpiece, and we sailed right in.

"You know him?" I said to Bobby.

"Not really. He knows I work for William Morris." As if that said everything. And I soon came to understand that it did. Everyone in L.A. was "in the business" in one form or another, or if not, they were trying to get "in the business" or they had a friend or sister or roommate who was trying to get "in the business."

"Wow," I said as we got into the bar. It was open-air, the sky above us black and sparkling with stars. On one side, the lights of Los Angeles burned orange, competing with the stars and winning.

Bobby soon scored a low table surrounded by white plushy couches. We stretched out on them, ordered vodka martinis, just like we always did when we were together, and proceeded to get pleasantly boozy. But we were interrupted on a regular basis.

The first time, it was a short, muscled woman with spiky, cherry-cola hair. "Are you Bobby Minter?" she said.

Bobby nodded, but didn't change his slouched position,

which I thought was rude. I sat up straight and smiled at her, waiting to be introduced.

"I'm Rachel Tagliateri," she said.

"Nice to meet you," Bobby said, although he didn't sound as if it was all that nice.

I started to hold out my hand, but the woman barely looked at me and charged on. "Look," she said, "I hate to interrupt you, but I was just wondering if I could send you my head shots and some tapes. I'm on a reality show, you know *The Rat Race?* I'm one of the few people left, right? But I want to bridge from this into acting. That's where my true passion lies…"

She went on and on until Bobby sat up a little and raised his hand. "Rachel, was it?"

She nodded.

"I'm sorry, but I'm not accepting new clients right now."

Her smile dimmed. "Okay, well, I'll just send you the head shots anyway, just in case—"

"Rachel, I'm sorry," Bobby said. "They'll just get thrown away. Best of luck."

Rachel Tagliateri ran her hands through her cherry-cola hair and said, "Right. Great, thanks!" as if Bobby had just offered to take her to dinner.

"That was rude," I said when she was gone. I watched her walk to a group of women and point to Bobby and me.

Bobby sighed. "Are you kidding? That was nice. I let her go on about that ridiculous reality show, as if she's ever going to get an acting job after that. She'll work for scale for the rest of her life."

"Why couldn't you at least talk to her, maybe give her some advice?"

"Because if I did that, I would have to do it twenty-four hours a day. Everyone is looking to get connected, Kyr. You have to know when to put your foot down."

I made a face to show I didn't agree and sipped my martini. I felt some kind of kinship with the cherry-cola Rachel, because although I wasn't trying to be "in the business," I was new in this town, and I already sensed how hard it was to break in, in any capacity.

But I soon saw what Bobby meant. Within fifteen minutes, one of Cherry-Cola's gang came to our table and introduced herself.

"Olivia Tenson," she said. "I'm on *The Bold and the Beautiful*. I'm looking for new representation." She got a little more of Bobby's attention, but he soon sent her packing. Same with the stunningly beautiful boy with the jet-black hair and the dimples as deep as craters. Same with the comedian who sidled up to us and launched into his stand-up act.

"You see why I'm so glad you're here?" Bobby said. "You're my one true friend in town."

So I figured when I phoned Bobby that day from Fred Segal that he would call me back, maybe come meet me, but his assistant, Sean, said he was in a meeting that would last a few hours. I finished my wine and watched the rest of the patrons gossip with their friends or yammer into their phones. I made my daily phone call back to New York, but couldn't get Emmie, Margaux or Darcy.

Finally, I left, strolling aimlessly, nothing planned for the rest of the day. I walked through Third Street Promenade and then down the Santa Monica pier. I waited for L.A. to seep into my bones.

When Declan got home that afternoon, we took a walk on the beach, making our way to the pier for sunset.

"What did you do today?" he said. He was always concerned about whether I was "fitting in," whether I'd had enough activity. Every evening, he peppered me with questions and made suggestions about what I could do that week.

I told him about my day.

"Are you having me on?" he said. "You *walked* to Fred Segal?"

"It's only a mile or two."

"Bloody right. I can't believe you walked."

"You know how I feel about all the driving out here."

In short, I wasn't a big fan. Constant driving was required, since L.A. is really just a string of suburbs, not a city at all, and yet the need to drive everywhere killed any chance of spontaneity. Even if you were lucky to be with friends, and have someone suggest dropping by a party or a bar, there was the inevitable meeting in the parking lot where many important topics would be debated: Should we all drive? Can we take the 10 or will surface streets be better? How long will it take at this time of day? Does anyone have exact directions? Who's going to be there anyway? Is the casting director from the WB really supposed to stop by?

"Love," Declan said, "you've got to learn how to drive."

"I will…someday."

We walked for a few minutes in silence, the pier a short distance ahead of us, the sand cool under our feet.

Declan suddenly stopped and turned to me. He took both my hands in his; he looked very serious, which freaked me out.

"What?" I said.

"Kyra Felis," he said somberly. "I have a question for you."

My heart began to pound. "What?" I repeated.

He dropped on one knee. He kissed my hand.

"Kyra," he said. He took a deep breath. "Will you have me as your driving teacher? Will you trust me enough to put your adorable bum on the driver's seat of my car?"

I burst into laughter. "I don't know. I haven't known you all that long, and I don't know if I'm ready. It's a big decision and—"

He stood and interrupted me with a big, Fred Astaire–like dip. "We can do it. We can make this work."

"The gas is on the right, Kyra! You have to keep your foot on it to make the car move!"

I shot him a murderous look, although I couldn't blame him for yelling. I tried again. I stepped tentatively on the gas, but when the car shot forward, it scared the hell out of me, and I hit the brakes. Once more, gas…whoo, that weird power of the car lurching, tying my stomach in knots…and I pounced on the brakes.

I put the car in park, peeled away my death grip on the steering wheel and dropped my head. We were in a parking lot of a vacant strip mall, the only place Declan could find where I might attempt to drive and not maim the few pedestrians. I snuck a look at Dec. His face was flushed, his hair a little sweaty and pushed up in spikes. He looked, as he would put it, "shaggered."

"I don't think I can do this," I said.

Dec didn't look as if he thought I could do it, either, but he said, "Of course you can, love. If I can learn to drive on the right side of the road, you can learn to simply drive. Now let's just sit here a bit and review the controls." By that time, we'd "reviewed the controls" at least thirty times, but I was grateful for a task I could handle.

"What's this?" He pointed to the dash.

"The gas gauge. It's half-full."

"Good, and this?"

He kept pointing to various instruments, and I answered dutifully. I knew what he was doing. He was trying to build up my confidence by mentioning things I knew and could answer. He didn't understand that while I could also probably learn the controls of the space station, it didn't mean I was ready to blast off.

"Okay, we're trying again," he said. He breathed out heavily, as if he was preparing to pick up a large couch and move it to a third-floor apartment.

I lurched and braked down the street, the car bucking like a rodeo bull.

"Get her to bloody go!" Declan yelled.

You can do this, I said to myself. *Just do it.*

With a burst of determination, I punched down on the gas pedal with my foot. The car shot forward in one swoop.

"Whoa!" Declan said. "Not so fast!"

Suddenly, looming in front of me was a yellow metal garbage can left too far into the street. I told my arms to turn the wheel, but I reacted too slowly, and the car hit the can with a loud thunk, sending it soaring into the air like a mini blimp.

I squealed to a halt as the can landed with a clatter behind the car.

With trepidation, I glanced at Declan. He looked as though he wanted to cry

"In my defense," I said, "that yellow was a hideous color."

He moaned. "Let's go again."

I sped forward in short bursts and halted with too much force all afternoon until, little by little, I could withstand the power of the moving car. Four hours later, I drove one block up the street, turned around and drove another block back to the parking lot. We practiced all the next day, too, when I advanced to going through stoplights and backing into parking spaces (I'm sure our neighbor didn't need that ugly planter in the shape of a grizzly bear. Why put it in the parking lot, anyway?).

Two weeks later, I took my driver's license test. In the

hopes of flirting with the tester for special consideration, I wore a pink tulip skirt and gauzy white blouse. Unfortunately, my tester was a mean little woman named Barbara who used to be a gym teacher and still wore a whistle around her neck. Anytime I made what she called "an infraction" she blew the whistle. Lucky for me, and to Barbara's chagrin, I passed by a hair. When I came into the waiting room, Declan was there, pacing like an expectant father.

"I got it!" I said. I waved my little plastic rectangle of a license, on which, I must say, was a rather fetching photo of me.

When we pulled into our parking lot at home, there was a car in our spot. A tiny, old, rusted, green convertible. I couldn't have told you what type it was at the time; I still wasn't so good at judging the makes or models of automobiles.

"Should I call someone?" I said, staring at the car, annoyed. I wanted to get inside our apartment and celebrate. I wanted a glass of wine or three, and yet here was this car, delaying my intended intoxication.

I glanced at Dec, who was staring at the car with a strangely fond expression. He reached into his pocket and took out a set of keys I'd never seen before.

"It's for you," he said.

"That car?"

He nodded.

"You got me a car?"

He smiled.

"We can't afford that."

"I got my check for *Tied Up*." *Tied Up* was the movie Dec had shot that summer in Manhattan, but I knew that money had been earmarked for other things—paying off credit card bills, new head shots—and I told him that.

"That can wait," he said. "My colleen has got to have her own wheels."

I glanced back at the car. It now looked not so much old and rusted as it did charmingly antique, not so much tiny as it did delicate, and not so much green as it did jade.

I shrieked with delight, then crawled all over my new toy. Dec stood by, beaming.

"Wait right here," he said after a few minutes.

He emerged from the house a moment later with two bottles of beer, and we sat inside my new car, top down, and toasted to us.

chapter 9

After a few weeks in L.A., the weather shuddered and stopped. Fog blew in from the ocean. It looked like wet smoke, and became thicker and thicker until I could only hear the waves. Next came a misty rain, skies that hung low and looked like powdered ash. Everyone I met commented on how bizarre the weather was, how it was sure to change, but it dug in its heels and clung to Los Angeles like an unwanted lover who refuses to give up.

The lack of sun seemed to steal some of the magic from my everyday life, although I suppose it could have been other factors, too. Declan had been cast in a voice-over role in an animated film that required him to act the part, at least vocally, of a sprightly Scottish chicken. He was so excited when he got the call from his agent.

"Kyr! Kyr! I got it!" he said, holding his cell phone aloft like a trophy.

"The Edith Wharton movie?" My voice matched his glee, although I suspected that Dec had auditioned for the adaptation of *Old New York* more for me than himself.

"No, no!" he said. *"MacDaddy."*

"The one where you'd have to be a hen?"

"A rooster! The *main* rooster."

"Well, congrats, baby!" I hugged him. Absently, I thought about telling Emmie and Margaux that my new boyfriend had a part as a barnyard animal.

I must not have appeared suitably impressed, because he said, "Kyr, this is massive. It's a Disney film. You've seen *Shrek* and *Anastasia,* haven't you? Lots of adults love them."

"Yeah, absolutely," I said. I was sure that the only adults who "loved" those movies were parents who knew they had to see the movie thirty more times before their kids left for college and were, therefore, deluding themselves in order to stay sane.

The role seemed somehow ridiculous, and every morning as I watched Declan go through his vocal exercises, chanting, "O-hello-oooo, Om, om om," I found it more silly. It seemed beneath his talents, or at least the talents I assumed he had. But Max, his agent, had convinced Dec that this was a plum assignment, and Bobby, when I asked him, agreed. So I kept out of it, kissing Dec before he left, trying not to imagine him as a chicken. And then the whole dreary, powdered-ash day would open before me. I signed up with two temp agencies, but with all of the actors in town who also wanted temp work I rarely got any calls.

I tried to sleep. I *love* sleep. Have I mentioned that before? And I used to be very good at it. In New York, if I wanted, I could sleep for an entire day. I've always been that kind of person, even with the horns blaring outside my window in Manhattan, the scrape of metal cans in the alley. But in L.A., despite the crappy weather, I was restless.

I talked to Bobby nearly every day. He called me when he was having his morning coffee at the office, and I phoned him incessantly throughout the rest of the day for no reason, except that I was bored.

"Kyr, take up exercise or something," Bobby said, exasperated with me one afternoon. "Your metabolism is bound to catch up with you, and you're going to gain two hundred pounds."

And so I started jogging. Another concession to the L.A. lifestyle. I'd never really worked out before. In New York, walking around the city and running after cabs was enough exercise. But it was hard to live near the Venice boardwalk with its in-line skaters and weight lifters and runners without joining them once in a while. I ran from our house down Washington, even in the rain, and then let myself get lost around the little side streets and the canals of Venice. On the way home, I usually ran along the sand. I watched the surfers, all of them in black bodysuits, bobbing on the water like a pack of beetles.

Jogging allowed me to explore Venice, an area I came to love, but I wasn't very comfortable with the other places in L.A. There were too many people in the same biz, struggling for the same jobs. There was too much flesh, too much perfect skin, too many full heads of hair. But I liked Venice. It reminded me of New York—a ragtag amalgamation of people. Poor and rich; writers, artists and lawyers.

Still, I had too much time on my hands. Emmie told me I should sketch, that I should work on my designs, but new ideas, images, hemlines and sleeves stayed hidden from me.

I knew Emmie was right, though. Even if inspiration eluded me, I needed to find a new pattern maker, a new cutter, a new manufacturer for my designs. It's not particularly difficult to locate these people. They are there for hire. Whether you ever sell your designs after they make them is irrelevant. But it's important that you trust them, and that they don't rob you blind.

I made a few calls to Manhattan and soon I had appointments in L.A.'s fashion district with a host of people. I drove the surface streets in my new car, too anxious to get on the highway. The fashion district was bordered by an industrial section of downtown that could've been Anywhere, U.S.A., but the district itself had sidewalks crowded with hot-dog stands and displays of luggage, nylon dresses and athletic shoes. Most of the people I met there weren't right for me, or I for them. They were either astronomically expensive, or they specialized in sportswear, things with Lycra in it, while I designed with chiffon and silk and linen.

Finally, on a Tuesday afternoon, I found a pattern maker named Rosita, a sweet, kind Puerto Rican woman who had years of experience yet charged rates I could afford. Rosita then made a call and hooked me up with a cutter named Victor, and Victor, in turn, recommended a small factory that agreed, at a reasonable rate, to make my designs. That is, whenever I got my ass in gear and decided what my next line would be.

Poet's blouses had been my thing for a long while—silky slips of fabric with my circle of fake diamonds pinned at the cuff of one puffed sleeve. I'd sold a few lines to Neiman Marcus, and a couple others to a boutique, but for the last few years, no one seemed interested. Ditto for the line of trumpet skirts I'd designed last spring. But my real passion was in the even girlier stuff—the halter dresses, the flounced party skirts, the elegant gowns. I wanted to design clothes I would wear myself. But in L.A., would I ever wear those things again? When we walked the beach, I wore a casual skirt and T-shirt. When we went to dinner, most places were much more casual than New York.

Yet as I pulled into the apartment parking lot after meeting Rosita and Victor, I remembered that I did have something to dress up for very soon. The premiere for Declan's movie, the one he'd filmed with Lauren, was only a few weeks away.

I began to rework a dress I'd designed years ago in preparation for the premiere. Unfortunately, the work didn't exhaust me as I'd hoped, and sleep continued its elusive hide-and-seek. Insomnia, I learned, is one of the most ghastly of all medical conditions.

People who can sleep through tornadoes, the way I used to, have no capacity to understand this. "You're a little tired, huh?" they might say. "Well, just get some rest tonight."

You consider strangling them, but then you would go to prison, and it would be even harder to sleep, so you just give them a patient, bleary-eyed smile.

I was committed to L.A., for Dec's sake, and yet it was difficult for me to get accustomed to the way the city looked. It was something to do with the constant mix of the ugly and the beautiful: the beige-painted concrete buildings next to the natural loveliness of the palm trees; the homeless man with soiled plastic bags for his pillow, passed out next to a boutique on Third Street Promenade, where girls emerged with their own plastic shopping bags, their eyes lined with kohl, their lips pearly pink.

But surely, I told myself, this was purely American—the way the ugly and the beautiful converge. New York had its own mix, its own ugliness, ugly people. In Manhattan, for instance, there were the bond traders, brash packs of men talking too loudly and smoking cigars ("Cubans!" they told anyone who would listen). In L.A., the traders were replaced by thin-hipped boys in their twenties, smoking French cigarettes, claiming to be movie producers. *Produce, production, producers*—these words, I've decided, are the most vague in the entire English language.

The newness of the city bothered me, too. There were no turn-of-the-century monuments, so few prewar buildings. The city lacked, for me, a certain antiquity of character. It seemed a city without a soul. Or maybe I was losing mine.

Jack Nicholson took me to the bathroom one night.

Dec had come home early from his Scottish-hen job and, sensing that I was restless, he took me to Shutters to have a drink. It was a New England–style hotel with gray shingles and little white balconies overlooking the ocean. Inside, the lobby bar had overstuffed leather couches and chairs surrounding a crackling fireplace.

We sat near the fire and ordered a bottle of wine with a big cheese board. We cuddled and talked, and he made me remember why I was there with him, in that city.

After an hour, I went looking for the ladies' room and got turned around. I stopped to ask directions from a guy in a sport coat.

"Let me walk you there," he said in a mischievous and strangely familiar voice.

I glanced at him as he led me down a marble hallway. He looked familiar, too. A second later, I realized who he was. I felt like gushing. He was one of Emmie's favorite actors, and I debated telling him that. I actually considered the dreaded line he'd heard a million times—*I really enjoy your work*—but I'd been in L.A. just long enough to know better.

So I did what any good Los Angeleno would do. I pretended not to recognize him.

chapter 10

I didn't know what to expect of Declan's first movie premiere, but I knew I liked the sound of…the *red carpet*.

My gown was a black halter style with the circle pin at the base of a very deep V-neck, which came almost to my waist. Dec looked dashing in the Hugo Boss jacket we'd found for him on sale at Daffy's. I was a little more dressed up than Dec, but isn't that usually the case with women? Yet, when we arrived at the theater, I realized I was more dressed up than nearly everyone. Many of the women wore jeans and stilettos. The men were in everything from khakis to tracksuits.

There was indeed a red carpet stretching from the street to the theater's entrance. The carpet was rather short and thin, and looked somehow plastic, but the theater was ablaze in lights, and there was a buzz from the crowd behind the barricades—reporters, photographers, TV cameramen and a few fans. Hip-hop music pumped from speakers. The rain had stopped for once, and it was balmy under all those lights.

How wonderful it was to hand the car keys to the valet

and walk those twenty or so feet, knowing this was Declan's first big movie. Declan was unrecognizable to most people, and so we moved down the carpet in a leisurely way, answering a few questions from the reporters who were asking everyone the same thing. "How do you feel tonight?" "What do you expect from the movie?" "Was this a tough shoot?" Declan did a great job, though of course there wasn't much to say. In between the questions, we giggled like two kids who'd crashed a party.

"Who are you wearing?" a reporter asked me (finally!). She shoved a microphone in my face. I could tell she was asking for the sake of asking, because there was no one important around at that moment, but I was thrilled.

"It's my own," I said proudly. Declan squeezed me around the waist.

"But who designed it?" the reporter said. She had brassy, blond hair and green eyes that continually swept the place, even as she spoke.

"I did."

"Oh." She turned to face me for the first time, then gave my dress a once-over, followed by a nod, as if to say, *Not bad*. "So you're like Versace," she said.

"Well, thank you, but I consider myself more Armani than Versace."

"Sure," she said, clearly not understanding the distinction. She looked up at the crowd again, and suddenly her eyes went wide. "Lauren! Hi!" she said.

I glanced over my shoulder to see Lauren Stapleton hovering there. She wore a wrap dress with a splashy Kandinsky print on it and high, high sandals that made her skyscraper presence even more imposing. Her whole sartorial package was perfect—a blend of casual and glamorous.

"Declan," Lauren said, muscling her way between Dec and me in one fluid movement. "How are you, doll?"

"Fine, Lauren. And you?" Declan said, although I could barely see him. Lauren was towering over me, blocking me from Declan. The cameras flickered wildly as she hugged him. A number of TV cameramen began running. Suddenly, a crowd of reporters and photographers were in front of us, shouting questions.

"Are you two still an item?" one yelled.

"Oh, in some ways, I suppose we'll always be an item," Lauren said. She stroked the back of Declan's hair for an instant, but it was long enough for the photographers to capture it. "This film we made is truly special," she said, "and it's going to live in our hearts forever."

By then, Declan had made his way around Lauren and back to me. I slung a tight arm around his waist, determined not to lose him again.

"Lauren! Declan! Get together for a shot!" one of the photographers called.

Declan leaned toward Lauren but pulled me with him, so that the three of us squashed together. The cameras flashed like crazy. When they were done, Lauren seemed to notice me for the first time.

She gave me an annoyed glance, and without offering her hand said, "I'm Lauren Stapleton."

"Kyra Felis. We met in Vegas."

"Oh. Is that right?"

"I was with Bobby Minter."

"Ah. Bobby. Sure." She looked from me to Declan and back. "And you two…"

"Kyra's moved to L.A. now," Declan said, pulling me even closer to him.

"How nice," Lauren said. "And did I hear you say something about how you'd designed your dress?" She looked down at my hem, then her eyes moved painstakingly slowly up my body.

"That's right."

"Yes," Lauren said, dropping her voice so the reporters couldn't hear. "I thought it looked homemade."

She kissed Declan on the mouth before either of us could respond. A flood of flashes went off and when the white disappeared from my eyes, Lauren was gone, too.

"How could you let her do that?" I said to Declan as we took our seats.

"Christ, she's unhinged," he said. "I didn't even see it coming. Sorry, love."

I stewed over Lauren's "homemade" comment throughout the entire film. Luckily, I could honestly say that her acting was wooden and one-dimensional. This wasn't her usual romantic comedy, but a drama about a CIA agent (Lauren) who chases a nuclear device that has fallen into the hands of a terrorist organization. Without the pratfalls and the goofy dialogue that usually filled her movies, Lauren seemed out of her element. Declan, on the other hand, who had a smaller part as her CIA handler, was outstanding. This was the first time I'd seen him in a movie, and to my mind, he was clearly the best actor in the film. You felt the pain of his unrequited love for his agent but his devotion to his country. When his character committed suicide toward the end, I blinked away a tear and squeezed his hand.

After the movie, we went to a party given by Lauren's manager at his home in the Hollywood Hills. The party was held alongside a monstrous pool, which had a ring of tall silver candelabra surrounding it and a marble, cherub-ridden fountain in the middle. The effect was overdone but eye-catching—two adjectives that often go together in L.A.

I made the rounds with Declan. Later, at such a party, I would have noted precisely who was there, who wasn't. I would have noticed the producer who was considering Declan for a part and the actor he was up against. I would have wondered why Declan's manager was talking to that director. But I knew no one at this party, and Declan didn't even have a manager yet.

The topic of every conversation was how great the film was, how well it was sure to do at the box office. The mood was decidedly self-congratulatory. Whether this was a defense mechanism because the movie wasn't particularly fabulous, or whether these people truly believed it, I couldn't tell. I had just slipped away and ordered a dirty martini from the bartender, when I saw Bobby step through the sliding doors onto the patio. He looked handsome in tan linen pants and a black sweater that set off his black curls. He scanned the room, no doubt trying to decide who he should talk to, who he could ignore. When he spotted me, he smiled and headed for the bar.

I ordered another martini, and Bobby and I huddled together.

"Okay, here's the deal," he said. "I couldn't make it to the premiere, but I have to pretend I was there."

"Why?"

"Because I represent the guy who played the Russian general who helped the terrorists."

"The one with the cleft chin?"

"Right."

"He looks more Italian than Russian," I said.

"He is Italian. How was he?"

"Not bad."

"But not good, either?"

"Definitely not."

Bobby sighed. "And the movie?"

"Well…" I said, trailing off.

"Did it suck?" Bobby said.

"Pretty much."

Another sigh. "What about Lauren?"

"Oh, she *really* sucked," I said with relish.

Bobby took a sip of martini and glanced at me over the wide rim. "Do I detect a catfight?"

"No, I just think she's a bitch."

"Of course she is."

Bobby and I went on gossiping like that for the next ten minutes. I've read books that say gossip is destructive and dangerous. I don't doubt this is true, but there's no denying the pleasure of a good, mean chat with a friend. When Declan found us, we were on our second martinis and laughing about Bobby's Italian client whose next role was as a Polish prince turned deli owner.

Declan and Bobby shook hands. "Can I steal her for a second?" Declan said.

"Sure," Bobby said. "I've got to make the rounds."

When Bobby was gone, Declan led me by the hand down the length of the pool and through a small opening in the tall hedges that surrounded the property. The foliage back there was thick and untamed.

"Where are we going?" I said. "My shoes can't handle this." I was trying hard to lift the hem of my gown and walk on tiptoe so my heels wouldn't sink into the earth.

"Just a little farther," Declan said.

I held tight to his hand, ducking under low-hanging trees and stepping over rocks. We climbed upward through a rough-cut path.

When Declan stopped, I straightened and looked around. "Oh, my gosh."

We were standing at what must have been one of the highest points in Los Angeles, the sparkly orange lights of the city below.

"Now don't say anything," Declan said, "or I won't be able to finish."

And then he was on one knee in the dirt, fishing a velvety nugget of a box from his pocket.

The fresh air swirled around me at that moment. The lights of the city sparkled brighter.

"What are you—" I started to say.

"Please, love," Declan said. "I have to get this out."

He opened the black velvet box, and I gasped. Inside was a small, round diamond set high above a platinum band that was studded with tinier diamonds. It was exactly like the one my mother had worn, the one that had been buried with her, the one I used to study in photos and wish I'd had.

"How did you…?" I said.

"Emmie helped me. Now, let me talk."

Declan held the box higher and looked up at me. "Kyra. My mother always says you can't plan love. Jesus knows, that's true of she and my da." He shook his head. "What I'm trying to say is that I never even prayed for someone like you, because I didn't think you existed. But if I could have written a script for myself, it would have starred a woman just like yourself—someone smart and sweet and heartbreakingly gorgeous; someone who eats peanuts and pickles for breakfast and likes to put on a dress to go to the shops…"

I laughed.

"I would have scripted someone," he continued, "who would put up with a daft eejit like me." He paused, looked down. He took a deep breath. "We haven't known each other for years, Kyra Felis, but I know I want to spend every second, of every minute, of the rest of my years with you. Will you marry me?"

The air swirled again. I felt my hair caress my neck. I

blinked and gazed at Declan, at that perfect ring. Time seemed to swoop away, as if years had passed, but then I was back again, here with Declan still on his knee.

"Love?" he said.

"Of course I'll marry you!"

He put the ring on my trembling finger, and then I tackled him with a hug.

After we'd brushed the dirt off ourselves and hugged again for what seemed like thirty minutes, we made our way back to the party. I could barely believe what had just happened. I kept slipping on the path, because I couldn't stop looking at my ring.

When we reached the hedges and ducked under them to the pool, the party was even more crowded. Declan's agent, Max, hurried up to us.

Max was a diminutive, blond-haired, bearded man, who seemed to burn calories just by moving at such a fast pace. He wasn't one of the well-known agents in town, but from what I could tell, he honestly liked Declan and worked his butt off to find him parts.

"So, so?" he said, smiling.

Declan nodded.

"Yeah?" Max said. "Congrats, you two!" He embraced me and turned to the crowd. "I have an announcement!" he yelled, tapping his wineglass with a spoon.

I looked at Declan and opened my eyes wide. He had barely just put the ring on my finger and already we were making announcements?

Declan whispered in my ear, "Sorry, but I needed his help to find that spot up there. Let Max have his moment, then we'll get out of here." He put his arm around my shoulders.

"Ladies and gentleman," Max shouted, still clinking his glass. "Your attention!"

Soon, everyone was facing us, the sounds of the party dying away.

"Listen up," Max said. "Declan McKenna, who played the part of Frank in tonight's wonderful film, has done something even more wonderful. He has just asked his girlfriend, Kyra, to marry him!" Max gestured to us with a swoop of his arm. "Let's give them our congrats!"

The room burst into applause, and I felt a warmth I hadn't known since the sun left the city a few weeks before.

chapter 11

The next day, the sun really did come out. Maybe my mood had willed the clouds away. Suddenly, I had so much to do—a wedding to plan, a dress to design—and every day I awoke with a sense of purpose.

We didn't want to wait long to have the wedding, we decided. All we wanted was a small, simple affair with a few key friends and family. It would have to be somewhere in California, because Manhattan would be entirely too expensive.

Margaux screamed when I called her and said that of course she'd come out whenever I wanted her there. "God, you move fast," she said.

"I know, I know, but don't give me crap. I'm one hundred percent about Declan."

"Nope. No crap. Just don't make me wear a teal taffeta gown."

"You got it. So what's the news from there? I miss Manhattan."

"Ugh, don't. It's dirty and it's loud, and well…I do have some news of my own."

"What? What?" I said excitedly. I missed my talks with Margaux. "You didn't sleep with the massage therapist, did you?"

"No. It's a little different news." She paused. "I'm trying to get pregnant."

"You're what?" My voice went from excited to confused, almost mad. Margaux and I were a team of sorts, the ones who weren't going to have kids. You needed someone on that team to back you up against the wave of societal guilt-tripping that inevitably soaked you on occasion.

"I know it's weird to hear," Margaux said, "but Peter and I need something new. We're bored with each other."

"So learn how to play tennis! But a baby?"

"Well, it's not for sure we'll have a baby. We're just trying."

There was a silence that was uncomfortable and unusual for Margaux and me.

"At least you're having sex with your husband, right?" I said, trying to make light. Margaux was always complaining about the lack of coital relations between her and Peter.

"Yeah," she said, "but it's rather militaristic. You know, charts and stopwatches and all that."

"Ah."

"Enough of that topic. What did Emmie say about your engagement?"

"I haven't talked to her yet. We keep missing each other."

But an hour later, Emmie called me back.

"So it happened," she said. "Oh, my."

"Emmie, what's wrong?"

"Nothing, nothing, dear."

"Emmie," I said in a tone that said *spill it*.

"Well, it's wonderful," she said. "It truly is. I knew it

would happen soon, I just never imagined the exact moment." She coughed.

"Are you sick?"

"I don't get sick," she said. Which was what she always said, and, thus far, had blessedly been true. "Kyra, you deserve to be married to a man as delightful as Declan. Every woman deserves that."

I knew she was probably thinking about Britton Matthews.

As an early wedding gift, Emmie gave us a small donation to help with the costs. I told her no over and over, but she wouldn't relent, and secretly I was relieved. Declan had received only a small advance for the Scottish-hen job, and we had so little money to throw this party ourselves.

The exact location was also a problem. Although Declan had been raised Catholic, he found the concept of going to mass every Sunday (or even every month) as mystifying as American football. So no church wedding for us. We investigated a few restaurants, a few hotels, but we'd have to go deep into debt for those places, not to mention we couldn't book them for another year.

One Sunday, we drove to La Jolla to attend an outdoor concert of some band that Dec had followed in Dublin and that was playing at a music festival. We sat on the field of rich green grass alongside a thousand other people. We drank beer and got sunburned and made out on our blanket. A few times, Declan pulled me up to dance to his favorite songs, but I always laughed so hard at his bunny-hop dance style that I'd have to sit down and have a slug from my Miller can.

When the next act came on, some grunge garage band, we took a walk. On the other side of the park, we found a small pond. The surface gleamed light green and mirrored the yellow willow trees hanging over it. To the side, we spotted a white pergola with vine-covered latticework for its roof.

As we walked toward it, Declan squeezed my hand. "Love?" he said.

"Yes," I said. Somehow I knew what he was saying without him having to speak it.

We walked under the vines of the pergola. It was cool and airy.

"Can't you see it?" Declan said. He led me to the center and took both of my hands in his.

"Yes," I said again.

We stayed the night in a motel, and the next morning we tracked down the city's park manager. At three o'clock on Monday afternoon, we were handed a permit, which allowed us to have our wedding under the pergola in six short weeks.

The flurry of wedding planning left me so stimulated during the day and so exhausted at night that I finally started sleeping again. My days fell into a routine. Early morning, I'd throw on shorts, a tank top and my New York Fire Department cap, and I'd take a run along Venice Beach, the canals or the ocean.

Late morning, I'd work on my wedding-dress design at Cow's End Coffee. I usually sat at one of the dark wood tables in their loft, which felt like someone's open-air living room. I wanted a girlie dress, but it had to be elegant, too, something light and flowy, but not too princessy. I drew hundreds of designs, studying each to determine what I liked, then moving on to integrate that detail into a new sketch.

There were so many other issues to decide, too. Did we need flowers when the ceremony and cocktail party would be outside in the middle of all that nature? And what kind of cocktails should we have? Guinness for Dec, vodka for Bobby and me, and champagne for Emmie, of course, but what else? And then there was the issue of food. A small buffet or passed hors d'oeuvres?

In the afternoons, I usually headed back to the apartment, ready to spend hours manning the phone, trying to nail down the wedding details. One day, when I got home from Cow's End, I was wrestling with our mailbox in the lobby, pulling out the thirty or so flyers from San Diego caterers and the three bride's magazines, when I heard a little laugh behind me.

I turned to see a woman in a pair of tight white yoga pants, stretched across her full hips, and a blue camisole top that barely contained her breasts. She looked a few years younger than me. She had streaked hair in a ponytail on top of her head and a tiny, pushed-up nose, with a sprinkle of freckles across it. She looked like a 1970s *Playboy* bunny named Barbi.

"Getting married?" she said.

"How could you tell?"

She laughed again. "I just did it myself last year. It's a part-time job. I'm Liz Morgan. I live on the first floor." She held out her hand.

"Kyra Felis. Third floor."

"Oh, you're with the Irish guy, right?"

"Yeah. Declan."

"He's a cutie. Congrats. Isn't he an actor?"

I nodded.

"Is he getting any parts?" Liz crossed her arms and brought one thumb to her mouth, biting at the flesh by her nail.

"He is, actually. He was in that Lauren Stapleton movie that just came out."

"Oh, that's right. I've seen the pictures of them. And I've heard she's impossible."

"She is." I told Liz about the comment Lauren had made about my "homemade" dress.

"That fucking wench!" Liz said.

"Completely," I said, pleased. "But, anyway, Declan's got two other movies coming out, too. *Tied Up* he filmed this summer, and *Normandy,* he filmed a year or two ago, but it's going to be released in a few months."

"Hmm. A long release date like that usually isn't a good sign."

"I've heard, and it's too bad, because it's his one leading role."

Liz shook her head. "God, I would kill to have *any* role." She filled me in on the auditions she went to weekly, usually without callbacks, the few commercials she'd shot, and the one role on a sitcom as the main character's crazy cousin.

"It's a shitty business," she said. "So, anyway, when's the wedding?"

"Three weeks, five days, and—" I checked my watch "—two hours." I felt a flush as I spoke. Why had we decided to have this thing so fast?

"Wow," Liz said. "Are his parents coming in?"

"No, unfortunately. We only gave them a month and a half notice, and the airline tickets are all sky high. They really don't have the money, so we're going to visit them in Dublin over New Year's."

"Are you ready for everything?"

"Not at all. I mean, we've got the place and the guest list and a bartender and a band, but there's so much still to do."

"What about invites, did you send those out yet?"

"Well, most people know the date." I slumped against the bank of mailboxes. "To be honest, I haven't even picked out the invitations."

"Oh, honey. You better come with me. I've got a friend who's a graphic designer, and she can do them for you cheap and fast."

Liz took the stack of magazines from my hand and led

me down the hall. Her place had the same layout as ours, but Liz's apartment was painted bright white and filled with such a proliferation of white wicker—wicker chairs, wicker couches, wicker lamps, wicker picture frames—that it seemed as if the wicker had somehow mated and reproduced.

She directed me onto her balcony and sat me at the table made of—what else?—white wicker. "My God, your balcony is huge," I said. It was at least three times the size of ours.

"I know," Liz said. "It's the only one like it. Apparently, they built this one first, then started running out of money, so they scaled back the others."

"How long have you lived here?"

"Almost seven years. Jamey moved in last year when we got married."

"And what does Jamey do?" I wondered what her husband thought of living in a Pier One Imports store.

"He's a deejay. Need one for the wedding?"

"We're going with a jazz trio."

"Too bad. Well, here's Bridget's card." She handed me a heavily embossed business card in pale blue. "We'll call her while you're here. Do you know what style of invites you're looking for?"

"Definitely ivory, heavy paper, simple, elegant."

Liz went back inside to find her own invitations. She brought them out with a pitcher of iced tea and a basket of cookies in—surprise!—a wicker basket. A half hour later, we'd talked to her friend Bridget, who promised to meet me the next day and get the invitations done in a week. I pulled my dress designs out of my bag then and showed Liz. She gasped appreciatively at all of them. I smiled and thanked her for her help with the wedding, but silently I also thanked her for acting like a girlfriend, my first one in L.A.

★ ★ ★

We got it all done, somehow. Or I should say *I* got it all done. It wasn't that Declan didn't want to be involved, but he had the voice-over job, and even when I did give him a project to handle, it was never done exactly right.

"Sure," he'd say as he talked on the phone to the bartending service. "A hundred dollars a head sounds all right."

"For the booze?" I yelled from across the room, where I was on my cell phone with Rosita discussing the pattern for my dress.

I wasn't sure if he still had trouble converting dollars or if he just didn't have a good sense of negotiations (the latter, I learned, was the truth and the reason why actors have agents). I would have to grab the phone out of his hand and argue with the bartending service (or the limo company or the San Diego B and B) until we got a price we could afford to put on our credit cards. And so in the end, I did most of it myself.

Four nights before the wedding, Declan's best friends, Tommy and Colin, whom he called the Evil Twins, arrived from Dublin. Tommy and Colin weren't really twins but they looked very much alike—wiry, rock-hard bodies, sharp jawlines, green eyes—except for the fact that Tommy had red hair and Colin black. The resemblance between the two was helped out by the fact that they dressed, acted and talked precisely the same. They both had big, raucous laughs too booming for their bodies. They both wore faded jeans and big black boots. They were both outrageously flirtatious and could melt the hearts of even the coolest L.A. women (which they did continually during the days they were in town). And they both loved Declan like a brother.

"I can't believe you're marrying this jumped-up piece of shit," Tommy said to me the first day I met him. He had Declan in a headlock and was pounding on his shoulder in a way that looked painful, but Declan was only too happy to take their punishment.

"He's a little feck, he is," Colin said. Both he and Tommy let forth with their operatic laughs, punched Declan some more and kicked off their black boots.

It was the Evil Twins who indirectly caused the first real fight between Declan and me and made me realize that it's no fun being in a skirmish with Declan. Absolutely no fun. Not that I ever thought brawling with my old boyfriends was, technically, a walloping good time, but there was some satisfaction there. They would actually fight with me. Steven, especially, in his coked-up, alcoholic way would dramatically throw gin bottles and smash framed pictures. There was an order to our fights—the initial accusations, the yelling, the smashing, the crescendo and then eventually the promises to change and the electrifying make-up sex.

Declan, on the other hand, merely listened to me rail, announced that I was right, and promised that things would change. Where's the gratification in that?

The day the Evil Twins arrived, the four of us hung out on our balcony drinking beers and trading stories, but I could tell they needed guy-time, so I sent them off into the night and told them to have fun. At two in the morning, I woke up and started to wonder. At 4:00 a.m., I started to worry. By six, I was in an utter panic. It's the usual story—I called his cell phone and left ten million messages that progressed from a chipper, if slightly nervous, *"Hi, give me a buzz,"* to a bellowing, *"You asshole! If you don't call me to let me know you're okay, I'll call off the wedding!"*

By the time he strolled in with the Evil Twins at seven in the morning, all of them reeking of cigarettes and alcohol and Mexican food, I was on the phone with the police department, sure that he'd either been arrested for DUI or was in a body bag waiting for me to identify him.

The Evil Twins took one look at my bulging eyes and the prominent veins in my neck and ambled right back out the door to get coffee.

"Where the hell were you?" I screamed.

Declan paused, as if considering what the right answer might be. "Well, uh…" He stopped and began to yawn, but when he caught my expression, he clapped his mouth shut. "We went to the Whiskey," he said, "and then some other bar on Sunset, and then we left and got something to eat at—"

"I don't care where you were!" I yelled, although I realized somewhere in the back of my mind that I'd just demanded that information. "I want to know why you didn't call me to tell me you weren't dead! I thought you were on the side of the fucking road!"

For emphasis, I picked up the coffee mug Declan loved so much, the one that had been his grandfather's, and hurled it across the room. (It landed short of the wall and bounced lamely on the carpet, not even chipping). And then I waited for Declan to pounce back at me. I was a boxer in a ring, having landed the first blow, waiting to take one myself.

But instead, Declan said, "You're absolutely right," while he rubbed his red eyes in a desultory way. "I should have called. God, I'm sorry I made you worry."

"You should be!" I said, still yelling, although there was no reason.

"I'm so lucky to have you," he said, completely undefensive.

There was little else to say except, "Mmm, hmm. That's right. You *are* lucky." I looked around, but there was nothing else in proximity that would break if I threw it. And then I looked at Declan, who was so hungover, it was painful to gaze at him. "So anyway…" I said, itching for another point I could bring up, something I could shout about.

"You're the best, love," he said, pecking me on the cheek before he hustled into the bathroom to throw up.

chapter 12

On the morning of the wedding, Margaux came to my room. We were at the bed-and-breakfast, where most of the guests were staying as well. I felt as if I was hopped up on speed. My eyes were too big when I looked in the mirror; I was too aware, moving too fast.

"What's going on downstairs?" I asked her. The B and B served breakfast in their sunroom, and I knew Declan was probably there, along with our thirty or so guests.

"The twins are in the kitchen bugging the cook, and Declan is pacing around the lawn."

I peeked out the curtained window of my room, hoping for a glimpse of him, but saw nothing except the rubbery grass of the backyard.

"So are you sure you're ready to do this?" Margaux said. She flopped onto my bed and leaned back on her hands. She was wearing jeans and a white tank top over her too-thin frame, her fuzzy blondish-brown hair tousled around her head.

"What are you talking about?" I said, skittering around the room.

"You know. Do you want to do this so fast?"

I froze with my hand on the closet door, then spun around to face her. "Are you kidding? You *know* I want to do this. Why are you asking me this now?"

She shrugged and picked at the bedspread.

"Is it Peter?" I'd been friends with Margaux long enough to know that she often projected her worries, her concerns, her neuroses on to other people and their situations. We'd had fifteen years of friendship at that point, fifteen years since Margaux first cozied up to a bar stool near mine and gave me her story.

It was Christmas Eve, and we were both home from college in our junior year. We'd grown up only blocks from each other, but because she'd attended private schools and I public, we'd never met. I had gone to the bar that evening after the solitary celebration Emmie and I shared. Emmie had four brothers, and often we went to one of their places for the holidays, but she wanted to stay home that year. Having nothing better to do, I walked into the chilly night and landed at the corner bar, sitting on a stool, eating peanuts, making sporadic conversation with the bartender.

I was just about to leave when Margaux burst in. "I'll have gin and tonic," she said to the bartender, throwing her slouchy brown purse on the bar.

"Lemon or lime?" he said.

"Neither, and now that I think about it, hold the tonic, too."

The bartender gave her the drink. She took two gulps and turned toward me. "I hate my family."

I would later learn that her dad was a meek science professor at a private boys' school in the city, and her mother a perpetually depressed, passive-aggressive woman who said little, but was able to make scores of people unhappy. Her mother was the one with the money, having inherited it, and so the whole family kowtowed to her.

"Bad night?" I said.

"My mother is a freak. She wears her perfect dress and her perfect smile, but she's seething underneath, and we all tip-toe around her, hoping she won't blow. My father doesn't say a goddamn thing!" She took another sip of her drink. "Bad night for you, too, huh? Your parents are assholes, right?"

Before I could say that it wasn't so much bad as unevent-ful, maybe lonely, she was off again, complaining about her sisters and her paternal grandmother who all catered to her depressed, wealthy mother. By the end of the night, when Margaux had calmed down, I would tell her why I was there alone. I would tell her about Emmie and my parents' acci-dent.

Margaux and I moved from there right into a best-friend situation, as if our friendship had been sitting on the cor-ner of 92nd and 5th waiting for us to find it all along. She would go from college to traveling the world and finally to law school, where she would meet Peter, her Chinese hus-band, who was a brilliant man and an amazing dresser but had little sense of humor. I would attend my master's pro-gram and struggle with my designs. We would grow into adulthood together. But Margaux always had that same ten-dency I'd noticed that first night, to assume her problems were shared by most of the world.

So now, in my room on the morning of my wedding, I said, "What's up with Peter?"

"He's not coming."

"What?" Peter was supposed to fly in that morning, in time for the afternoon ceremony.

"He's got post-trial motions due. He says he can't get away. I'm sorry."

"It's okay," I said, which was absolutely true. Peter and I hung out when we had to because he was married to Margaux, but we would never have been friends without that connection. "I'm sorry for you," I said. "I know you were looking forward to getting some time alone with him."

"I was looking forward to getting pregnant!" She swiped away an angry tear. "How in the hell am I supposed to get knocked up if he's not here for me to have sex with?"

Silently, I wondered what kind of father Peter would be since he was never around. I sat next to Margaux on the bed. I rubbed her hand.

"We've got issues," she said.

"Then why are you trying to get pregnant?"

"Because it could change everything. I know that sounds crazed, but I think if we had a baby, everything would have to change."

"Maybe it should change *first*."

Margaux looked at me with a forlorn face. She had green-blue eyes that seemed as if they might spill over with more tears any minute. "I'm sorry," she said, starting to cry in earnest now. "I'm such a bad friend. It's your wedding. My God! Why didn't you tell me to shut up?"

I smoothed her hair. "Don't worry about it."

She brusquely wiped her eyes with her fingers. "All right. Enough of that. You're getting married today!"

"I know!" I shot up from the bed and back into my speed-addict mode. I dug in my suitcase for my earrings, but then remembered my mother's blue handkerchief I wanted to wrap around my flowers, and I ran over to my other bag and started rooting around for that.

"Kyr," I heard Margaux say from the bed.

"Yeah?" I had just remembered my new lacy, white La Perla underwear. Where was that? Had I unpacked it already?

"Kyr, stop," Margaux said.

I swung around. "What? What?"

"You're going to be a stunning bride, you know that? And you and Declan are going to live happily ever after. You're going to be the ones who do it."

"I know," I said.

Margaux shot off the bed and hugged me.

You've probably seen the wedding photos already. It was that asshole photographer who sold them to the magazines.

He was a short little guy, who was insistent in terms of price and his "vision" for the photographs. I didn't care about his height, of course, and I took the insistence in stride, assuming that he, like Dec and myself, was trying to make a living at his art. I wanted to help him out, and honestly, I didn't care what angles he shot the photos from. Yet later I would see him not so much as short and insistent but as a Napoleonic, wheedling, opportunistic prick. He showed us the proofs about four weeks after the wedding, and he actually sent all the photos we picked out, but the negatives were absent. When Dec hit it big with *Normandy,* the Napoleonic photographer stopped answering my calls. A few weeks later, the photos appeared in three magazines.

So, you've probably seen the shot of me walking down the aisle with Emmie, who was leaning heavily on her cane and dressed in an ivory cashmere sweater and a long golden skirt I'd designed. You might have seen the shot of her leaning in to kiss my cheek and whisper in my ear, "My sweetheart, my little girl, I want you to always hold on to the love you two have. Hold on very, very tight."

You've probably also seen Declan standing by his best men, the Evil Twins, all three of them handsome in rented black tuxes, the twins with green-and-yellow-plaid bow ties I couldn't talk them out of. And you've probably seen

Margaux, as my matron of honor, and all the guests like Bobby and Aunt Donna and Declan's agent, Max. Although I was horrified when those photos were splashed across the magazines, I secretly hoped that people at least liked my dress, with its gathered chiffon bodice and silky, flowing skirt. I hoped everyone noticed how happy we were in those photos, how our eyes gleamed bright, our smiles stretched wide.

The photo I often study most is the one of Declan and me during our first dance on the lawn. In the background, you see our friends—Emmie holding Bobby's arm for support, Margaux laughing with the Evil Twins, Liz Morgan and her husband—but most importantly I hope you see how blissful we were as we looked into each other's eyes, how content. I stare at that photo often because I am now acutely aware that it was one of the few moments of peace Declan and I had before the circus invaded our lives.

chapter 13

After the wedding, a whole new kind of busyness set in. We had a short honeymoon at the B and B in La Jolla, where we talked of little else but the wedding and the shenanigans at the reception. (Like Margaux getting rip-roaring drunk and propositioning Tommy. In the bathroom, I had to convince her that her plan to get "knocked up" by the carrot-topped Tommy and then trying to pass off the baby as her Chinese husband's wouldn't be prudent.) When we got home, we had thank-you notes to write, we had unpacking to do, we had backloads of laundry to haul to the basement washer.

We also had to devise a plan to dig us out of debt to the caterers, the band, the B and B and, of course, the Napoleonic-asshole-photographer-who-would-later-betray-us. In order to do this, Dec's friend who managed the Groundlings theater gave him a job working the box office. For my part, Rosita helped get me a freelance gig at one of the fabric trade shows downtown. Mostly, I stood behind a booth of suede swatches and looked pretty, but I felt happy to be anywhere near the fashion world, happy to be contributing incomewise, happy to be married. In the downtimes, I sat behind the booth and scribbled menu items for a Thanksgiving dinner for Declan and me. I thought about Christmas coming up in a month, how I would decorate the whole apartment with all the kitschy holiday crap I'd collected over the years.

The premiere for *Normandy* was imminent, too, only a few days after Thanksgiving, although Declan was expecting even less from this film than the recently released one with Lauren Stapleton. (That movie had completely tanked at the box office, which saddened me on behalf of Declan yet made me maliciously gleeful when I thought of Lauren.)

No matter what Dec said about *Normandy,* though, I was looking forward to it, because for the first time, he had the lead role. *Normandy* was a World War II movie that was actually made before the film with Lauren, but wasn't released until later because of concerns about the political climate in the U.S. and whether the public would embrace a war story. The director, Kaz Lameric, is a big-name Hollywood director, but for some reason he had a hard time getting a studio interested in the film. He'd put up a large sum of his own money, took a risk on a relative unknown like Declan, spent years making it, and now the movie was finally opening.

In short, life had returned to blissful normality following the wedding. I've gone back and counted the days. There were sixteen days when we were like anyone else—planning the holidays, worrying about money, juggling our opposite schedules. I can't say that everything shifted massively when *Normandy* came out, but certainly that was the cataclysmic event in our lives. Did we sense it even a little as we got ready for the premiere that night? Did I notice any tremors in the earth as I applied pink lip gloss with a tiny wand? Did I feel it even a little as I put on my vintage 1940s dress with the atomic print, which I thought might be perfect for the event? Did Declan know when he came behind me in the mirror and kissed my neck?

I think the answer, unfortunately, is no. But I wish we had wondered that night. I wish we'd had some inkling that it was all about to change. Because I might have stopped worrying about my shoe choice. I might have taken one last look around the apartment before we left so I could remember the basic, boring, *wonderful* life we had just started to create.

The premiere for *Normandy* was similar to the one for Declan's movie with Lauren, in that the red carpet was rather short (it was also rather orange-looking and thin, too), and although there were photographers and reporters and a few curious fans lined up outside the theater, it wasn't out of control.

Maybe it was simply that Declan and I were slightly more used to the flashing cameras, the shouted questions, the occasional scream from a fan. I felt perfectly comfortable in my atomic-print dress, knowing Lauren and her oatmeal skyscraperness weren't about to swoop in and insult me.

Declan, too, had prepared better for this premiere. I noticed that he had answers ready for the reporters. Yes, he said at least fifteen times, it was a privilege to work with someone like Kaz Lameric. It was an experience he'd never forget. And yes, it was an honor to play the part of a heroic World War II veteran, and then he'd quip, "Although I wasn't so thrilled to be playing a Brit." That got smiles from the reporters, while I stood to his side, chuckling each time like a trained monkey.

This time, no one asked who I was wearing, but that was fine with me. It was Declan's night, and I was content in the background.

We were shown to our seats in a special section of the theater. Kaz Lameric was already there, and he and Declan hugged and thumped each other on the back enthusiastically. Declan introduced me as "his wife," which made me stand taller. I loved it when he said that. I was throwing around the word *husband* like crazy, too. I whipped it out in grocery stores ("Can you please give me a little more turkey? My husband goes through it like crazy") and whenever people complimented me on my ring ("My husband chose it himself"). *Husband* was a magical word, I'd discovered. Simply say it, and I perked up like a cut flower placed in water.

Kaz Lameric and I made brief conversation before the movie started. He was a shorter, powerful-looking man with gray hair combed back and thick, black eyeglasses. "Kyra, it's lovely to meet you," he said, holding my hand lightly but looking into my eyes with an intensity that was gripping. "And let me tell you something about your husband." That word again. I nodded eagerly and leaned toward him.

"The movie is better than they think," he said, "and *he's* better than they know." He nodded sagely at Declan. I could see that the rumors about Kaz's magnetism were true, but I found his spin doctoring a little sad. There weren't big hopes for the movie, after all. It seemed as if he was trying to convince himself.

I told him how nice it was to meet him and took my seat next to Declan. When the movie started, I was thinking about the fabric show, and what time I'd have to get up the next morning. The opening credits didn't help—white letters on a black screen, while classical music, which was haunting and fairly sleep-inducing, played in the background.

I was rooting through my purse for lip gloss when I

heard a collective gasp from the audience. I looked up to see the opening shot—a panoramic view of a battlefield littered with bodies of soldiers, while one British soldier stood alone. Slowly, the camera closed in on him, on Declan, and his weeping face.

Declan's voice, in a British accent, filled the theater. *Five days can change a man,* he said. *It can rip from his life what he holds most dear, and yet those days can teach him something. Powerful lessons he might never have learned.*

The camera swept away, the image of the battlefield twisted and swirled and was replaced by a scene of joking British soldiers preparing to leave for the shores of Normandy. Declan's character, William Huntington, is quickly established as the smiling, laughing life of the party, the one the other soldiers respect and emulate. He is shallow, the early scenes show, and somewhat haughty and quick to judge people, but a good guy underneath.

The happy scenes quickly end when the troop tries to reach the shores of Normandy. William's best buddy, Randolph, is killed, along with many others, a loss that turns William violent and angry. After much bloodshed, they finally make their way to land, where William is sent off by his commanding officer to take a message to an American general. William resents the assignment, which he sees as making him simply an errand boy. He wants to stay with his platoon and fight, but the commanding officer insists. William stomps off into the French countryside, handsome and angry.

It was at this point I dragged my eyes away from the screen and glanced at Declan, because the man on-screen didn't look like my husband. I looked back and noticed how his face was scrunched up in an irritated, British sort of way. I had assumed, by that time in our relationship, that I knew every expression Declan possessed, but I barely recognized the man in that shot.

I turned to Dec again. "You're amazing," I said. "I'm in awe."

Declan's face broke into a huge grin. "You like it then?"

"It's stunning."

This wasn't some statement made by a wife to bolster her husband. The film was shot beautifully, and the editing was perfection—the touching scenes lingering, the battle scenes choppy and harsh. Most of all, Declan was unbelievable. He was evocative, he was gorgeous, he was real. The movie with Lauren hadn't allowed him much range. I'd had no idea how fantastic an actor he was.

The movie continued. Trials and tribulations abound while William tries to locate the American regiment. When he does, the Americans encounter gunfire, and William is forced to fight side by side with the foreign troops. Without the men he was trained with, he feels lost, and he has to learn to rely on the American men. In a particularly poignant scene, William puts himself in the line of fire to save Tim, an American who had befriended him. Unfortunately, he fails to save him, and Tim dies in his arms. William, himself, suffers a shoulder wound, which he nurses as he eventually makes his way back to his own unit. When he reaches them, he finds that they have all been killed. He would have died as well if he hadn't been sent on that mission.

The movie ended where it started—with William's voice-over, while he gazes at the sea of bodies, wondering about the randomness of life and the lessons that one is sometimes forced to learn. The last shot of William's face tugged hard at my insides, not because my husband was weeping on-screen, but because it *wasn't* my husband. Declan had transformed himself, somehow. He was William Huntington. He was a heartbroken shell of a man.

When the lights went on, I covered my face.

"What is it?" Dec said, putting his arm around me.

I didn't want to cry, but I couldn't help it. Partly it was the movie, the staggering losses that William went through, but partly it was Declan, too. I was so proud of him, so unbelievably proud I thought I might combust. I couldn't believe I was married to him.

"Tell me," Declan said. "What do you think? Did you like the ending?"

"You were amazing," I said.

"Yeah?" His golden-brown eyes were glittery, excited. I knew how much this meant to him. Although he wanted fame and fortune, it wasn't as important as critical acceptance.

I glanced around at the rest of the theater and saw a number of people dabbing at their eyes, saying, "Oh, my God." I think I knew then that Declan would get everything he wanted.

Part Three

chapter 14

Lydia, one of my New York friends, called the day after the *Normandy* premiere. She had given birth three weeks before, and although I'd been leaving messages, this was the first time we'd spoken since she'd become a mom. She was mostly elated, she said, but she was exhausted and overwhelmed, too.

"Sometimes, I just want to throw him across the room," Lydia said, "and other times, like when I watch him sleep, I could cry because I'm so overwhelmed with love."

"I feel that way about Declan," I said.

"Which part? The throwing across the room or the crying with love?"

"Both."

There was silence. "I think it's a little different," she said.

"Maybe." But I didn't think so. I was as proud of Declan, as enamored with him, as if I'd created him myself.

A couple of days later, *Normandy* had its official box-office release. On that Friday morning, Dec and I got up early, knowing the reviews would be out. We bought every newspaper we could find on our way to the coffee shop. Since my work at the fabric show had ended the day before, I was back to taking care of loose ends, glad to have a purpose.

"I'm dying to look," I said to Dec as we stood in line and ordered, an espresso for me, a regular black for him.

"I feel sick," he said.

He was a little pale that morning, the way he got when he was truly nervous. He'd been running on a high since the premiere. I had loved the film, everyone at the premiere had loved it, but Declan knew that his wife and the people who attended it were *supposed* to love it. They were supposed to tell him what he needed to hear. Now, he wanted the official nod from the critics.

We took our drinks and our stacks of papers to a sidewalk table. It was vividly sunny. Because we both wore sunglasses, I couldn't see his eyes.

"Now?" I said, holding the *New York Times*.

Declan rubbed his jaw. He took a sip of his coffee. "Fuck, that's hot."

"Honey." I leaned over and took the coffee away from him. "Can I look?" I was bursting to read the reviews.

"All right, love. You look. Tell me if there's anything I need to see."

"Got it." I gave a sharp nod of my head, like a sergeant who's just received an order from his major. I flipped and found the section I needed, then flipped again, looking for the review.

"Oh boy," I said when I saw the headline.

"What? What? Is it bad? It's horrible, isn't it?"

I skimmed the article, my pulse pounding faster.

"Read it," I said, handing it to him.

Will Oscar Come Calling?

Normandy is the gut-wrenching chronicle of William Huntington, an upper-class British soldier who learns lessons about humanity and acceptance when he's made to fight alongside American troops. This could be trite stuff, but Declan McKenna, an Irish actor new to American films, plays the part of Huntington to sheer perfection. We laugh with him when he's a cad, we feel enraged for him when he loses his best friend, and we can't help but bat away a tear when he discovers what awaits him after he makes his way back to his brigade…

…Adapted from a quiet novel of the same title, which was only released in the U.K., *Normandy* should bring a wave of Oscar nominations, not only for the infamous Kaz Lameric, who poured so much of his directorial soul (and his own hard cash) into this film, but also for newcomer McKenna, whose acting is subtle and yet complex. He paints a harrowing individual picture of war and heroism, which calls to mind Tom Hanks and Daniel Day-Lewis.

"I'm subtle and complex?" Declan said. He waved the paper around like a winning ticket at the horse track.

"You're harrowing!" I said.

"Shit. Holy shit." He bounced in his chair. He gulped the coffee, seeming not to notice the scalding heat this time. "Find another one."

I leafed through *Variety*.

A Gloriously Bloody Mess

Normandy, Kaz Lameric's long-delayed epic, takes on culture clashes, politics and friendship during the Normandy invasion and ends up a gloriously bloody delight. In short, posh Brit William Huntington, played by Irishman Declan McKenna, takes an assignment to deliver a message to an American general—a task that seems to him cowardly and distasteful—but his journey to the American troops and back is anything but spineless. The film, which was more than three years in production, falls somewhat short in the history department (example, one of the American soldiers is wearing eyeglasses that weren't stylistically born until the 1960s, and a visit by General Eisenhower is premature since he wasn't at Normandy until many days after the invasion), yet this is still a richly impressive and densely realized work that opens the eye and mind to the often overlooked aspects of a soldier's life. By far the best performance in the film is delivered by McKenna, who has the wit and charm to play the early hapless soldier, and the exceptional range to play a man changed and aged after only five days. He surely deserves an Oscar nomination.

Declan put the paper down and gazed at me across the table. "Holy shit," he said again.

"Yeah," I said.

We read through the rest of the papers as fast as we could. Without fail, they all praised Declan.

"What do I do now?" Declan said. He sat amid a pile of newspapers. "I mean, what am I supposed to do now?"

We were both so excited that we were looking around at the other patrons, looking back at each other, looking at the papers.

"I feel like we should tell someone," I said. "Let's call your parents." We'd planned a trip to Dublin to visit them soon, but I still hadn't had much contact with them.

"Good," Dec said, seizing on the idea. But then he glanced at his watch. "It's Friday. They'll be at the pub."

"We have to do something to celebrate! Is there a pub open around here?"

We glanced up and down Washington Boulevard with its

surf shops and convenience stores and restaurants. Many of the restaurants were closed until lunch.

"I got it," I said. I gathered up the papers and led Declan to a convenience store where I bought a bottle of champagne. We brought it to the beach and popped the cork.

"I hope we don't get arrested," Dec said, drinking from the bottle and passing it to me.

"Who the hell cares?" I took a gulp and nearly coughed up champagne foam. "You're 'subtle and exceptional'!" I yelled.

"I deserve an Oscar nomination!" Dec shouted.

We passed the bottle back and forth and finally lay back on the sand, letting the sun shine happily upon us.

An hour later, we walked back to our place, tipsy and lazy and floating on Dec's new success. We decided we would take a nap, then have a late lunch at C&O's on Washington, followed by shopping at Fred Segal (where I wanted to use some of the money I'd earned at the fabric show to buy Declan a celebratory present).

By the time we got back to the apartment, there were eighteen messages on our machine and another ten on Declan's cell phone. Some were from friends who had read the reviews, a few were from newspaper reporters, and most were from Declan's agent, Max.

"Christ, you'd think he'd be happy," Declan said, listening to the fifth voice mail from Max.

"Why? What's he saying?" I was sitting on the couch clipping the reviews from the papers.

"He's in a bloody panic." Declan shook his head and dialed a number. "Max? It's Declan," he said. "Yeah, well thanks, I thought they were great, too, and..." He trailed off, nodding as he listened to Max. "Why would I need a publicist? Hmm. Okay." He listened some more, pacing around the living room. "Right. Well, I think that's premature, don't you? I've got you for that." Another pause. "Well, if you think so. I'll make some calls on Monday." More pacing. "Today? I suppose so."

Eventually, he got off the phone and sank onto the end of the couch. I had most of the reviews cut out by then and arranged in a pile on the coffee table.

"He's hired a PR firm for me," he said.

"Wow. That's incredible. But shouldn't Kaz and the movie do that?"

"Too small a budget, and Max says he's got more requests for appearances than he can handle."

"What do you mean, appearances?" I said, folding a newspaper back into order.

"TV shows, I guess, like *The Tonight Show.*"

I dropped the newspaper and looked up at him. *"The Tonight Show?"*

Dec nodded. His eyes were big and unblinking, as if his pupils had suddenly been dilated. He looked slightly scared.

"Oh my God!" I leaped over the papers and jumped into his lap.

"I can't believe it," he said, "and Max thinks I should get a manager. He says it won't be just about blind auditions for me anymore. He says I need a manager who can produce for me and think more globally about my career."

"So you're going global?" I teased, nibbling on his earlobe. "I think we should celebrate that."

He growled and kissed me, and soon we were half-naked on the couch. But then Dec's cell phone rang. We ignored it. It rang again, and again.

"Christ," Declan said, raising himself off me and looking at the display on the phone. "It's Max. He's never going to stop."

He flipped open the phone. "Yeah," he said. He nodded while he listened to Max. "I will, I will," he said. "Yes, I'll do that right now." He sighed and sank back onto the other side of the couch.

"You are *not* going to leave me in this condition, are you?" I said. My bra was hanging around my neck and I had only one leg of my running pants on.

"I'm sorry, love," Dec said. "Max says I've got to call these managers today and get interviews with them, and then talk to the PR person he hired."

"Okay, you can do that in five minutes." I pulled him by the hand back to my side of the couch. "I'm fast when I have to be."

"God, you make me crazy," he said, the weight of him falling on me again, his lips on my collarbone. The sun was streaking in the sliding glass doors. The apartment was deliciously hot.

But then the phones started ringing again. Both of them this time.

I laughed. "The sex gods apparently want us to wait."

"They're such arseholes," Dec said, reaching for his cell phone and looking at the display. "Max again."

I got up and showered. I cleaned the apartment while Declan's phone conversations went on and on.

Finally, he took a break. "This is mad," he said. But he looked thrilled, standing in the kitchen shaking his head.

I went to him and kissed him on the nose. "I am so happy for you. Now, can we go to C&O's? I'm starving."

"Love, I can't. Max has already set up two interviews for me, and I've got to meet with those managers. You'll have to go without me."

"What about Fred Segal? I want to buy you something ludicrously overpriced."

Dec looked at his watch. "How about I meet you there at six? In the café?"

"Deal," I said.

On my way downstairs, Liz Morgan popped her head out of her apartment. "Kyra!" she yelled. "Declan's reviews. They're amazing!" She was wearing a suit in an angry red-orange color with a horrible boxy cut. In her hands, she held a copy of *Variety.*

"I know," I said. "We can hardly believe it."

"Where's Declan? I've got to congratulate him."

"He's on the phone. He's got a million things to do today."

"Well, tell him I'm thrilled."

"I will. Do you have time to get lunch at C&O's?"

"Oh, honey, I wish. I've got this audition for a commercial. I'm supposed to be a businesswoman with constipation. What do you think?" She twirled around in the angry, boxy suit.

"Perfect," I said honestly.

I spent a lazy lunch eating outside and scouring the papers for any other reviews of *Normandy.* I still had hours until I had to meet Dec at Fred Segal, so I drove to Abbot Kinney Boulevard and spent a few hours strolling. I liked the street with its antique stores, trippy little clothing boutiques, pizza stands and vegetarian restaurants. I bought a large old hatbox papered in blue-and-white toile so we would have some place to keep Declan's reviews. I put it in the trunk of my car and headed to Fred Segal.

I was a half hour early to meet Dec, so I ordered a glass of wine and called Bobby from my cell phone.

His assistant answered, but he put me through right away.

"Kyr," Bobby said, "I've been meaning to call you all day. The buzz about Declan is off the hook."

"I know. Can you believe it?"

"No, I mean seriously off the hook," he said. "Everyone over here is talking about it, and you better tell Declan that I'm calling him soon. William Morris wants him."

"But he's already got an agent. He has Max."

Bobby scoffed. "Max is two-bit. Declan needs to be with a big-time agency now."

I squirmed uncomfortably in my chair. "I don't think he's going to make changes like that anytime soon."

"Are you kidding, Kyr? *Everything* is going to change for him. It's a whole different ball game."

"Not necessarily."

"Trust me on this. I know what I'm talking about."

I took a sip of my wine and didn't say anything.

"Look, I don't mean to freak you out," Bobby said, "but don't be surprised if Declan's not around much anymore. He's going to be pulled in a lot of different directions."

"Jesus, Bobby. It's a movie! Just a movie. And he was great in it. He'll have some different opportunities now, but we'll take it one day at a time." I glugged more of my wine.

"All right. Whatever you say. Hey, what are you doing tonight? I can get out of here in about fifteen minutes. Want to have a drink?"

"I'm meeting Dec, but thanks. I'll call you tomorrow."

"Tell Declan I'll be calling him, too."

After I got off the phone with Bobby, I ordered another glass of wine for myself and one for Declan.

Six o'clock came and went, and still Declan wasn't there. The café was full by then. "Would you like to at least order appetizers?" the waitress said, annoyed, no doubt, that I was commandeering the table only to swig sauvignon blanc by my lonesome.

"No thanks," I said. The thought of food was wholly unappealing. It would sober me up.

As six-thirty neared, I pulled Declan's glass of wine toward me and dialed his cell phone number. It went to his voice mail.

At six forty-five, I paid the bill and drank the last of Dec's wine. Feeling light-headed and drunk and pissed off at being stood up, I wandered through the stores. I was in a destructive mood. I fingered a hand-blown glass bowl with a price tag of six hundred dollars. I was torn between smashing it or buying it.

Behind the counter, the clerk was watching a small TV while she folded linen napkins. I was about to turn away, when something caught my eye. I focused in on the TV's tiny screen, and saw my husband's face.

chapter 15

I was sitting on our balcony, another glass of wine in front of me, when Declan bounded noisily into the apartment.

"Kyr!" he yelled. "Kyra?"

I heard him tromp into the bedroom, then the bathroom. I stayed silent, fixing a steely, *you-asshole* expression on my face. Finally, he peeked his head out the sliding glass doors.

"I am so sorry, love," he said. "You have every right to leave me for good, but please, please don't." He walked around the table to my chair and sank to his knees, clasping my hands.

I stayed silent, watching him. He looked freakishly alive and legitimately remorseful at the same time. His hair was a little crazy, his eyebrows furrowed and…did he have makeup on?

"Look," he said, "I've been in meetings all day with managers. And I have to decide which one I want to go with. *I* have to decide. I mean, do you get that? I've never been the one to decide anything since I was in this business. You just beg people to take you on, and they say, 'We'll see.' But here are these guys who've worked with everyone, asking *me* to work with *them*."

A little flame of happiness flickered at his news, but I mentally extinguished it. "So what does this have to do with the fact that you stood up your wife?"

"Okay, get this. After I met with all these managers at Max's office, I went to the *Entertainment Tonight* set and…" He got off his knees and stood up with his hands outstretched, as if he were singing the last number of a Broadway musical.

Again, that flame of excitement. "And?" I said.

"I did an interview!" He opened his hands wider.

My heart leaped for him. I wanted to squeal. But I couldn't let him off the hook. "And?" I said again, a little testier this time.

"And my cell phone died, and then after I left, I had to meet the publicists. They were making all these plans. It's crazy what they're saying, and the time just got away from me. I'm so sorry, love. I truly am. I wish you could have been with me."

"Yeah, me, too," I said sarcastically.

"I'm an egregious arsehole. I don't deserve you. Please forgive me."

I sighed. I pined for Steven, who would defensively throw a lit candle at my head. "I saw part of the interview."

"You did? What did you think?"

"You were handsome and charming," I said grudgingly.

"Thank you, Kyr. And I honestly am sorry. Will you forgive me?"

I crossed my leg and swung it back and forth, turning to stare out at the ocean. "I've got one question for you," I said. "Did you meet Mary Hart?"

As an adolescent, I hadn't watched much television, since Emmie didn't own a set, but I had a junior-high friend named Colleen, who'd been strangely fascinated with Mary Hart. It had something to do with the rumors that the sound of Hart's voice could send dogs barking and electrical equipment malfunctioning. Whenever I was at Colleen's house, we watched *Entertainment Tonight,* and held Colleen's little terrier in front of the TV to see if he'd go insane. The poor dog was annoyed, but never suicidal.

"I met her briefly," Declan said.

"What's she like?"

"Unbelievably, scarily positive. I wonder what she's like at funerals."

"What about her hair?"

"Rather like a helmet, but quite nice."

"And what did you tell her about your love life?"

"Well, I didn't tell her anything, she didn't do the interview. Some bloke did. But I told him that I had a wife who was a brilliant fashion designer and the sweetest, most adorable woman on the planet."

I stood up. "All right, now you can take me to dinner."

On Monday, Declan hired a manager named Graham Truro. Graham had started his career as an assistant for a very young Robert Redford. He eventually rose to the role of Redford's manager, and later took on everyone from Goldie Hawn to Brad Pitt. Graham looked more like a school principal than a Hollywood manager. He wore suits that appeared to have been bought off the rack at Target and ties that were perpetually stained with coffee. He was balding like a monk, and he had a large red nose, which made me wonder if he put too much Kahlua in his coffee. And yet Graham Truro had shrewd eyes and, I would later learn, an even shrewder mind.

Graham's skill was not just in handling actors or considering what projects might be good for them. No, the skill

Graham Truro was known for was being able to chart the potential trajectory of a star and being able to take that star even higher. He mused over what role a star should have next, then packaged that movie and made sure the star got it. He glad-handed and wheeled 'n' dealed and sold his soul to get his stars the roles, the movies, the images he thought they deserved.

The first thing Graham did for Declan was work with the PR people and Kaz Lameric's company to set up press junkets for *Normandy,* which would allow TV and newspaper reporters to interview the actors and directors. Normally, such events would have taken place before the movie came out, but because of the low budget and the low expectations, none had been arranged. Now there would be a local one in L.A. After the holidays, international junkets would follow in Tokyo, London, Rome and Cannes, all accompanied by premieres in those cities.

The first one took place at the Beverly Hills Hotel. I spent most of that week watching the interviews of Declan on TV. He was on the morning shows; he was on the noon news; he was on the entertainment "news" programs. I taped these shows religiously, marking each one with the name of the show, the date and the approximate time Dec was on. Meanwhile, I sat on the couch and perused magazines and newspapers, clipping out items about Dec and how he was the "new hot property" in Hollywood.

I was thrilled for him, but I missed him. Between Max and Graham and the PR people and the seemingly hundreds of others who now wanted a piece of him, he was busier than he had ever been in his life. I grew lonely in the apartment, but it wasn't solely because I was there by myself. It had more to do with the chilly realization that I didn't know my husband as well as I had thought. Oh, I don't mean that he wasn't devoted when he got home, or that he was acting differently. What I mean is that I truly didn't know as much about Dec as I'd assumed I did, and this became painfully obvious watching him being interviewed on all those shows.

"What is your ultimate goal, in terms of acting?" he was asked by the *Today Show* correspondent.

"Theater is my passion," Declan answered. On the screen, he sat on a black director's chair, a *Normandy* movie poster behind him. "And so my ultimate goal would be to write a play and star in it."

I blinked a few times from my position on the couch. *That* was his big acting goal? Why didn't I know that? Or had I heard it and forgotten?

"And in your dream world," the interviewer continued, "what theater would be lucky enough to get this play?"

Somewhere on Broadway, I thought.

"Somewhere in Dublin," Declan said.

And later, I saw Declan being interviewed by the blonde on *E! News Daily*. "So, Dec," she said chummily. I had noticed that chummy and irreverent was this woman's M.O. "You've been linked with Lauren Stapleton, who's such a great actress."

"Ha!" I shouted from the couch.

"And I know you've worked with her," the chummy blonde said. "But if you could work with any actress in the world right now, who would it be?"

Declan made a show of pulling on his chin as if this was a tough, tough question. Jesus, if he says he wants to work with Lauren again, I thought, I will move out right now.

"Katharine Hepburn," he said with finality. "I wish I could have been acting while she was here."

"Huh," I said. I had no idea he was a fan of hers. I apparently had no idea about so many things in Dec's head.

"But wait a minute," the chummy blonde said, interrupting Declan's poetic riff about the late Ms. Hepburn. "I said, 'right now.' If you had to work with any woman *right now,* who would it be?"

"*Any* woman?" Dec said, shifting in his seat. Was he flirting with the chummy blonde? "Well, then I'd have to make my wife an actress, because truly she's the only woman I want to work with."

I sat up straighter on the couch and smiled. Maybe I didn't know everything about him, but I'd heard what I needed.

Two weeks after *Normandy* came out, I got a call from my ex-boyfriend, Steven. Emmie had given him my number. Emmie always liked Steven because he was charming and would stay up all night listening to her stories about working with authors like Britton Matthews and Mackenzie Bresner. I realized later that Steven was probably so charming and able to stay up so late because of the coke habit he hid relatively well, but I never told Emmie that. And I never told her about that last big fight Steven and I had.

In fact, Steven and I hadn't spoken since two weeks after that fight when I went back to his apartment to gather my shoes from his closet, my makeup from his bathroom drawer.

"Don't forget this," he'd said with sarcasm, holding aloft a lace thong with one finger. He was dressed all in black that day—black pants, black long-sleeved T-shirt and a black baseball cap. He looked like a modern-day Satan.

When I went to take it from him, he held it high over my head.

"Jump," he said, a sneer on his face.

"Fuck you." I turned and left the apartment.

But years had passed by the time I got his call in L.A. It was one o'clock in the afternoon, and I had just come in from visiting Rosita with a design for a gauzy slip dress. I told Rosita that the dress was something I wanted to wear to one of the many events Dec now had on his calendar, but the truth was, I hoped to try to make the dress part of my new collection. I hadn't admitted that to Rosita, though, and not even to Declan, because it was such a toss-up as to whether the line would sell. I would develop it—maybe four dresses, three different blouses, a few skirts and some pants. I would beg and plead buyers from department stores, boutiques and catalogs to view the clothes. And then I would wait to see if anyone was in a buying mood. If not, all that work would have been for naught, something I was all too familiar with.

When I came back from seeing Rosita that day, I couldn't stop thinking about all the collections I had designed before that didn't make it. Would this be yet another in that long tradition?

I took off my structured white shirt and black gabardine slacks. I changed into a pair of shorts and one of Declan's T-shirts and sat on the balcony. I had the phone on the table with me, but lately I'd been letting voice mail pick up. The calls were so rarely for me. Yet I felt a deep desire for human contact of any kind right then, so when the phone rang, I snatched it immediately.

"Felicity," Steven said. It had been his nickname for me, a play on my last name.

"Jesus, what are you doing?" I said. I couldn't help but smile a little. I was needy, and I was all too happy to let time work its magic, leaving behind more good memories than bad. In that instant, I remembered when Steven and I first dated, and how his voice on the phone could make me smile. I remembered how he used to study my designs and make incisive comments I didn't expect from him. I remembered the linguine with lemon cream sauce he would make for us when he got home from the bar.

"I'm calling you," he said. "It's been too long."

"Oh, I don't think it's been long enough."

He laughed. "God, you were always a pain in the ass."

"Me? Don't get me started, Steven."

"Yeah, right. So what's going on out there? I can't believe you abandoned New York."

"Love makes you do strange things."

"So you're in love, huh?"

"I'm married."

"Maybe you're not aware, but love and marriage don't always equate."

"In this case they do."

"Yeah?"

"Oh, yeah."

"Well, I'm glad for you, Felicity."

"Thanks," I said, because I believed him. He sounded calmer than I remembered, somehow older and wiser.

We talked for at least twenty minutes. We caught up on each other's friends and families. Steven promised to look in on Emmie for me. I told him about L.A., how I loved certain things—the ocean, my jogs around Venice, Declan. I told him how I *didn't* love so many other things—the driving, the annoying newness of the city, the "business" everyone was in but me.

"You'll just have to come back to New York for a visit," Steven said.

I'd been thinking the same thing. I wanted to take Declan to visit Emmie. I wanted to wash L.A. from my hair, even if it was for only a few days. The problem was that the holidays were looming, we were leaving for Dublin after Christmas, and Declan had so many other things on his plate right now. But Steven's words had struck their mark.

"Maybe we will," I said. "I'm really dying to get back to Manhattan."

"Absolutely. Come home for a while, and come to my place."

"You've opened a new bar?"

"A bar *and* restaurant," he said proudly. "It's called Jasmine. It's French Vietnamese. You've got to see it."

"That's fantastic. I'd like to check it out."

"You'd bring Declan, too. Right?" It was the first time that Steven had said my husband's name, and something about his simpatico tone rang false.

"Most likely," I said, wary.

"It would really help me out, Kyra."

"What would?" I stood up from the table and put a hand on the balcony railing, feeling a sudden alarm.

"If you could bring Declan here, I'd get a lot of pub, you know? It would mean a lot to me."

I brought the hand to my head, and squeezed my eyes shut. "You're unbelievable. You know that? You called me because of Declan, didn't you?"

A tiny pause erupted in the conversation. I knew I was right.

"No," Steven said. "I don't even know what you're saying."

"Yes, you do! Jesus, Steven!" I don't know why I was so hurt. I shouldn't have expected any more from him, but a zing of pain hit me just the same.

"Kyra, don't get all emotional. I'm just asking a favor."

"And I'm just telling you to fuck off."

A couple days later, Dec and I attended a cocktail party in Malibu thrown by his new manager in Dec's honor. It was so exciting to be there, with Dec in the spotlight among all these important Hollywood types, but all night I noticed something different about the way Dec was speaking. Too quickly, it seemed at first, then with more of an Irish lilt than usual. But I was being towed around by Graham's wife, Sherry (a woman who had to be a few years younger than I and, therefore, about thirty years younger than Graham), introductions were being made, and so I really only orbited Dec during most of the party.

Finally, I was able to excuse myself and go to the bathroom, a stark white space with a wall of windows overlooking the Pacific. I stared outside for a while, wondering at the velocity with which Declan (and by default, I) had been invited to a place where even the toilets had ocean views.

When I came out, I saw Declan talking to Max and three other people. One guy, who was in his forties and bore a resemblance to John Belushi, I'd been told was a studio president that Declan had always wanted to meet. The woman next to him was his wife. The other man was in his sixties, someone I didn't recognize, which was not surprising since I know so few people in this industry.

The whole group was laughing at Declan, at a story he was telling. Dec quickly introduced me to everyone, and went back to the story.

"It's the truth," he said, "people in Dublin can swear better than any people on this earth."

I'd heard him say this before. In fact, Declan could rattle off strings of profanities in the most creative ways, and he insisted that his talent was minimal compared to the rest of the Dubliners. But it was the way he had spoken the sentence that was odd. "Truth" sounded like "troot," and "Dublin" sounded like "Dooblin." And suddenly his speech was peppered with questions instead of statements. ("Didn't I, now? Didn't I grow up only a stone's throw from the River Liffey?")

But why was he doing it? To entertain the crowd? That seemed to be it. Max chuckled happily. The studio president gestured toward someone else at the party ("Ya gotta hear this!" he said), and soon there were four other people huddled close to Declan. People cocked their ears because when that brogue got heavy it became even harder to understand, and yet they were all smiling that isn't-he-charming smile, giving each other looks, knowing they would be relating this story to everyone they ran across tomorrow.

How strange it was to listen to him talk like that, as if someone else, some enhanced version of my husband, had inhabited his body.

At one point, the studio president's wife, an elegant woman in her late forties, turned to me and introduced herself as Leila. "Do you know how rare it is to find someone like your husband in Hollywood?" she said. "I mean, do you really get it? He is just wonderful."

"Yes," I said simply, trying not to make a face. What would she have done, I wondered, if I had said, *He is wonderful at oral sex, but he can't clean a kitchen to save his life.*

In my head I imagined the other questions I was surely about to hear from Leila. *Do you know how amazing he is? God, do you realize how lucky you are to have him?* These were the type of questions people constantly asked me since *Normandy* came out. Speaking in low, hushed, reverent tones, the person was always completely unaware of how insulting these queries were. They assumed, first of all, that I was some poor, pathetic woman who would have lived a life of misery and destitution had it not been for some cosmic alignment that brought me into Declan's world. Secondly, they presupposed that I didn't know the man I'd married, that maybe I actually found him stupid and slow and idiotic, and only through the words of these people would I wake up and recognize my accidental good fortune.

"My God, do you hear him?" Leila said. "He is so hysterical."

"That he is." *And you should hear this story when he's not doing his Paddy McIrish imitation.*

"You must be so proud."

"I am," I said truthfully. Despite it all, I was immensely proud of the way Declan held his own in that crowd. He more than held his own, actually. He was the star.

"I love your dress," Leila said. She reached out and touched the skirt. I was wearing one of my fifties swing dresses, but I'd had this one made with a wild seventies Pucci print.

"It is fabulous," said a voice from behind me.

I turned. It was Kendall Gold.

Even *I* knew Kendall Gold. She was the daughter of a famous comedic actress, who had made her own name by taking on quirky roles and period pieces until she won an Oscar last year. Her face was ubiquitous on every magazine rack. With her sunny blond hair, and her allegedly sunny disposition, she was America's "It" girl of the moment.

We introduced ourselves, and Leila, Kendall and I drifted away from the group around Declan. We talked fashion. I told them how I'd designed my dress. As they oohed and aahed over it, I found myself experiencing a rare, happy moment that had nothing to do with Declan. I gave them each one of my new business cards. *Kyra Felis, Designer* the cards read optimistically.

"Let me know if I can design something for either of you," I said. Immediately I felt like a door-to-door salesman, pitching vacuum cleaners to housewives.

I had to drive home that night, because Dec had had way too much to drink. Maneuvering the car at night, in unknown territory, was even more terrifying than usual. I was hanging over the wheel, peering into the darkness at the curves in the road.

"So what was that back there?" I said to Declan. "Were you trying out for the part of a leprechaun?"

"What do you mean?" I noticed the brogue was much lighter now that we were in private.

I started faking his accent, mimicking a few of his phrases. "You might has well have done a jig," I said.

He laughed. Yes, he admitted, he was putting on a bit of a show, but he really wasn't faking it. That was how he used to talk when he was young. He brought it back occasionally, usually when he'd had a few drinks. People liked it. They responded to it, and he missed home. It made him happy to talk like a real Irishman once in a while.

"Does it bother you, then?" he said.

I hesitated, still squinting at the road.

Finally, I said, "Yeah."

"Why?"

"Because you're acting. And yet there were no cameras, no one to call 'cut' or 'action'. You were doing it on your own."

"So what?"

A decent question. Why was it annoying me? Finally, I figured it out. "How am I supposed to know if you're acting with me?"

"Ah, love, because you know me." He leaned over the console and rubbed my arm. "You knew then I was just pretending. You'd always know. And besides, I'd never act with you. I don't have to."

We'd come into some area of civilization again, and I stopped at a light. He leaned farther into my seat, nuzzling my neck.

"You should be kissed, and often, and by someone who knows how," he said, using a Clark Gable voice.

I pulled back and looked at him.

"See," he said. "You knew. You'll always know."

chapter 16

It was ten in the morning, a few days after Graham's party, and I'd just gotten in from a run, when the phone rang.

"Please hold for Kendall Gold," said a woman, who sounded very busy.

"Excuse me?" I said into the phone.

No response.

I panted and used the bottom of my T-shirt to wipe sweat off my forehead. I shifted the phone to the other ear. When nothing happened for a few seconds, I was about to hang up.

But then I heard, "Kyra? Are you there?"

"Kendall?" I said.

"Yeah, hi. I met you at that party in Malibu."

"Sure," I said. "Are you looking for Declan?"

"No, no. I wanted to talk to you."

I pulled the phone away and stared at it for a second. Why was Kendall Gold calling me?

"You there?" I heard her say.

I put the phone back to my ear. "Yep, right here. Uh...how are you?"

"Fine, great. Well, you know, the usual bullshit. I've got ten scripts to read, and one of my personal assistants mistook me for David Spade and tried to attack me. Goes with the territory, right?"

"Does it?"

"Well, you know how it is with personal assistants. They're loyal until you can't get them an audition. I mean, how many has Declan gone through?"

"Declan doesn't have a personal assistant."

"Are you kidding me?"

"I don't even know what a personal assistant does." I went out on the balcony and sat in the sun.

"My God, they do *everything*." Kendall ran down an exhaustive list of duties her PAs did for her, which included returning her phone calls, reading e-mail, answering fan mail, buying her underwear and protein bars, picking up her dry cleaning, making her travel plans and coordinating her household staff.

"But look," she said, "I didn't call to talk about PAs. I called because of that dress you wore in Malibu. Are you selling it anywhere?"

"I wish. No, I made that for myself."

"Would you be willing to make one for me?"

I sat up straight. Did I just hear Kendall Gold asking *me* to make her a dress? "Of course," I said.

"I've got this charity luncheon at Tom and Rita's, and I thought it would be perfect. Half fifties-suburban, half Studio 54."

I laughed. She'd described the dress perfectly. "I'd love to make one for you. When is the luncheon?"

"Well, that's the hitch. It's next week. Is that too soon?"

I calculated everything I would need to do—get her

measurements, cut a new pattern, find the material, beg the factory to make it for me ASAP. One week was technically and entirely not enough time.

"I can do it," I said.

I was still on the balcony—scribbling notes, sketching Kendall's dress—when Declan came in.

"I'm out here," I yelled.

When he came though the doorway, I jumped up. "Guess what? Guess what?"

"You're cooking dinner?"

I scowled. He knew I never cooked, and yet he was always making light of it, which sometimes made me wonder. Did he wish he had a more stereotypical wife, one who would clean instead of calling Angel Maids, one who would whip up steak tartar instead of speed-dialing sushi takeout?

"Kidding, love," he said. He dipped his head down and put his forehead on my collarbone, his arms around my waist. "What's your news, then?"

I pushed him back slightly so he could see my face. "Kendall Gold asked me to make a dress for her!"

"What?" His face was elated. "You're kidding? Which dress? The slip dress with the satin straps, or maybe that draped one with the bias cut?"

When I met Declan, he could barely distinguish between the words *sleeve* and *hem,* and yet here he was talking bias cut with me. I hugged him again.

"No, the fifties one with the Pucci print that I wore to Graham's."

"God, that's brilliant!" He lifted me off my feet.

When he set me down, we heard a strange whir and then a series of clicking sounds. We both looked to the alley below the balcony. A man stood there with a camera and a black bag slung around his body.

"Hey, there!" Declan called down to him.

The photographer let the camera drop for a moment. He had a sharp, pointed face like a ferret, but friendly eyes. "How about a smile from you two?" he said.

Declan looked at me. He shrugged in a "what do you think?" kind of way. He appeared pleased with this development. I shrugged back.

We turned to the street and put our arms around each other. We smiled wide for the photographer.

That was a mistake.

Anyone who has lived in Manhattan knows that where there is one cockroach, there are others. Declan and I soon learned that the same axiom applies to photographers.

Two days after that first photographer appeared in our alley, we found three more outside our front door.

Declan was thrilled. "Hey, what's this?" he said in a happy voice. We had just stepped out onto the front stoop. I blinked at the bright false sun, tightening my arms around myself in the surprising chill.

Declan was dressed in new black Joseph Abboud slacks that Graham's assistant had bought at Graham's instruction. Declan had to "stop looking so MTV and start looking more old-school movie star," Graham had said. Graham's specialty was molding an actor into a persona. Declan, he had decided, wouldn't dress in skull caps and baseball shirts like that other Irish actor, and Graham had put the kibosh on Declan's own jeans and loose, oversize shirts, too. Rather, Graham had decided that Declan would wear crisp white shirts and Italian leather shoes and soft-as-silk pants. He would be a throwback to James Cagney and Spencer Tracy.

It irked me a little when Declan had come home wearing such an outfit, boasting that Graham had paid for the whole thing. The clothes were great—it wasn't that—and the charity of the situation didn't bother me. On the contrary, I think I had a strong sense, even then, that Graham, as well as many others, would make scads of money on Declan. What rankled was that if anyone should be selecting clothes for Declan, it should be me. Graham may not have even known that I was a designer at that point, but the new clothes felt like a slam somehow.

Anyway, the morning of the three photographers, Declan was wearing one of his new outfits, while I was in running pants and my old faded jean jacket. I had only gotten out of bed to walk Declan to his car. Our time had become that scarce. I so rarely saw him that in order to spend time together, I walked him to the parking lot, or he sat on the edge of the tub when I took a bath at night. Moments together had become as precious as pearls.

So I was blinking furiously in the sunlight when we saw those photographers. "Hey, what's this?" Declan said, and they shouted, "Declan! Declan!"

They didn't know my name yet, or they didn't care, and either way that was fine with me.

At my side, Dec preened. These photographers signified that what was happening to him—the acclaim from *Normandy,* the ridiculously huge advance he'd just gotten for a new film, the multiple offers that were pouring in—was real. These photographers, inadvertently, told him that he deserved the reviews and the new, massive money we had in the bank. I thought to remind him of that other axiom—*Never believe your own press*—but in his case, the press was true. Declan was fantastic in *Normandy.* He did deserve millions of dollars for feature films and car commercial voice-overs.

But within days those three photographers turned into six. Then they morphed into a pack of ten. And soon, they weren't just lingering outside our apartment. They followed Declan in his car. They shot us sitting outside at Cow's End when we could find time for coffee. I tried running from them once, when we turned a corner and saw them lurking, but I tripped and skidded onto my knees on the asphalt. Those bloody scrapes on my knees stuck with me for weeks. Every time I looked at them I felt like hunted prey.

In New York in the evening, I had always left my lights on, my curtains open. I really didn't think anyone would take the time to watch my dim form from across the street. But now in L.A., I was always drawing the curtains, peeking out for the familiar shape of a telephoto lens.

As I said, at that point it wasn't me they wanted, which was relieving and yet vaguely insulting. They wanted Declan. They wanted shots of him buying a paper, saying hi to someone on the street, and putting gas in his car, just as bad as they wanted those red-carpet shots, those photos of him pumping Brad Pitt's hand, the ones of him mugging with Geri Halliwell.

But even though it wasn't me they wanted, I was affected. It was hard not to be. When I walked out of the house, when they were still waiting for Declan to appear, they would shoot a few desultory shots of me, for something to do. I didn't know their names, like Declan did. I didn't see their presence as anything more than an uninvited guest at the foot of our marriage bed. Yet still I knew they were there. I couldn't help but set my face in a somewhat nice expression. I couldn't help but throw my shoulders back, and affect nonchalance as I threw my vintage Margaret Smith bag onto my other shoulder. Like never before, I noticed my own posture, my expressions, my movements, my car with its layer of dirt, my black Versace sling backs that were fading at the toe, my halter dress that had produced a black thread dangling from its hem, my too-faded navy running pants, my sand-caked Nike shoes, my fake Gucci sunglasses, my brand-new zit on my cheekbone, my eyebrows in need of waxing, my chipped fingernail polish.

I was always aware of the photographers, and therefore, I was hyper-aware of myself. It was as if the Kyra of old, the one who'd lived in Manhattan and been content with her small life, was watching the new Kyra, and unsure what to make of her.

chapter 17

The pictures that were taken in those initial few weeks cropped up first in the tabloids, then in *In Touch* magazine, then in *Us Weekly*, and eventually they spread to other glossies. Every day, Graham's assistant sent over a packet of Declan's press clippings from the previous day. At the beginning, Declan and I went over them together in bed. We spread them out around us, like pirates with their booty. We exclaimed over this picture and that caption; we laughed at the ones where he looked overexcited, his eyes wide; we groaned at the ones where he'd been snapped with his mouth open like a caught fish.

Those were good days. True, the photographers were always around, and yes, we had only minimal time together. But Declan had found the success he deserved, and my own career was finally kicking into place, at least for the week I was working on Kendall's dress.

I found the perfect fabric. It was lighter than what I'd used for my dress, the Pucciesque print even more splashy. Rosita worked her magic overnight from my sketches, and she got Victor to cut the fabric in two days. I'd decided to sew the dress myself, and I worked on it constantly. I had a purpose now. I was designing, and I would make some money on it. There is no better feeling than doing something you love and getting paid for it.

I called Kendall Gold when the dress was done and scheduled a fitting.

Her place was in Bel Air. I pulled up to the black iron gates, which stretched skyward, and gave my name to the person whose voice came over the intercom. The gates slowly opened, and I drove up a long brick driveway until I came upon Kendall's house. It was a huge yellow stucco home with a wavy, Spanish-style roof. Despite its monstrous size, the house had an inviting, happy look about it.

Kendall herself came to the door, dressed in gray workout shorts and a white tank top.

"Hi!" she said, giving me a hug. "I'm so excited to see it!"

She led me into the foyer. My shoes clicked on the Spanish tiles. Above my head, an iron chandelier about as big as a tractor wheel hung from the high, high ceiling.

"Will this work for our fitting?" Kendall said. She took me into the living room beyond the foyer, which was decorated with yellow walls, slouchy, slip-covered sofas and rattan tables. Sunlight streamed from open French doors, a huge pool and veranda beyond them. The effect was casual, elegant.

"Perfect," I said. "Are you ready to see it?" I had forgotten to attempt nonchalance; instead, my voice came out high and fast.

Kendall clapped her hands and nodded, even though this couldn't have been a unique experience. The top designers in the world had made gowns for her.

I slowly unzipped the garment bag. As I did this, I experienced a pang of nervousness. *I* loved the dress. I thought it was exquisite, but what if it wasn't the dress she remembered? What if she despised it?

The zipper snagged on something and stuck. "Now, I can make alterations if you don't like it," I said, my hands tugging frantically.

"Sure, sure," Kendall said. Strangely, she sounded as excited as I felt. "And I swear, I'll tell you if I don't like it. Believe me, I'm honest to a fault."

I finally jerked the zipper free and removed the dress, holding it out.

She squealed. "It's fantastic! Brie, come here!"

"Who's Brie?" I said.

"My assistant. Can you believe that name?"

A girl who looked about eighteen stepped into the room. "Wow!" she said when Kendall showed her the dress. "Cool!"

"I've got to try it on," Kendall said.

She stripped off her tank top, dropped her shorts and slipped the dress over her head. I was used to seeing people naked for fittings, but I was overly aware of the fact that this was *Kendall Gold* that I was seeing naked. She was at least five foot seven and had large, tanned breasts (implants, perhaps?), but there was something pixie-ish about her. Besides the breasts, she was whippet thin, and then there was that frothy gold hair and the impish personality.

The dress fell onto her frame and draped over her shoulders perfectly. It hugged her breasts and her waist just the way it should, and flared flawlessly around her hips. The oranges and yellows of the fabric complemented her sunny coloring. A circle pin of fake diamonds—I had brought boxes of them from New York—glittered from the center of the waist. Kendall skipped to a mirror hanging on the wall and squealed again. "I love it! Now, who should I say

I'm wearing? I saw from your business card that you go by Kyra Felis, not Kyra McKenna, right?"

"Right," I said. I couldn't stand the thought of giving up my parents' name.

"Kyra Felis, it is." She twirled around so that the skirt lifted and swung. "Kyra Felis, you are fabulous!"

I watched Kendall Gold, movie star, spinning around in a dress I'd designed, and right then I felt fabulous.

"So how is Declan handling all the press?" Kendall asked me. We were seated at the island of her kitchen, having tea from two mismatched mugs. The kitchen probably could have held fifty people, but with its pine furniture, Spanish-tiled floor and wide bay window it exuded comfort and charm.

"Declan loves it," I said. "This is what he's always wanted."

"And you?"

I sighed. "I'm happy for Declan, but I'm having a hard time with it. I don't like the feeling of being watched all the time, and the paparazzi make it hard to go anywhere."

Kendall nodded. She was back in her tank top and shorts, her wavy blond hair in a ponytail on top of her head. "Are you starting to do the separate-entrance thing?"

"What do you mean?"

"Well, you know, there're tons of ways to manage the paparazzi. That's really what you *have* to do. Use them when they can help you, avoid them when you need to be on your own."

I must have looked confused, because Kendall kept talking. "For example," she said, "you've got to start picking the spots you go based on the way they handle celebrities. Go to the places that have VIP rooms, or the ones who will let you come through the kitchen door. You know, go to Mr.

Chow's and Spago. Those are cliché, but they'll help you out. Or another trick is that you and Declan can leave separately and arrive separately, too. That cuts down on the photographers. You scatter them. You can also get look-alikes to act as decoys."

I put down my mug and stared at her, shaking my head. "This sounds like espionage."

She laughed. "It is in some way, I suppose. But it's what we signed up for. You can't complain about getting something you wanted. You can only learn how to control it to your advantage."

"I didn't sign up for it." I noticed, vaguely, that I sounded like a child forced into a soccer game.

"Are you going to keep designing clothes?" Kendall asked.

Her question surprised me. "Of course."

She lifted her eyebrows. She sipped her tea. "Well, you've got real talent. And you married Declan, who's a celebrity now. If I were you, I'd learn how to roll with it."

Kendall was right. I had married Declan, I had signed up for better or worse, and I should make the best of our new life.

I started smiling more when we saw the paparazzi. I didn't complain when our sunset walks were photographed by at least four people who scurried around us like vermin at our feet.

But it became tougher, because Declan now had fans, real live people who wanted to know him, love him, for better or worse, just like me. He'd been getting bags of fan mail since *Normandy* opened. Since I had so much more time on my hands, I'd been reading the mail and sending out the head shots with his autograph, which seemed to be what most people were after. But the bags got larger, and then the letters got stranger. Women started sending nude photos of themselves ("We should send these to the twins," Declan said), and a few people claimed to be his long-lost sister, cousin or uncle who could use a little help with their cash flow. And then he started getting letters from Amy Rose.

Dear Declan, the first one said, *I've watched you through the curtains with that woman...*

"'That woman? That woman?'" I said. "What the hell is this?"

Declan took the letter from my hand and read it, chuckling. The rest was about how much she loved Declan. "She's full of it," he said. "Graham warned me about these people. They latch on to some celebrity and get attached."

"Yeah, attached is one way to put it." I moved to the window and peered out onto the alley. No sign of anyone, but was she lurking out there in the shadows? I yanked the drapes closed.

A few days before Christmas, Graham called the apartment.

I assumed that after our usual pleasantries I would hand the phone to Declan as I normally did. But Graham said, "Kyra, I'm glad you answered."

"Oh?"

"Yes, I was calling to talk to you." He had a deep, raspy voice that always made it seem as if he was calling from a jazz club, a whiskey in hand.

Graham and I were on pleasant terms. I respected his work on Declan's behalf—it certainly seemed as though he was working very hard, an impression that would never be sullied—and I think he respected the relationship Declan and I had at the time. Still, Graham never called to talk to me.

He got right to the point. "I wanted to make sure you saw the *People* magazine that just came out."

"The one with the picture of Declan and Kaz?"

"No, the one with you in it."

"Oh, is that the shot where Declan and I are standing outside Capo?" Dec and I had taken to eating frequent dinners at Capo, an upscale Italian restaurant in Santa Monica. Though neither of us wanted to admit it, we liked Capo because it could only fit a small number of patrons, thereby reducing the number of people who would now look at Declan in an I-think-I-know-you-but-I-can't-place-you kind of way.

"Capo?" Graham said. "What the hell is that?"

"A restaurant."

"No, no," he said impatiently. "There's a fashion page in *People.* In this new issue, they wrote about your dress. Kendall Gold has it on. Some loud print."

My belly fluttered with excitement, my mind flickered with optimistic pride. "What does it say?"

Graham cleared his throat. "It says, 'The Winner's Circle' and then it reads, 'Kendall Gold wears a fifties-inspired dress designed by Kyra Felis, wife of Irish hottie Declan McKenna. "These dresses are comfortable and hip," Gold says. "They're the next big thing." We agree.'"

I squeezed the phone. I thought about Declan and how he must have felt that night at the *Normandy* premiere. Like he was on the verge.

Captain Christmas. That's what my friends in Manhattan used to call me, because of all the holiday junk I gathered like a bag lady at a Salvation Army clearance sale. As long as it had something to do with the Christmas holidays and it was kitschy, chipped, garish and wasn't part of a matched set, I wanted it.

The few pieces of Christmas stuff I'd received from my parents' estate had begun the whole fascination. There had once been an entire place setting of red plates with a roughly painted Christmas tree, a whole set of hand-painted miniature ornaments and an eight-piece set of silver candles that looked like wreaths. But Aunt Donna wanted all these things—she had bought them with my mother, she told Emmie—and Emmie, who felt bad for Donna, even after the custody battle, agreed to give them to her, as long as I got to keep one of each.

So started my Captain Christmas collection. I never wanted a set of anything from then on. Even as a teen, I would scour flea markets and New Year's Day sales for anything else to add. At first I kept it respectable enough. I purchased the odd red-and-green candle or a drinking glass with a holly pattern around the mouth. But then I became drawn to the Christmas junk—angel dolls with heads that bobbled, a mug depicting Santa peeing on a roof with a caption that read, "Where icicles come from."

Every year in New York, the minute I got back from Emmie's Thanksgiving dinner or the visit to one of her brothers' homes, I would pull out my boxes and decorate my apartment. I would string copious amounts of colored lights until the place screamed with color and blinked like a Vegas casino.

I had a cocktail party every year, where guests were asked to bring along a piece of Christmas crap to donate. Usually I wore a skirt and knee-high boots with one of my obnoxious Christmas T-shirts, like the one where reindeer diarrhea flies into the face of Santa, who remarks, "That's the last time we stop for Mexican food." My friends loved the party each year, and my collection grew.

I got a late start that year in L.A., what with *Normandy* coming out, and Kendall's dress and all the hoopla surrounding Declan. But finally, a few days before Christmas, I lugged the boxes from the back of the closet and decked our halls with synthetic garland and lights that played "Grandma Got Run Over by a Reindeer."

"Oh, Christ, love," Declan said when he came home at seven that night. "This is fecking hideous. It's brilliant."

"I know!" I said, pleased that he got the concept.

I poured us wine into two mismatched ceramic chalices, one red and gold, the other a lurid green.

Two nights later, we had a Christmas Eve dinner for Bobby, along with Liz Morgan and her husband, Jamey, and Brandon, Declan's friend from acting class, with his wife, Tara, the woman who had sent me to Fred Segal that first time.

Bobby thought my crappy decor was "fucking awesome."

"Leave it to you to turn super kitsch into super keen," he said, handing me a bottle of merlot. "How are you?"

Bobby and I had a moment alone because Declan had run out to the store to pick up paper towels. He'd worn a baseball cap and sunglasses, even though we hadn't seen many photographers for the last day or two. It seemed that even the paparazzi celebrated Christmas.

"I'm great." I kissed Bobby on the cheek and poured us wine. "Did Kendall say anything to you?"

Kendall used to be one of Bobby's clients until she defected to CAA but they still kept in touch.

"She loved that dress," Bobby said. He hitched himself up on a stool, jingling the bells that I'd hung around the base. "She's been talking you up everywhere. I think you and Declan are going to be the new power couple."

"I don't want power, I just want to have someone buy my designs."

"You're going to do it, Kyr. Just grab the bull by the horns and run with it."

"Thanks for the encouragement. Now where's your date? Stella, was it? Or Kris? I can't remember."

Bobby dated a revolving series of women who were nearly impossible to remember. They were all gorgeous, all in their twenties, and Bobby seemed attached to absolutely none of them.

"It was supposed to be Kris," he said, "but I told her to go home to Kansas."

"Why?"

"I didn't want to lead her on by bringing her here and making her think we were spending Christmas together for a reason."

I started to set out cheese on a green-painted wood board that had a grimacing snowman in the corner, who looked drunk or possibly just ill. "So you got an attack of the conscience," I said.

"Exactly."

Declan came in and hugged Bobby, clapping him on the back. "Merry Christmas, you tosser," Declan said.

Liz and Jamey arrived next.

"Wow," Liz said, blinking. Jamey's eyes darted about the room as if he was in a fun house and expected someone to jump out of the shadows.

Brandon and Tara were there shortly after. They were both clad in cashmere sweaters. They brought a bottle of Dom Perignon and a large box of chocolate truffles from K Chocolatier in Beverly Hills.

"My, my," Tara said when she walked in. She pursed her lips and shifted her bag to the other shoulder. "This is quite the place."

I could see that they had expected so much more. Certainly from the house—Declan was a movie star now, after all—but also from the decorations.

"Kyra is Captain Christmas," Declan said.

"Yeah, she does up her apartment like this every year," Bobby added. "She's legendary in Manhattan."

"Ah," Tara said, still clutching her box of truffles.

I tried to explain. I told them about my collecting over the years. "It's not supposed to be beautiful. It's just..." What was the word? I looked around at the apartment. It had looked fantastically trashy an hour ago, now it just looked like trash. "Fun..." I said, finally, my voice tapering off.

"Absolutely," Liz said. She glanced around. She nodded. "I get it. I love it."

I squeezed her hand. I liked her more and more all the time. Bobby had been my only real friend in town, and since *Normandy* came out, I'd spent hours with him on the phone deconstructing what was happening with Declan, telling him about the photographers and the weird letters that continued to arrive from Amy Rose. (*We should be married as soon as you get rid of her,* the last one said. Amy Rose always called me "her" or "that woman" in her missives. In another letter, she'd written, *Thought you would want to see a recent picture of my parents.* Paper clipped to the letter was a photo of side-by-side tombstones.) But Bobby had helped me to try and laugh at the letters. He got the fame thing. He'd lived on the fringes of it for years. He understood the paparazzi, the press. He gave me advice on avoiding them, and told me different tips to pass on to Declan about handling interviews. But Liz was more of a regular girlfriend. We got coffee together; we ran through the halls to borrow a purse or a book.

"Right," Tara said, finally relinquishing the truffles into Declan's hands. "It's really...interesting. I love it, too." She was obviously trying to suck up but doing a poor job of it.

"It's bloody great," Declan said, his voice defensive on my behalf.

"It's perfect," Bobby chimed in.

But it didn't help. The forced jocularity and apparent distaste of Brandon, Jamey and especially Tara were evident throughout dinner. I could almost hear Tara telling her friends tomorrow how sad it was that someone as amazing as Declan had to be married to someone as pedestrian as me. In a bout of passive-aggressiveness, I gave her the tiniest helping of mashed potatoes. I restrained myself from spitting in them.

I escaped to the bedroom at one point to phone Emmie. She'd refused my invitation to come to L.A. for the holidays, saying somewhat secretively that she had "plans." It made me think that she had no plans at all and simply didn't want to travel. I offered to fly to New York for a day or two, even though Dec wouldn't be able to get away, but Emmie insisted that Declan and I spend our first Christmas together. I had felt guilty for days, wondering if she was alone in her apartment, but she had called earlier when I was out, leaving a phone number I didn't recognize.

A man's voice answered.

"This is Kyra Felis," I said. "Is Emmie Franklin there?"

"Well, of course she is," the man said. He had a smooth, cultured voice that sounded familiar.

"Who is this, if you don't mind me asking?" I said.

He chuckled. "Emmie didn't tell you?"

"She said she was visiting friends."

"That she is. This is MacKenzie Bresner, Kyra."

"MacKenzie! Oh my God, how are you?" As far as I knew, MacKenzie was married and living near Saratoga Springs, surprisingly close to where Emmie was raised.

"How is your wife, MacKenzie?" I asked.

He cleared his throat. "She died about six months ago."

"I'm so sorry."

"Yes, so am I. But Emmie is keeping me company."

"Oh. Well, that's…that's wonderful. Is she there?"

Emmie quickly got on the phone, as if she'd been standing next to MacKenzie the whole time.

"Merry Christmas!" she said.

"Emmie," I said, ignoring her greeting. "Do you have a boyfriend?"

"I have to run, darling," Emmie said, but then she did something I'd never heard before. Emmie giggled.

It was enough to make my Christmas a happy one.

chapter 18

The day after Christmas, only a few days before we were to leave for Dublin, *Us Weekly* ran a photo of Kendall wearing my dress on its "Hollywood 'Have to Haves'" page. I was thrilled about the coverage. The problem was, I was unsure how to capitalize on it.

This time I called Graham. He'd told Declan and me that he wanted to be informed of everything we did in our lives, adding that he would always help us in any capacity that he could.

"Nice clip in *Us*," he said when I reached him. The man missed absolutely nothing.

"Thanks. Look, Graham, I know you work for Declan, but I wanted to ask you a favor."

"Shoot."

"I need a sales rep to sell my clothing. I know a few people here in the fashion biz, but they're pretty low profile," I said. I filled him in on Rosita and Victor. "Basically I'm wondering if you might have any contacts I could talk to."

"I know fashion about as well as I know Russian, but I'll make some calls."

That afternoon, I was contacted by three freelance sales reps. When I was back in Manhattan I had tried, unsuccessfully, to get a rep to work for me. These people usually took on ten to twelve designers and made the rounds of the boutiques, department stores and trade shows trying to sell their clients' lines. Now, even though I didn't have a collection ready, I had three who were willing to consider me.

Suddenly, I was a flurry of activity. In order to see what they would be selling, and, therefore, to decide if they wanted to work with me, I had to have a collection, or at least a few items and sketches for the rest. Meanwhile, our trip to Dublin was looming. This was the first time I would meet Declan's parents, and I was nervous.

I scrambled to put together the line. I spent an afternoon in the fashion district picking out new material for what I'd started to call the "Kendall dress." I'd decided that I would make that dress in at least four other colors and fabrics. I called Rosita and Victor and begged them to clear their schedules. Then I called the plant manager, who promised to make me samples immediately. Next, I had to decide what else would go in the line. Whatever the garments were, they had to complement the Kendall dresses. I sketched and sketched; I pulled out my old dolly and draped fabric every which way, until I came up with an A-line skirt that would be made in a stiff, white cotton covered with geometric black shapes and the circle pin on the hip. And pedal-pusher pants with jeweled cuffs. And light blouses that tied at the waist. And long, thin clutch purses with a circle-of-diamonds clasp.

I stayed up late to get it all done. I got Rosita to make the patterns and, as promised, the plant manager pushed through the designs in a few days. I chattered to Declan about this fabric and that pattern. He offered to wear the dress when he went on *Conan* if it would help me. We packed for Dublin and checked our tickets and talked to Graham about how to get to the airport without photographers following us.

On the day we would leave for Ireland, I showed my line to the three different sales reps. I was tense and edgy, like a kid dressed up as a reindeer, ready for the Christmas play.

But to my surprise, it was easy. Almost too easy. Every rep wanted to take me on. They barely had to look at the garments to decide this. I went with Alicia, the one who had the most questions, the one who said that she didn't like the cuffs on the pedal pushers. She seemed the person who would be most honest, and honesty was a trait that I sensed would become more and more scarce in our world.

I called Emmie again as I waited for Declan to get home and our car to arrive. I hadn't been able to get ahold of her since our Christmas phone call, and I wanted desperately to talk to her before we flew to Dublin.

This time she answered. "Hello, hello," she said, her elegant voice chipper, the way it used to be.

"Where have you been?" I settled onto the couch, surrounded by my new red matching luggage and Declan's duffel bag, which he refused to toss, even though we had money now to buy him better stuff.

"My dear, why do you sound like a warden?" Emmie said.

"Why didn't you tell me before that you were dating MacKenzie Bresner?"

"Oh, dating. *Please.* You don't date at my age."

"What do you do then, become sex buddies?"

"Kyra!" Emmie said in her fake-shocked voice. Then she chuckled. It was very hard to shock Emmie, although I'd been trying most of my life. "We are old friends who are spending some time together," she explained.

"Does he have an apartment in the city?"

"No."

"So, does he come and visit you?"

"Yes."

"And so," I said, "is he sleeping in your room or mine?"

"That's enough of this conversation, I'm afraid. I don't kiss and tell."

"Then you are kissing him!" I stood with my finger pointed to the sky. I was triumphant, like a lawyer on cross-examination who's just gotten the witness to admit where the body is buried.

"Aren't you supposed to be on your way to some Irish hamlet?"

"His parents live in Dublin."

"Ireland is one big hamlet," Emmie said. "Now, just find me some twelve-year-old Tullamore Dew and call me when you return."

I checked my watch after we hung up. Declan still wasn't home, and the car service wouldn't be there for ten minutes. I dialed Margaux's home number. No answer. I tried her at work.

"You're there," I said when she picked up.

"You know me," she said. "Typical lawyer—I came back the day after Christmas. What's up with you two? I can't turn a corner without seeing Declan's face these days."

"I know. It's nuts."

"Well, I'm not complaining. I've been milking the fact that I was at your wedding. My clients think I'm so very hip now."

"You've always been hip."

"True," she said. "What else is up?"

"Emmie has a boyfriend. MacKenzie Bresner."

"What? That is so unfair!" I could almost see her throwing a file at her big office window.

"How do you figure?"

"Emmie is getting laid at age eighty-three by a brilliant author, and I can't even get my husband to sleep with me!"

"No luck with the baby thing?"

"You have to have sex to have a baby thing."

"Right. Sorry."

"Oh, don't be. Tell me something exciting to take my mind off it."

"Well, we're supposed to be on our way to the airport." I got up from the couch and peered outside for the car service. Shit. Three photographers, back from holiday leave. They were chatting up a young woman who I'd noticed outside a few hours ago. She wore faded baggy jeans and a purple T-shirt. I knew that the moment we stepped outside, the photographers would drop their friendly banter with her and spring into action. Despite myself, I went into the bathroom to check my makeup.

"Have I given you my tips on Dublin?" Margaux said. After college, Margaux had floated around the world, searching for herself, for some direction in her life. She was forever sending postcards from Paris, Rome, New Delhi, Sydney. She had lived in Barcelona for a short while with a painter named Miguel. She had marooned herself on a Greek island for a few months with an American roommate named Casey. Margaux was, without a doubt, my travel guru.

"Hit me," I said.

"Okay. Here's the deal. Everyone says to stay out of Temple Bar—it's a neighborhood, by the way—but the fact is it's a blast. You've got to get drunk around there at least once."

"Got it."

"The Irish put sausage in everything, which will be weird at first, but it makes all their food taste better, so just eat it."

"Done."

"And lastly, don't talk about politics. They know so much more than we do, even about American policies, and you'll never get them to shut up once they start."

"Excellent." I heard Declan's key in the door. "Gotta go," I said.

"Kisses to Declan," Margaux said. "And luck of the Irish to you."

When we got outside, we struggled with our bags. I had massively overpacked as usual, and Declan was trying to carry his duffel, while pulling one of my little red suitcases with wheels, and balancing my new Prada bag on top of it. I labored behind with my big suitcase.

The photographers ran to us and began clicking off shots. They were only a foot from our faces, making it hard to see around them. In the round, warped glass of their lenses I could see my own fun-house image. I tried to smile but lost my grip on my luggage. When I bent down to grab it and readjust, two photographers leaned with me, shooting me from that angle. I straightened up and matched Declan's stride, yet still the photographers hung with us, getting off one shot after another, walking backward—an art form they've perfected—their lenses rarely farther than ten inches from us.

"Hey guys," Declan said to the photographers. "How about a little help?"

They laughed and kept shooting.

"Seriously," Declan said, sounding annoyed with the paparazzi for the first time. "Give us a fecking break." It was bright out, and we were sweating in the sun.

The driver of the town car popped out of his seat and began assisting us.

"Declan! Declan!" one of the photographers called. "Where are you headed?"

"Oh, we'd never tell," Declan answered.

"He's going to Ireland."

Who said that? Both Declan and I swung around from the car. The woman in the purple T-shirt, who'd been talking to the photographers, stood slightly to the right, wearing a pleased little smile. She had long brown hair that looked as if it needed a trim, and she wore frosty pink lipstick.

"Isn't that right?" she said. "You're going to visit our family in Dublin."

I glanced at Declan. How the hell did she know about Dublin? On the Internet, there were a few unofficial Declan McKenna Web sites, which had all sorts of random information. Had our trip to Ireland somehow made it onto one of them?

"Well, I'm visiting *my* family," Declan said. His voice was laden with feigned pleasantness.

"Our family," she said with eerie simplicity. She didn't blink. Her eyes were dark, dark brown, almost as if she had no pupils.

"What's your name, then?" Declan said.

"Amy Rose."

It took a second for the name to click, but then it reverberated in my head like a gong. Amy Rose. The woman who'd written those letters. I'd been trying to take them in stride, to laugh at them the way Declan and Bobby did, but the sight of her terrified me. I took a step closer to Dec.

"Can I sign an autograph for you?" Declan said.

"Oh, I've got that already. I'm here to go to Dublin, too." She gestured toward her feet, where a small, brown leather bag sat waiting. She apparently traveled much lighter than I.

No one seemed to know what to do or say. The photographers got off a few shots of her, then lowered their cameras and watched the exchange. The driver stood near the trunk, frozen.

"Well, we'll take you along next time," Declan joked, but I could hear the strain in his voice.

She took a step toward him. I flinched.

"Let's go then," the driver said. He slammed the trunk and shooed Declan and me into the car. He nearly dived into the front seat and started the engine. We looked out the window and saw that Amy Rose had moved closer to the car, a creepy smile on her face.

"Go," I said to the driver. "Please go!"

When we got to the airport, the gate agent read Declan's passport, then glanced up with a look of interest.

"Mr. McKenna," she said. "It's such a pleasure to have you flying with us today."

"Thank you," Declan said.

I stood next to him, holding out my passport, which the agent ignored.

"I loved *Normandy*," she gushed. "It was so visually stunning, and you were magnificent."

"Thank you very much," Declan said, and I could see the strain of the Amy Rose encounter starting to dissipate under her praise. It took that little for him.

After rambling on about *Normandy* for another few minutes, the agent finally deigned to take my passport and finished checking us in. Then she called a porter to escort us to the first-class international lounge. I had never known that airport porters existed, and I had never traveled first-class before, so this momentarily lifted my spirits, too.

The lounge was lovely—muted tan walls, groupings of gray chairs and couches, an array of food and drink. If the room had been in someone's house it would simply be a nice living room, but plopped in the middle of LAX, it seemed like a palace ballroom.

At least half the people in the room looked up from their laptops or magazines when Declan and I walked in. No one bothered us, though, as we got a few triangles of cheese and a drink from the bar. We took a seat near the plate-glass window that overlooked the tarmac. Declan picked up the courtesy phone and dialed.

"Graham," he said. "Sorry to bother you at home." He paused. "Yeah, we're on our way, but we had a spot of trouble getting here."

He told Graham the story about Amy Rose, the words she had said. "Kyra is really freaked out," he said. "And to be honest, I am, too." He glanced over his shoulder, lest any reporter be lurking. You never knew.

After a moment, Declan gestured for me. I sat on his lap, and he held the phone close so that we could both hear.

"Listen, kids," Graham said. "I think it's time to get you out of Venice."

I shot Declan a look. Venice Beach was the one place in L.A. I felt attached to.

"I know you love it," Graham said, as if sensing my thoughts. "But it's really not a secure place. Sure, there are some nice big houses on the canals, but any Tom, Dick or Harry could trot right down there and jump your fence."

"What about a place on the beach?" I said. I adored the ocean, especially viewed from the Venice boardwalk.

"Those places are worse. You've got tourists from South Dakota walking by all day, and the houses are smashed close together. It'd be easy to stand out on the beach and point a telescope, or something worse, right into your windows."

I had a flash of Amy Rose in her purple T-shirt, standing on the beach with a hunting rifle.

"What do you suggest?" Declan said.

"Here's what I'll do for you. While you kids are gone, I'll get a real estate agent looking for something more private. You've got the money now. You might as well stop throwing it away on rent and get someplace safe for the both of you. How does that sound?"

Declan looked at me. I nodded. I was already dreading going back to our apartment with Amy Rose lurking somewhere outside.

"Sounds good, Graham," Declan said.

"Great. Call me when you're in Dublin and give me a fax number. I'll send you listings, and I'll personally start looking. We'll find you a new home."

Another one, I thought.

chapter 19

Despite the relative luxury of first class, with its hot, white towels and unlimited cabernet (which I made good use of), I felt trapped and restless the entire time. I couldn't stop seeing Amy Rose, her face leaning close to the car window. I kept hearing her matter-of-fact voice saying, *You're going to visit our family.* What was wrong with that girl? And how many times had she watched us through our windows?

It wasn't hard to figure out how she had learned our address. After *Normandy* came out, we got an unlisted number, but there were still millions of phone books out there that said precisely the street and apartment number of our place in Venice.

The flight was interminable. While Declan snoozed with his chair fully reclined, his black shoes poking out from under a blue blanket, I drank one glass of wine after another. Instead of making me mellow, my anxiety grew. The plane felt like a flying lipstick tube where I was trapped against my will.

When we arrived in Dublin, Declan was fresh and keyed

up at the prospect of seeing his family and friends. Meanwhile, I was about to meet my in-laws with a hangover and a bad attitude.

As it turned out, the twins picked us up. "Hello, pet," they said to me, hugging me roughly and messing my hair. Instantly, my mood improved. I wasn't sure where the term *pet* had come from, but I loved it. It made me feel like somebody's little sister.

Their car was tiny and cramped and dirty, shades of Declan's old car in L.A. (Since receiving the huge advance for his new film, he'd gotten a gold Jaguar sedan.)

"Christ, man, we can't turn on the TV anymore without seeing your bleedin' face," Colin said to Declan. The twins seemed not so much impressed by Declan's success, but rather found the whole thing hysterically funny.

"And then there you are on this fecking interview, all straight-faced and such, talking about your *inspiration*." This again from Colin, who rolled his eyes and wiggled his shoulders.

"Yeah," said Tommy, raking his hands through his red hair, "like you've ever had any inspiration other than a properly poured pint of Guinness."

Declan put his arm around me in the back seat and took their ribbing in stride. He swung his head constantly, looking out the windows. "God, it's good to be home."

"We're taking your girl on the scenic route," Tommy said.

Ten minutes later, Tommy told me to start paying attention. "This here is O'Connell Bridge," Tommy said as we passed over a four-lane bridge. People packed its sidewalks. "And you can get a view of the River Liffey." The river was a wide stretch of placidly flowing brownish water. I didn't admit to the twins that I had somehow expected it to be green.

The buildings in the area were tightly packed brownstones or brick apartment buildings with storefronts at ground level. It was a real city, unlike L.A., and I got a twinge of excitement to be there. We turned right at the end of the bridge and drove along the river's edge.

"Here's Temple Bar," Declan said, gesturing to an area with cobblestone streets and shorter, quainter buildings. "Boys, Kyra's friend, Margaux, has told her we've got to get her pissed in Temple Bar."

Tommy swung around from the front seat, a lascivious grin on his face. "How is Margaux?"

"Now listen up," Colin said from the driver's seat. "See that across the river there?" He pointed at an impressive white stone building with a colonnade and a shallow green dome. "That there is Four Courts. That's where Declan's da works."

"I can't wait for you to meet my parents," Declan whispered in my ear.

"Me, too," I said. Truth was, I was nervous again. I wished I'd slept or at least washed my face on the plane. I felt like a human grease slick.

Declan's parents' house was in an area called the Liberties, a more suburban part of the city. Rows of squat cottages were all connected together, but each was painted a different color—brown, yellow, cream, red. Short stone walls and diminutive iron gates gave the illusion that they protected the cottages. Lace curtains hung in nearly every window.

"The neighborhood is getting all posh now," Colin said, "but we're fighting it."

Declan's parents greeted us at the door. His father, Liam, was a barrel-chested man with graying black hair and the red nose and tired eyes of a career drinker. His mom, Nell, was the one who looked most like Declan. She had his chestnut hair and his golden eyes, although her eyes bore a certain tiredness that I'd never seen on Declan.

I knew that Nell's life with Liam had been a long haul. Liam's constantly drunken behavior and dalliances with other women had sent her first into rages and then into a separation of sorts. While Declan and his younger sister, Brenda, were in their teens, their parents lived together, but they had different lives. Every so often, Liam would move into the apartment of one of his girlfriends, but within months he would be back in his bedroom down the hall from his wife.

They were one of the first couples to get a divorce when the divorce laws changed in Ireland. Declan said he couldn't have been prouder of his mom for giving Liam the heave-ho, but within six months they were spending all their time together, more time than they had spent when they shared a home. Seven months after that, they remarried, and that was precisely when Declan left for L.A. His father didn't deserve his mother, he said, and he couldn't stand to see it.

"Declan!" Nell threw herself into her son's arms.

She had tears in her eyes, which almost made me cry, too. She had told Declan that his father's drinking was better— not perfect, but better—and that she was happy now with her husband. I knew, though, that she missed Declan immensely. He had been her main friend and support for all those years. Declan's sister was one of those quiet kids who kept to herself and her few friends, and so it was Declan who had gotten his mom through the tough times.

"Kyra," Nell said, turning to me. She grasped my hands in both of hers, then gripped me in a sudden, tight hug. "We're so happy to meet you."

"It's wonderful to meet you, too."

I shook hands with Declan's father, who patted me on the arm. "Sure, aren't you the loveliest girl that Declan's ever courted?" Liam said.

"Oh, thanks, I—"

"And he's courted many," Liam said, cutting me off.

The twins guffawed and started rooting through the kitchen cupboards.

I exchanged a quick hug with Brenda, a slight girl with a very fat baby on her hip. "Nat," she said to her child, "this here is your aunt Kyra."

My heart jumped and spun around at those words. I hadn't thought of it before, but I was an aunt now. A member of the family.

"Can I hold him?" I asked.

She handed Nat to me. He had fuzzy blond hair and too-blue eyes, a string of drool from one corner of his mouth. I bounced him on my hip, the way Brenda had been doing, and I felt another jump of my heart. He wasn't crying! The kid *knew* I was family.

Declan was across the room, accepting a bottle of soda from his dad, nodding at something he was saying. It had never been particularly smooth between them, mostly because Declan felt the need to protect his mother, but there was an apparent ease now. Declan was talking, explaining something about *Normandy,* while his dad beamed appreciatively.

I continued to bounce Nat on my hip. I asked Brenda how old he was. As she and I talked, I glanced once more at Declan. He caught my eye and beamed at me, and right then Los Angeles and Amy Rose seemed far, far away.

Declan and I spent the afternoon sightseeing around Dublin. He was hopped up on some kind of energy. He couldn't wait to show me everything.

We went first to Christchurch, stunning in its size and splendor, then to Dublin Castle, a King Arthur–type castle with moats and spires, plunked incongruously in the middle of the city. I put my hand on a mammoth stone door, marveling at the other people who might have touched that same stone seven, eight, even nine hundred years ago.

"It's amazing, right?" Declan asked me at least five times.

Declan wanted to talk to everyone we came across. Only a few people recognized him, and he seemed not to care in the slightest. We met people in cabs and in coffee bars and in line at the National Museum. How sexy and full of character the Dubliners seemed to me. It had something to do with the Irish accent, so much more friendly and interesting than the British, so much more approachable. A British accent comes from the nose, but a brogue rolls out of the chest with a laugh waiting behind it.

In the early evening, as the sky turned a blue-black, Declan and I walked the lawns of Trinity College.

"God, it's amazing to be back here," Declan said. He hadn't attended Trinity but he'd taken a playwriting seminar that had been held in one of the classrooms. "What do you think, love? Do you like the city?"

"I adore it," I told him honestly. I felt comfortable in a way I hadn't since I left Manhattan.

"I miss it so much," Declan said fervently. "So fecking much."

"But you love L.A.," I pointed out.

"I love L.A. the way I love my sister," he said, slinging an arm over my shoulder. "But I love Dublin the way I love you."

The next day, Dec's mom took me shopping on Grafton Street, a tight-angled avenue paved with brick and lined with shops and bars.

Shopping is something I love but I've mostly done alone in my life. As a kid, Emmie took me to Bergdorf's and sent me off with a salesgirl. Later, as an adult, she would take me back there when I was depressed, but it was always to choose between a few items she knew I wanted but couldn't afford—a Pucci scarf, a Louis Vuitton bag. Once I'd made my selection, we were gone.

So it was strange but marvelous to be with Nell on Grafton Street. She picked out clothes for herself, but she was looking for me the whole time, too.

"Kyra, girl," Nell would yell, gesturing for me to come to her side. "Sure, aren't these marvelous?" She handed me a pair of very cute powder-blue pants with tiny flowers embroidered along the cuff.

"They're great," I said. "What would you wear with them?"

"Oh, not for me!" She laughed. "No, no, my dear. My backside would look enormous. I thought these would be lovely on you."

I took them and studied them, struggling to hide how pleased I was by her mothering.

"Oh, I have to see them on you." She hustled me off to the fitting room, where she stood outside until I came out to model for her. "Adorable!" she proclaimed.

I told the saleslady to ring them up. Even if I'd hated them, I think I would have bought them just to see Nell smile.

I took a nap when we got back from shopping that day. When I woke up, Declan was sitting at the kitchen table with piles of paper surrounding him.

"Graham already has ten houses for us to think about," he said. "He faxed us the listings to the corner store."

Nell came in the kitchen, and together we starting looking through them with Declan.

"Glory be to God!" Nell said. "These must cost a fortune. They're right mansions, they are."

She wasn't far off base. These were real houses. Some had five bedrooms, some boasted four to five thousand square feet.

Then I looked at the list prices and nearly gasped. When Nell left the room for a moment, I whispered, "Dec, we don't need a million-dollar house."

"A million won't get us anything," he said, holding out a listing. It showed a white ranch house with a roof that looked more weather-beaten-gray than a nice Ralph-Lauren-paint-kind-of-gray. The bushes out front were bedraggled; the sidewalk leading up to the house was broken in places. It had three bedrooms and 1.5 baths, and the description said it was "cozy" with "knotty pine cabinets." The list price was $990,000. Was that all a million dollars bought these days?

"It's in Bel Air," Declan said, pointing to the picture "but it's in a neighborhood, right next to a bunch of other houses. We might as well stay in our apartment. Now, this is something that might work for us."

He gave me another listing that showed a Southwestern desert–style home with adobe walls and a large arched front window. *Holmby Hills, Luxury Living at Its Finest!* the description boasted. It went on to brag about the four bedrooms and three and a half baths, the location at the prestigious Bel Air Crest, the pool, the spa, the "grand, sweeping staircase." Finally, at the end, it mentioned the price tag of well over two million dollars.

"Okay, I'm not even commenting on the price right now," I said to Declan. "We just don't need something this big. It's only the two of us."

"Not really," he said. "I've got to get an assistant, and they'll need to work there. And you need a proper office, and I'd like to have someplace to review scripts and such."

"Ah, you're so grand, are you now?" Nell said, coming back into the kitchen and putting a kettle on the stove.

"No, Ma, it's just how it has to be. Besides, the most important point is the security. This place has an alarm system, a gated entrance and a safe room."

"What do you need all that for?" Nell said.

Declan glanced at me. I knew he liked to protect his mother from any unpleasantness in his life. He felt she had enough of her own.

"We just have to be careful now," he said. "That's all."

I thought of Amy Rose for the first time since we had arrived. I wondered if she was watching our apartment in Venice, waiting for us, for Declan, to come home. The concept of tall gates and a red light on an alarm system made me feel safer at that moment. I picked up the stack of faxes again.

That night we went with the twins and Dec's family to the Octagon Bar in the Clarence Hotel, which was apparently owned by some of the members of U2.

Declan adored U2. Our apartment always pulsed with their music when he was home. He was forever talking about the Octagon Bar and how "brilliant" it was, and so I'd expected something impressive, or at least impressively hedonistic in a rock-star kind of way. But really, it seemed like a rec room in somebody's basement. There were the intriguing octagonal contours, of course, and there was an octagon-shaped bar in the center, but the ceilings were low, the lighting bad and patchy, and the bucket chairs dated-looking.

Declan's mom was nervous as we took our seats. "I haven't seen anyone yet," she said, "but if I do you can be sure it will be ugly, now, won't it?"

Nell had been the former head of housekeeping at the Clarence before leaving for the Shelbourne. She seemed to think that she might be bodily thrown out of the Octagon Bar once someone spotted her. In fact, she seemed upset when she didn't get tossed. No one recognized her at all.

Wonderfully enough, since we'd been in Dublin, only a few people recognized, or at least admitted to recognizing,

Declan, either. Oh, there was a sole photographer who approached us on the street, and asked, politely, for a photo. We obliged, he snapped two shots, and was gone. A short article had also appeared in the *Irish Times,* which mentioned that "Ireland's new top gun in Hollywood" was back in his native city for a visit. Other than that, our time in Dublin had been spent blissfully without the press, without fans.

There was one guy, though, who approached us that night at the Octagon, as we sat in the bucket chairs near a table that was too small for all our drinks.

"Declan McKenna," the guy said in a disappointed voice, as if to really say, *I thought I told you not to show your face around these parts anymore.*

"Yes?" Declan said. He looked up with his now-practiced, yes-it's-me-I'm-a-celebrity-you're-right face.

"Declan McKenna," the guy repeated. He was standing still, but the top half of his body swayed like a tree in the wind. It was at that moment, I think, that we all realized the guy was blotto. The twins tensed, sat a little taller in their chairs.

"Ya come back to conquer the homeland, did ya?" the guy said. "Think you can swing in here on your vine and we'll all dance a jig for ya?"

"No," Declan said, perfectly pleasant. "No, not at all. Just visiting."

"Visiting? Ha!" The man ran a hand over his beard. He wore a triumphant expression as if he'd just figured out Declan's real intentions. "We're not impressed by you, ya hear that?"

"Sure," Declan said.

"You're shite, that's all. You're a fecking pissant Yank bastard now, don't pretend you're not."

"Okay."

"I want you out of town as soon as you can get on your horse."

"I thought it was a vine," Declan said.

The man looked angry, then confused, as if he'd been caught making a big mistake. "Just leave soon!" he said.

"Sure," Dec said. "Thanks for stopping by."

The guy meandered away, his tree-trunk upper body undulating slightly. Dec and the twins and his father burst into raucous laughter.

"What?" Nell said. "Sure, you're not all laughing, are you? The cheek of that nutter! He insulted you!"

"Christ, that was a brill slag," Colin said, wiping his eyes.

"Brilliant," Declan agreed. "It's just like Bono said. 'When there's a big house on a hill in America, people walk by and say, "That will be me someday." But when they're in Ireland, they look up at the house and say, "I'm going to get that guy someday."'"

The week in Dublin sped by. We visited aunts and uncles of Declan's, we baby-sat for Nat, we drank too much with the twins. Despite the change of scenery, our days felt the way they had before *Normandy* came out. Life was effervescent, wonderful, somehow normal. But on the afternoon before we were supposed to leave, Declan went out to the corner store to get another fax from Graham.

When he came back, he hustled me into the tiny guest bedroom we were sharing. "Look," he said, handing me a few sheets of paper.

Stunning 1926 Old Hollywood Spanish on Mulholland Drive. Panoramic canyon and valley views. Gated entrance. Ultimate privacy. Ballroom-size living room. Gorgeous master suite. Media room. Exquisite kitchen, pool, spa.

Then my eyes found the price tag. $4,100,000.

"You've got to be kidding me." I looked back up at Declan.

"Hold on there," he said. "That's not quite the price."

"It says four million dollars."

"Listen, love, it used to be four million, when it was listed last year. The owner took it off the market right quick when he became ill. He died a month ago, and the estate lawyer is selling it. He just called Graham's agent yesterday and said he'll punt it for 2.7."

"Two point seven million," I said. I was somewhat used to hearing about other people paying outrageous prices, especially in Manhattan, but I'd never myself had to bat around such figures before.

"It's a bloody steal," Declan said, his voice getting more excited. "We're the only ones who the agent has told, but we have to let her know today."

"What do you mean? We haven't even seen it yet!"

"Graham said that's how these estate sales go sometimes. You've got to jump on it. He's been there with Sherry, and they both love it. They say it's perfect for us."

"How do *they* know if it's perfect for us? We can't buy a house without seeing it first."

"Look, love." Declan sat on the bed and pulled me down next to him. "I'm trying to save money because that's what you want to do, and I agree we should watch it. But we *do* have the money now, and we're not going to get a deal like this ever again. This is a half-price home, for Christ's sake!"

"A half-price home we haven't seen yet." Was I the only sane one here?

"Well, look at the rest of the pictures." He pointed to photos of a charming kitchen and two offices ("one for each of us," Declan said) and a sunroom that looked over the valley and the canyon.

"It's beautiful," I said, "from what I can tell, but I haven't seen it with my own eyes. How am I supposed to move in there?"

"Hold up," Declan said. He picked up the phone on the white wood nightstand. "Graham," he said after a few seconds. "Yeah, it's Declan. Listen, can you tell Kyra about the house?"

I shot Declan a look, but took the phone.

"Kyra," Graham said. How soothing and confident that voice of his was. "This place has you two written all over it. It's just beautiful. It's not too overstated, but it's very lux. The living room is huge yet it's comfortable and casual, too. There are two offices. It would be a perfect place for you to work on your designs. The master is stunning, with closets bigger than your kitchen."

I admit I perked up at the part about the closets.

"I know this is a strange way to do things," Graham said, "and I wouldn't even mention this to you two if I wasn't absolutely positive that you'd love it. I tell you what, even if you get home and you hate it, or you just want to live in it for a few months while you're looking at another place, you could turn this puppy around in a few months and make a mil easy. I'd do it myself if I didn't have money tied up in other places."

I was silent. The part about being able to sell helped, but was that true? I knew nothing about real estate.

"Kyra," Graham said, "I think you know that you can't stay in that apartment. That woman who was outside when you left for the airport—I've seen her type before. She makes me nervous."

"Me, too."

"Look, talk to Declan some more and let me know, okay? The agent is breathing down my neck, but I'll hold her off for a few more hours."

"Thanks, Graham."

I hung up the phone. Declan watched me with expectant eyes, like a kid waiting to find out if he can stay up late.

Crazy, ludicrous, stupid, some woman was saying in my head, but I kept hearing another voice, this one stronger. It was Amy Rose saying, *You're going to visit our family in Dublin... I'm here to go to Dublin, too.* And I could see her neat handwriting on the letters—*I've watched you through the curtains with that woman.*

She scared me—there was no way around it—and the thought of constantly looking over my shoulder for her was unbearable. Then there were the photographers camped out in our alley or near the front door.

"I guess it would be better to get out of the apartment soon," I said.

Declan nodded. I got the feeling that he was afraid to say anything, lest he break the tentative spell Graham had cast over me.

"If I hate it, we're looking for something else right away," I said.

"Right. Right. Perfect."

We sat in silence. In the other room, I could hear Liam talking to Nell and her childish laugh in return.

"Are we doing this, love?" Declan said.

I groaned. I rubbed my forehead. Finally, I looked up at Dec. "Okay," I said. "We're doing it."

Declan and the twins and I went out to celebrate our new house that night.

"I want to hear some music," I said in the car. "Some Irish music."

"Oh, she wants Irish music, does she?" Tommy said.

"Let's go to Temple Bar," I said, thinking of Margaux. What would she say when she heard about our house?

"You were in Temple Bar when we went to the Octagon Bar," Colin said.

"But that was a hotel! I want a real Irish bar."

"Well then, pet, we can't go to Temple Bar," Colin said.

"Ah, let's go," Declan said. "What my girl wants, my girl gets."

Fifteen minutes later, we parked and walked the crowded cobblestone streets of Temple Bar. The pubs and restaurants blared their music, as if the loudest would win the most tourists. We went to Oliver St. John Gogarty's, a busy three-story bar and restaurant.

"At least let's go to the upstairs bar," Colin said. "It's not as unhinged as the rest of this place."

The top-level had crackled, red brick walls and an old oak bar where whiskey bottles hung upside down at the ready. The bartenders were red-faced and friendly. And there was a band, just as I'd hoped, but they weren't onstage. Instead, they sat around a long, rectangular table, playing to themselves—for themselves, it seemed—although they were surrounded by watchers and dancers and drunks.

Declan and the twins refused to let me order wine and instead made me drink Guinness. Guinness, I learned, is a bit of a sneaker in terms of intoxication. It slowly made me loopy, happy.

"Anyone want to pop out for a bit of a smoke?" Colin asked, flashing a joint in his palm.

"Me, please!" I said. I hadn't gotten stoned in years, but it sounded as if it would complement my buzz perfectly.

"I'm driving," Tommy said. He picked up his pint of Guinness and kept drinking.

"Nah," Declan said. "I don't do that shit anymore."

Colin and I left the bar. He led me down the cobblestone street and over a bridge with iron railings painted white.

The lights overhead were bright. Cars sped by, crossing

the River Liffey. We leaned over the railing in the center of the bridge, watching the brown swirling water.

"Here you go, pet," Colin said, handing me the lit joint.

"Here?" I said. I swiveled my head around guiltily. "We're in the middle of a bridge."

"It's the best place. The cops think bridges are for lovers and jumpers, so as long as we're two people and we don't look ready to jump, they'll leave us alone."

I looked around again. A bundle of young guys walked past us, none of them glancing our way. The cars streamed by.

Finally, I took the joint from Colin's hand and inhaled big. I waited for the rush to hit my brain. Nothing happened.

"No offense, Colin, but your pot sucks."

"True, true. We only get shite here. But every once in a while something gives you a kick."

We leaned on our elbows and watched the water some more.

"It's been great craic having you two here," Colin said.

"Great *craic*. God, that term kills me! Maybe I should start saying 'heroin.' You know, 'It's been such good heroin having you around.'" I peeled off into a fit of giggles. Okay, possibly I was a tad baked.

Colin laughed with me. "Sure, but I'm serious," he said. "Declan is mad for you, and I just want you to know that Tommy and I approve. You get on with Declan better than any woman I've seen before."

"Well, thank God, because we're already married."

"Honestly, Declan is different with you."

"How so?" I turned to face him. This interested me.

Colin gave a lift of his shoulders. "It's like he's really Declan with you. The Declan I know and Tommy knows. Before, when he was with other women, he always seemed like someone else."

"What do you mean?"

"He was acting. Like he was in a film or something. But with you, pet—" Colin ruffled my hair "—what you see is what you get. You get the real Declan."

"Thanks," I said. "Thanks for telling me that."

We stood in silence a few minutes more before we walked back and joined Declan and Tommy. The bar seemed more golden inside now, the band louder than when we left, more lyrical, magical. The sound from the fiddles soared to the ceiling and floated back to my ears. I kissed Declan flush on the mouth, then wandered away without a word. Later— it could have been ten minutes or two hours—he found me at the bar, talking to a man named Mick, a fiftyish reporter for the *Irish Times,* covering the Middle East beat, and Morag, a nineteen-year-old girl who was out on the town for the first time since the birth of her eight-week-old son. Declan chatted with the three of us for a while. I can't for the life of me remember the topic, but I remember I was enthralled with my new friends, with that night.

Declan and I eventually drifted away to the window where we watched a soft rain fall on the shiny stones of the street below.

"How remarkable," I said.

"What's that, love?"

"I just had beers and great conversation with an unwed teenage mother and a Middle East reporter."

He kissed the top of my head. "That's Ireland."

Part Four

chapter 20

We got home from Dublin on a Tuesday night, where fifteen reporters greeted us outside our apartment.

"Look, why don't I go in first," Dec said, "and we'll have the driver take you around the block a few times until they leave."

I kissed him on the nose. "I'm too tired for subterfuge. I want my bed."

"And I want you *in* our bed. So let's go."

We opened the car door to the sounds of cameras popping and the glare of flashes.

The next morning we were on our way to see our new home with the real estate agent, a pert woman with a blond Dorothy Hamill cut and a bright yellow suit. Her name was Vicky and she would not shut up.

"You've got complete privacy up here," she said, swinging around from the driver's seat of her Lincoln Navigator to beam a tense smile at me. Declan sat next to her in the passenger seat. "I mean, I know that's what you need now. I deal with many celebrities, and this is just about one of the neatest properties I've seen. Not to mention the price cut. That's just loco, and I can tell you that I've got a host of other clients who would have jumped on it if I gave them the chance, but Graham told me you needed something quick, and Declan, if I can call you that, I hope first names are okay, so Declan, I can tell you something you might be very interested in. William Mulholland was an Irishman who brought the water supply to Los Angeles, and this road is named after him."

"Is that right?" Declan said when she finally took a breath.

"Oh, it's true." And she was off again.

I tuned her out and stared out the window. I'd never been on Mulholland Drive, the windy road that split the city from the Valley. I noticed that the trees grew higher and higher as we left the city behind. Lovely, for sure, but somewhat remote compared to our old place. Where, I wondered, was the neighborhood coffee shop, the little corner grocery store?

"Vicky," I said, interrupting her diatribe on the concrete aqueduct that Mr. Mulholland had built. "If you live in this area, where do you get coffee in the morning? Or go grocery shopping?"

"Oh, it's no problem, there are a few places."

"Anything in walking distance?"

"No, but hey—" she tittered nervously "—this is L.A., right?" She went back to discussing the history of the Los Angeles water supply.

"We're almost there," Vicky said five minutes later. She clapped her hands.

I felt a grip of excited nervousness in my stomach. We were about to see the house we'd bought, the house we would live in, the house we'd never seen. *I* was going to be living in a house worth millions! But what if it was ostentatious? What if it was a mini version of the Playboy mansion?

Vicky finally stopped at a tall, brown iron gate with elegantly twisted posts. She punched a series of numbers into a little silver keypad, as if she was at a drive-thru ATM, and then the gates parted in the middle and swung open.

The driveway was paved with yellow stones. "Follow the yellow brick road," Vicky said cheerily.

"Whoa," Declan said as we pulled up to the house.

"Whoa is right," I said.

The house soared above us, all white with rusty-red roofs. Many, many roofs. A roof over the doorway, a roof taller than that, one beyond that, a few to the right. My pulse picked up. This was *ours!*

"How many floors is it?" I said.

"It's interesting," Vicky said, jumping out of the car and leading us to the front door. "It was built in 1926, but different owners have added on different parts to the house, so now there are four floors and two wings."

Declan and I looked at each other. I shook my head. Were we ready for this?

"It's okay, love," he said, squeezing my hand.

Inside, the place was airy and bright. In the center of the house was an open space surrounded by railings where light poured through from above.

Vicky twirled around and ran her hand over the railing. "The last owner added this sunroof and light shaft," she said, "so that you have natural light all day. It really saves on electricity bills."

I grimaced momentarily. I'd been so focused on the price tag that I hadn't even thought about the astronomical utilities or taxes.

"Now come see the living room," Vicky said. "You will just die."

She led us around the light shaft and down a few steps into the most colossal living room I'd ever seen. The ceilings were pitched and beamed. The parquet floors gleamed like an ice rink.

"Stunning, isn't it?" Vicky said.

"God, it is," I said. *This was ours,* I told myself again. *All ours. We own this home.* But some part of my brain refused to register that information. What would I fill it with? The furniture we had now in our apartment would barely fill the foyer.

Beyond the living room, French doors led to a slate-floored sunroom that looked over the pool and the valley.

"I know you have security concerns," Vicky said, "but with this sunroom you can get the feel of sitting outside without worrying about photographers or intruders. There's even a state-of-the-art air system to give the feeling of fresh air." She flipped a switch, and a shot of lilac-scented air entered the room.

I nodded. It was a nifty technological accoutrement, but it made me feel like a gorilla caged in a zoo.

It took twenty minutes for Vicky to give us the rest of the tour. Declan was enamored with the media room, where a fourteen-foot screen popped out of the wall with a click of a button. We both loved the pool on the ground floor. There was a breathtaking view of the canyon and the city in the distance, and a Japanese-style waterfall where the water ran in a solid sheet down a slick marble wall, making a soothing, gurgling splash when it hit the pool.

The kitchen was massive but friendly somehow with a terra-cotta floor and huge stainless-steel appliances. "These are restaurant quality," Vicky said proudly, caressing the stove top.

"Mmm," I said appreciatively, although neither Declan nor I cooked, even a little.

We went next to the master bedroom, which was bigger

than our entire apartment in Venice. It had its own sun porch, its own living room and a bathroom that had five rooms of its own (a toilet room, a steam room, a linen room, and his and her closets that were each larger than our bedroom at the apartment).

"How do you like your new house so far?" Vicky said.

"It's beautiful," I answered.

"Love it," Declan said.

"Great, great!" Vicky said. "Well, let's go next to the south wing. I'll show you the guest bedrooms and the one office, and then we can see the north wing."

I trailed behind her, trying to grasp the fact that my new house had not just rooms but wings. *I have wings,* I kept saying to myself. *Wings.*

Graham took charge of the situation—he hired movers to pack and move us, he even dealt with the Venice Beach landlord—and so within a week or so after returning from Dublin, we were there, on Mulholland Drive, in that cavernous house.

I'm not a prima donna when it comes to my living space. I have lived happily in three-hundred-square-foot squares with nothing but an old trunk and a matchbox closet to hold most of my belongings. It's true I find the idea of camping absurd, and I consider the concept of going without a shop-bought coffee every day a major inconvenience, but I don't need luxury. I don't need an enormous amount of space. And so, when Dec and I moved into palatial luxury on Mulholland Drive, I felt uncomfortable. Logically—*intellectually*—I adored the house. It was a wonderful space. But it didn't feel like me or, more importantly, like Declan and me. I tried to fake it, thinking that I'd get accustomed to the sumptuousness, the seclusion, but instead, each day, I felt more unlike myself.

I'm making it sound as if our house was somehow empty, and although it's true we didn't have a hell of a lot of furniture, it was anything but empty. In fact, our new home was entirely overcrowded—with strangers.

The first new addition was a housekeeper.

"You guys are too busy to maintain this whole house," Graham said when he first raised the issue. "We'll get you someone to come in five days a week."

Declan and I were in our new living room as we listened to him on speakerphone. We were laying down newspaper in the shape of chairs and couches, trying to decide where we should put the furniture we had and what else we should buy. Graham's jazz-bar voice boomed off our blank walls.

"We just spent way too much on the house," I told him. "We can't afford a housekeeper."

"Believe me," Graham said, "the money you'll spend on a housekeeper will be cheaper than spending your own time trying to clean the whole place. But hey, Declan, maybe you should ask Jerry."

Jerry was another horse who'd been added to Declan's stable of "people." Jerry was a business manager who now took care of our finances.

"Jerry said we could swing it," Declan said.

"Well, there you go," Graham said. "I've got a service. I'll have them send someone over."

Soon, there was a woman named Trista who came every morning at eight-thirty. She was smoker-skinny and had a terrible mullet-style haircut and a sullen attitude, but she could clean like no one I've ever seen. She scrubbed the kitchen as if it were an operating room; she washed the wood floors by hand; she even polished my perfume bottles to a high shine. The best part was that she hated to talk. You got the feeling that Trista had experienced some decidedly crappy things in her life, but she wasn't about to tell you that and she didn't want to hear about the crappy portions of your life, either. So she went about her work silently. She slipped through the house like an alley cat grateful to be in from the cold.

Declan's assistant, Berry, was the next to arrive at our abode. She was twenty-three, with wide brown eyes, wavy brown hair and a turned-up nose that always made me imagine her in Daisy Duke shorts and a gingham top tied below her breasts. She had, in fact, been raised on a farm in southern Illinois before moving to L.A. when she was eighteen. She had never gone to college, but instead had been a personal assistant to the stunt double for Jennifer Garner and later an assistant to the star of a WB show. She was sweet and nice, but she could also get rid of un-wanted callers with ease and she was a scheduling wizard, always keeping track of Declan's many appearances, meet-ings, photo shoots and obligations. She worked mostly out of Declan's office in the north wing, but it seemed she was always underfoot. "Hey!" she would yell when she used her key to come inside each morning. The front door would slam shut. Soon, she was traipsing through the house in her clickety-clack wood sandals, rooting through the fridge and shouting, "Do you guys have peanut but-ter in here?"

There were others, too. Manuel, the pool guy, came once a week and worked with test tubes and powders like a chemist at a pharmaceutical company. The mysteriously named T.R., our landscaper, also arrived weekly with six Mexican men in one pickup. They fanned out and went about their respective jobs, so that if I looked out the win-dow of the second-floor hallway, they were indistinguish-able—six hunched backs clad in green T-shirts.

Since our house was built in the 1920s, there were often other tradesmen in the house. My favorite was our plumber,

Dan, who wore a yellow golf pencil behind one ear and red denim overalls. Plumber fashion. I liked it.

To add to our growing household, I finally got a call from my design sales rep, Alicia, who squealed into the phone that not only had she sold my line to Macy's, our target buyer, but there were six boutiques (two in L.A., three in New York, one in Chicago) who wanted the line, too. I leaped onto the bed in our master bedroom and jumped up and down like a seven-year-old.

"Say that again!" I shouted into the phone.

"Your line has been sold!" Alicia said. "Isn't it fabulous? They'd all seen the photos of Kendall Gold, and they love your stuff and of course, they all know about your husband. Everyone is thrilled."

I let myself crumple on the bed, on my Zen-green sheets that I had thought were so "L.A." when I moved to the city. I wanted to focus on her words, *They love your stuff,* but instead I kept hearing, *They all know about your husband.* I had finally sold a collection, and not just to one store or a catalog based out of Lincoln, Nebraska. The sales that Alicia was talking about would bring me to the point in my career I'd always dreamed of. But were the buyers wanting the line because of me and my designs, or because of Declan?

"Kyra," Alicia said, "why so quiet? Isn't this amazing?"

"It is." I stood up again. She was right. It was amazing. I shouldn't go looking for trouble where there wasn't any.

When Trista walked in a minute later, I was still jumping on the bed.

Declan and I went to Il Cielo in Beverly Hills for a celebratory dinner that night.

It was a small place fashioned like a sparkling Italian garden. We were seated at a table near the front and ordered a bottle of champagne.

"To Kyra," Declan said, a raised glass of bubbly in his hand. "Soon to be L.A.'s most famous designer."

"I don't want to be famous," I said. "I just want to be the best."

He cleared his throat and lifted his flute higher. "Right. Here's to Kyra, the goddamn best designer in the world."

We clinked glasses. I leaned over the table to kiss him. And then I sensed it—a photographer outside who had caught our kiss on camera. It wasn't the first time, surely, and I knew that it wouldn't be the last, but even that one camera could color things. Eventually, the restaurant chased him away, but for the five minutes he was out there snapping shots, our dinner paled, at least for me. How can you be natural? How can you be a wife, a lover, in front of a camera, especially if you're not an actor?

It hadn't been all that long since *Normandy* came out, but I had already learned that every mistake, every triumph, every sullen look, every expression of joy, is amplified when you are in love with someone famous.

Soon, Alicia was also at the house every other day or so, to talk, to fill me in on details. And how could I tell her to back off? She had continued to sell my collection to others. Once Macy's was on board, three other department stores soon jumped on as well. I had to hire my own assistant then, a slight Japanese woman named Uki.

Tied Up, the movie that Dec had shot the past summer in Manhattan, was released early because of his notoriety. What had been the role of "Fifth Waiter in White Tie played by D. McKenna" became "Special Guest Appearance by Declan McKenna." Declan's publicist, Angela, a tall, excruciatingly thin and well-dressed woman with a beaklike face, stopped by the house a few times a week to discuss this PR angle and that, this promotion and that, this interview and that.

Bobby was at our house often, too. He was courting Declan for William Morris. Bobby tried to sell Dec on "the team" that would represent him at Morris, a different agent for voice-over, for TV, for "mo pic" (Bobby's lingo for "motion picture," which always made me think of the Three Stooges). But Declan refused to leave his original agent, Max, who spent more and more time at our house as well. And so Bobby came for Declan and stayed for me.

I missed Emmie terribly. She'd been impossible to get ahold of lately, because she was nearly always with MacKenzie, and whenever they were together they had no time for anyone else. Emmie seemed to be falling in love, for only the second time in her life, but I knew so little about it.

Meanwhile, I missed Margaux, too. This newly formed desire to bear spawn had become an obsession with her, which was strange since she'd previously regarded having a child as fondly as having a colonoscopy. We were in our own, very distinct worlds right now.

So I was grateful for Bobby. But at night, after he left, after all the others left as well, and when Declan wasn't home for one reason or another, I was nervous in that big house. I am the type of girl who feels safer at 2:00 a.m. on Houston Street in Manhattan than I do at 2:00 p.m. on a Main Street in rural Iowa. And at our new house on Mulholland Drive, sometimes I didn't feel safe at all.

I'd thought that once our address wasn't public information, the mail would wane, but with *Tied Up* just released and the international premieres for *Normandy* coming up, Declan was only getting more well known, and his mail—now sent mostly to Max—grew by the bagful. Every few days, someone from Max's office dropped off sacks of it.

Declan's assistant took over my old job of reading through the mail and sending out autographed head shots to people who requested them, but Berry was under strict orders to show us any menacing or otherwise odd correspondence.

After we moved into the new place, there were a few strange letters from a woman in Munich, who claimed to have had sex with Declan in the back room of the Hofbrau House and was now having his baby.

"Well, I hope I had a big draft in my hand," Dec said.

We sent those letters to Declan's new entertainment lawyer, who would handle it at four hundred dollars an hour. There were other letters from people claiming to have met Declan before and wondering why he was ignoring them. There were two men who wrote frequently to say that they knew Declan was gay, and they were appalled by the way he refused to come out of the closet, when the gay movement had come so far.

Then the letters from Amy Rose started again. She sent them to Max's office. In the first one we received after Dublin, she said that she was sure it had been an oversight not telling her that Declan had moved. *I have my bags packed, Declan,* the letter said. *I know how busy you are, but you'll need to let me know our new address soon. I've canceled my lease, but I need that address. I love you with all my heart, Amy Rose.*

As I looked over her letters, I wondered, had this girl actually canceled her lease? Did she honestly think she would be moving in with Declan, or was it just a ploy for attention? Graham told us to ignore her. "I know it's troubling," he said, "but the worst thing you can do is give her any encouragement."

We spoke to the police, but there was nothing threatening in the letters, they said, and from what they could tell, "Amy Rose" might be simply a first and middle name. They couldn't tell what her full name was, nor had she included a return address or a phone number. It was as if she assumed Declan knew precisely how to get ahold of her.

I tucked those letters in a box with the others from her, but they kept coming—usually at a rate of three a week— and Amy Rose was getting angry.

Declan, sweetie, the next letter said, *this is getting ridiculous. I've told everyone that we've bought a new place, and I'm moving soon, but I need you to pick me up, or at least send me the address of the new house. You know how much I love you.*

Declan's mom called one night from Dublin, saying that a nice woman named Amy Rose had called her, looking for Declan.

"I knew enough not to say anything specific," Nell said proudly. "Sure, hasn't Declan told me over and over how we need to be careful now? But I might have let slip that the house was on Mulholland Drive."

"Oh, no," I said. "You didn't tell her the address, did you?"

"Of course not. Didn't I just get done saying that I know how to hold my tongue? She was a lovely woman, that's all. Seems very enamored with Declan's acting ability, and that's hard for a mother to resist, now, isn't it?"

I got off the phone and called the police detective. Again, he said that without a specific threat or obvious harassment, there was little to be done. I hung up the phone and tried to console myself with the fact that there were thousands of homes on Mulholland Drive.

chapter 21

Nearly every other day, I left Uki in my office (in the south *wing,* that is) and drove to the fashion district in order to confer with Rosita or the cutter, or to beg the manufacturing plant to make the clothes for my line quicker. I liked the chance to escape the house, and I'd grown fond of the crowded streets of the fashion district with its packs of Hispanic teenagers, but the frequent trips pulled me away from other things I could have been working on at home. I mentioned this to Liz Morgan one day, who I still spoke to often, and she offered to help me out part-time.

"God knows I need some pocket change," she said. "I'm not getting any parts. At least not the ones I want."

Liz had just turned thirty, and she was starting to panic. If she didn't make it as an actor soon, she said, it would be too late.

"That's bullshit," I always told her. "Declan is in his early thirties and look at him."

"He's a man," Liz said, sounding resigned. "It's much, much different."

I hired Liz to come over a few times a week to pick up the slack. It was a balm to have her around. Between the ever chipper Berry, the sullen Trista and the overly deferential Uki, I needed someone I could truly talk to.

At first, I asked her to help Berry with Declan's mail, which was increasing exponentially by the day. The problem was, Liz spent way too much time on it.

"Listen to this," she'd say, reading from a letter. "'Declan, if you could just call my mother on her eighty-second birthday, it would mean the world to her. You remind her of my father who died thirty years ago.'" Liz would sigh and look at me. "Isn't that sweet?"

"It is," I said. "Where does the mom live?"

She looked back at the letter for a moment. "Bari. I think that's in Italy. But that's okay, right? I mean, we just have to figure out the time change."

"Head shot," Berry would say authoritatively from the other corner. "Put it in that pile." She gestured toward an already towering stack of letters.

Berry ran Declan's office like an army general, her sunny personality disappearing until she decided to bop through the house in search of food. (Peanut butter was her favorite, and so, just to tweak her, I often hid it in the back of the fridge behind gallons of milk and bottles of water.)

Another assistant was hired to help respond to all the mail. We now had people all over our house, all the time.

I've always liked being alone. Always. It's forever a source of amazement that so many people detest solitude. I suppose, on a clichéd level this means I'm comfortable with myself—and that surely was true for the few years before I met Declan—but that wasn't always the case. I've had many neurotic years. The post-college, I-am-such-a-fuckup stage;

the I'll-never-succeed-in-this-business stage; the why-am-I-dating-such-an-asshole stage. But even then, through all those years, I adored time alone. Maybe this has to do with being raised in Manhattan when one is so rarely by oneself.

But our lives required staff now, and so the new assistant came in, and Berry and I gave Liz other odd tasks to handle.

"Not a problem," Liz said. "This is better than the job I was going to take at Ed Debevic's."

Professionally, I was happy, too. The only exception was the fact that I had to drive in order to do my job, and I just couldn't get used to the whole driving thing. My license and my precious jade car from Declan hadn't changed that.

It was impossible to time anything accurately. If I gave myself lots of leeway to fight the gridlock, I might get lucky, but then I was thirty minutes early. More often than not, I wasn't so "lucky" and instead found myself calling Rosita or Victor on my cell phone and apologizing profusely for being late.

"It's this goddamn traffic!" I would say.

After my incessant complaints, Declan suggested I make a game of it.

"What?" I said, irritated to be pulled out of my rants about gridlock and asshole drivers who failed to give the thank-you wave.

"Look, love," Declan said, pulling out a Thomas guide. "Try to find a different way to take, okay? Look for little side streets and shortcuts. Then time yourself and give yourself a prize when you beat your record."

"A prize? Like what?"

"Well, I usually award myself a pint or two, but maybe you could give yourself a pair of earrings you've fancied."

"Hmm," I said. My competitive nature flared, even though it would be myself I would compete with.

The next day, instead of taking the 405 to Pico, I got off on Olympic and wound my way from 16th to Santee to 14th. I shaved off five minutes from the day prior. Another time, I tried taking Beverly Glen to Sunset to La Brea. A disaster—an extra twenty-five minutes. Once, when I tried to take a different route home at the end of the day, I made a wrong turn and came across a street seemingly in flames. I hit the brakes and leaned forward to peer through my windshield. The street was filled with trash cans, all ablaze and tended by homeless people, an eerie sight that could have been Manhattan during the depression.

Over the months, I awarded myself a Chanel bag and Yves Saint Laurent shoes and M·A·C lipsticks, all for good driving time. But it couldn't sway me. I still hated the driving.

Graham and Declan's PR agent asked if they could set up a few interviews for me. I told them I'd never been interviewed, and I didn't think I had anything particularly interesting to say. I wanted to dial down the media fracas, not crank it up. But Graham pointed out that this would help me as well as Declan. I could get my "message" out there about my designs. I didn't mention that there was no message, that I just designed clothes I liked, because I realized Graham had a point. Why turn down a chance to get my designs in the press?

I gave my first interview for a women's magazine called *Kate.* Just that one woman's name. I was never a big magazine reader, but the few times I'd seen *Kate,* I rather liked it. There was a certain irreverence about it because it didn't necessarily ass-kiss the makeup companies and the designers. Instead, it field-tested products and clothes and didn't hesitate to slam them.

"Normally, they have a three-month lag time," Angela,

Dec's publicist said, "but some story fell through, so this will run soon. They just want to know what it's like to be married to a movie star. It'll be a short piece."

What happened to my message? I wondered.

The reporter was young. When she arrived at the Starbucks in Santa Monica where we planned to meet, I mistook her for a high-school student. She wore low, tight jeans and thong sandals. Her skin was as smooth and creamy as milk. Carrie was her name, and she clearly thought that all my nice, planned answers about Declan and my informational speeches about my designs were insufficient, because she kept digging for something more. She smiled blandly when I talked; she made a few notes, but the same questions kept coming in varying forms: "Are you jealous of the attention Declan gets from other women?" (No, I said. I'm really not the jealous type); "Isn't it hard to watch him fool around with someone on-screen?" (It's strange, I said, but not hard. I know it's his job. And did I tell you about my Kendall Gold dresses?); "Well, I'm not much interested in Kendall Gold, but what about Lauren Stapleton? I've heard she wants Declan back." (I struggled not to make a disgusted face. Fact was, I'd been hearing the same thing when I snuck a glance at the tabloid clippings Max sent over. I affected an unconcerned shrug and told Carrie that Lauren had had her chance.)

The sun was beaming through the window at this point, right into my eyes. I was hot and cranky, and I wanted to be home, or at least inside my little green car.

Carrie asked me for the third time to describe what it was like to watch Declan kiss someone on-screen.

"Honestly," I said, trying to shift away from the sun. My chair scraped on the floor. "It's weird but it doesn't upset me."

Carrie sighed and ran a hand through her cropped black hair. "That's not exactly what I want," she said.

Here's where I made my mistake. I was annoyed. I thought I could loosen her up with some humor. "Well, I've heard a lot of women want to fool around with Matt Damon, but we don't always get what we want, right?"

It was meant to be funny. It was meant to be a light-hearted comment. It was stupid. I'd never even met Matt Damon, but Margaux had a crush on him, and there he was, his name flying from my mouth. Carrie scribbled notes in earnest then. I tried to take it back, but I only made it worse. Carrie left shortly after with a smug look.

When the issue came out three weeks later, the headline for the story read, *Declan's Wife Craves Matt Damon* with the sub line, *Declan Was Second Choice.* The article said little about my designs and lots about how I pined for sex with Mr. Damon.

Declan's response surprised me. "How could you?" He was brandishing a copy of *Kate* magazine like a sword.

It was six o'clock at night, and he'd just gotten back from Graham's office, where he'd been given an advance copy of the issue. We were in our new living room with the ice-rink floor. We'd gotten a few pieces of furniture—some fat leather couches by the fireplace, a coffee table—but still the room was too big. It bore a slightly hollow quality.

Declan huffed and paced around the room. This was the first time I'd seen him truly pissed off, but instead of scaring me, it made me want to laugh.

"How could I what?" I said.

He flipped open the magazine and found the article. "How could you tell this woman that you wanted to sleep with Matt Damon?"

"I didn't say that! C'mon, Dec, you know how it is. They take what you say out of context."

He sat on the couch and slammed the magazine on the coffee table for effect. The maple legs wobbled.

I flipped the magazine over, determined not to look inside at the picture of me. In the photo, which was taken during the interview, my mouth is wide open. I was in midsentence, but in the context of the story, it appears not only that I crave Matt Damon, but also I'm prepared to give him one hell of a blow job.

"Babe," I said, starting to get a little pissed off myself. "I'm sorry, but I didn't want to do that interview to begin with."

He stewed silently, the muscles in his jaw twitching a little.

"Hey," I said more softly. "What happened to 'Don't worry about it' and 'It doesn't matter'?"

This is what he'd been telling me for weeks when I got upset about the crazy media coverage, the articles about his alleged romances with Lauren Stapleton, Cameron Diaz and Tara Reid.

"It matters because it's you." He gripped my hand.

"What do you mean? They can say all sorts of things about you having a threesome with the Olsen twins, but they can't touch me?"

"That's right, love." He squeezed my hand harder. "I signed up for this. *I'm* the actor, for fuck's sake. I wanted to be famous, and I have to put up with this, but I don't want anyone saying anything about *you*."

I climbed into his lap. "Hey. I'm married to you for better or worse, right? I have to put up with it."

At the time, I meant it a hundred percent.

chapter 22

I admit, I was looking forward to when Declan left for Tokyo for the Japanese premiere of *Normandy*. I was relieved at the thought of having some time to myself. But when he was gone, it only reminded me that I was surrounded by near strangers in that house. At night, when they went home, I somehow couldn't enjoy that alone time I craved. Instead, I missed Declan. I watched him on *Extra!* as diminutive Japanese women screamed and cried and tried to break down police barricades with surprising force. Who are these people? I wondered. What do they want from him? What do they think they know of him?

London was the next stop after Tokyo. I was in my office with Uki when Declan called me from the airport lounge at Heathrow, where he was waiting for his escort.

"I'll be at the Savoy Hotel, love," he said. "Should be a quiet night. Tomorrow's the junket and the premiere."

"I wish I was there with you," I said. Fabric swatches covered my desk. I was working on a new line at Alicia's urging, and there was still so much to do to get the existing collection ready for the stores. There was no way I could have taken off ten days to travel with Declan.

"How are things there?" Dec said. "Is Berry around?"

"I think she ran out to get peanut butter."

"Well, when you see her, tell her to get back to my office and back to work." He knew how Berry's presence grated on me. Now, he had another assistant, Tracy, who was on the road with him. "I've got to go, Kyr. I love you."

"You, too."

Later that evening, after Berry and Uki and Trista left the house, I turned on the TV and flipped forever, finally landing on *Entertainment Tonight*. I sat through an exposé about the breakup of some boy band and a story about a radio shock jock who had nearly died pulling a stunt. Then the brunette who was sitting in for Mary Hart said, "Declan McKenna and Lauren Stapleton. Are they an item again? We'll have footage of their night in London when we return."

"What?" I said, uncurling my legs from under me. I turned up the volume.

Fifty or so commercials played for at least twenty minutes before the show returned. I sat there, muttering, "What the fuck?" and "Calm down, calm down."

The brunette finally came back on and reviewed the history of Declan and Lauren's "relationship," showing pictures of them from the movie set and the premiere. She then went on to briefly mention that Declan had married a fashion designer, without mentioning my name, before zooming into video footage of Declan and Lauren coming out of a London restaurant earlier that night. Declan was looking very Spencer Tracy in a suit and tie. Lauren wore a plunging red dress.

I shrieked and threw the remote against the wall. I picked up the phone and dialed the number for the Savoy Hotel.

"I'm sorry, madam," the male hotel operator said snippily. "Declan McKenna is not staying here."

"Yes, he is," I said, matching his tone. "This is Declan McKenna's wife."

"I'm sorry, but we have no one here by that name."

Of course. The goddamn code names Declan now used when he stayed in hotels so that fans wouldn't call him. He'd forgotten to tell me the one he was using tonight.

I tried the name he'd used in Tokyo—Tommy Colin—the first names of the twins.

"I'm sorry, madam," the operator said again, sounding very un-sorry.

"Give me a break here!"

He cleared his throat.

I tried the last names of the twins, Declan's parents' names and the names of U2 band members. All the while, I paced the gold-carpeted floor of the media room, which now seemed like a padded cell in an asylum.

"I'm his wife!" I yelled at the operator.

"Madam, if you only knew how many people have called here tonight claiming to be his wife."

"So you admit he's staying there!" I yelled triumphantly.

"No, madam. I didn't say that. We have no one named Declan McKenna here."

I slammed the phone hard enough to break the receiver. Unfortunately, it didn't. I thought about calling Graham but it was already past eleven. Berry might know the code name, but damn if I'd admit to her *I* didn't know it. She took a gleeful pride in knowing everything about Declan, which irritated the hell out of me.

I stomped out of the media room to our master suite and spent a mostly sleepless night imagining Lauren in Declan's plush bed at the Savoy. I trusted him, I kept reminding my-self, I did. I didn't *really* believe that he would cheat on me, but then what had he been doing at that restaurant with Lauren? Why hadn't he told me she would be there? Why hadn't he told me his fucking code name?

I finally fell asleep at 4:00 a.m. Three hours later, the phone rang.

"Morning, love," Declan said, cheerful as can be.

"Are you kidding me?" I screamed. I raged about Lauren, about having to see them on TV, about not knowing his check-in name.

"I'm sorry," he said, not quite yelling the way I was, but raising his voice. "I've got a bit of pressure, you know? And I've got fucking jet lag, too."

He had forgotten to give me the code name, he said, and as for Lauren, he had no idea she was going to be in London. She'd shown up at the restaurant, and when they left, they'd been hounded by reporters and paparazzi. He went to the hotel, alone, and went to bed, and that was that.

"Christ, love, I'm sorry," he said, "but it's just the media. Let it go."

I was so tired at that point, I broke down sobbing. But I knew it was more than exhaustion. I knew that I couldn't let it go, at least not for long, because this—this watching our lives on TV and reading about it in the newspaper—was here to stay.

While Dec was on the rest-of-the-world promotional tour for *Normandy,* I suddenly became a minor paparazzi target. The spotlight had shifted while he was gone, helped along by the *Kate* magazine article, the Kendall Gold publicity and the fact that I was selling my designs. Suddenly I was someone in the eyes of the media, where I'd been just a wife before.

Wherever I went, I felt like I was the actor, because it seemed as if I were onstage, with too many eyes on me.

"Kyra! Kyra!" they yelled, as I came out of Rosita's building into the twilight. They had finally learned my name.

"Hello," I said. I tried to maneuver around them, clutching my bag to my side. I always felt as if they might try to pickpocket me as well as photograph me.

"How about a smile?" they yelled.

I hadn't mastered the art of the quick-flash-fake-smile-that-looks-genuine the way Declan had, but I would try. I could feel the grin come out stiff and heavy. I would start imagining what my hair would look like in the picture, but then I would hate myself for caring, which would make me frown, and then the photographers *would* pounce, chasing me down the street and to my car, following me to the store where I bought my groceries and my wine. Within days, a picture of me wearing a massive scowl, holding a bottle of wine in a brown bag would appear in the tabloids with a caption like *Declan Drives Kyra To Drink*.

It became too hard to go out for the small things. I began to have Berry pick up my groceries and my wine, and when the workday was over, I spent my nights alone, unless Bobby could take me to dinner.

On those many nights at home, I turned to the TV more and more. I was watching it in earnest for the first time in my life. Emmie abhorred TV, and as a result, I never watched it as a kid, with the exception of *Entertainment Tonight* at my friend Colleen's house. In college, I was too busy getting stoned and lolling around my boyfriend's apartment. In grad school, I spent all my time at the drawing table. Later, in New York, I had too much to do to be enticed by TV. In fact, I didn't even own one.

But now, there I was, three thousand miles away from home, drinking too much red zinfandel from fat, bowl-like glasses and watching hour upon hour of the boob tube. Why had no one told me what garbage was on television? I couldn't drink enough to make it funny. I changed to cabernet, but still every show was so fucking stupid.

And yet, I couldn't stop. No one had given me a hint as to the complete inaneness of ninety-nine percent of TV programming, and yet no one had explained how compulsive it is. I was an addict. I could go cold turkey for a while and swear to quit. But then I would itch, I would twitch, until I could find out who had received a rose on *The Bachelor,* whether they were going to convict that guy on *Law and Order.*

When Declan got back from the tour, he was in meetings all the time. Meetings with the producers of this film, meetings with the directors of that. Declan had literally gone overnight from an actor who had to beg his way into auditions, to an actor who rarely had to read for anything or anyone. They could meet with him, they could talk to him, but it had to be big to get him to read from a script. He was now considered that good, or at least that bankable.

One afternoon when he left Studio City, he thought he saw a black car following him. He got a call on his cell phone then, a call from Max he was waiting for, so he took it and soon forgot to pay attention to the black car. When he got to Mulholland, he noticed it again, he told me. The car's windows were tinted, making it impossible to see who was inside. He took the curves faster than usual in his new Jag. He punched up the gas and ran through yellow lights. But it was still there, always behind him like a shadow. It was right on his bumper when he got to our gates. He punched in the security code, wondering if he should confront them or just get through the gates and shut them out. He wondered why he felt so anxious and thought it might have something to do with too many spy movies. His hands were wet on the steering wheel as he waited for the gates to open. Surely the car would back up now and drive away, but they were right on his tail, and they came right into our driveway.

Declan stopped his car short of our house and jumped out of the car, angry and nervous.

"Get out!" he yelled, rushing up to the car. "Get the fuck out of there and tell me what you want!"

The car idled. It seemed to him like a black cat waiting to pounce. Declan stalked up to the driver's side and pounded on the window. He wasn't sure if he was being brave or stupid. Still no reaction from inside, but he thought he heard the sound of more than one voice, and he thought he could see more than one person inside.

Declan pounded on the window again. He said he was intent on breaking it if they didn't show their faces.

But finally, the window rolled slowly down. And revealed four teenage girls, terrified, but clearly thrilled to be in the driveway of Declan McKenna.

Before I met Declan, I had always thought the concept of celebrities with bodyguards sublimely ridiculous. These people weren't visiting dignitaries, after all. They weren't leaders of a troubled nation.

And the first time Declan's manager suggested it, shortly after we returned from Dublin, I said never, ever was I going to have some beefy bohunk trailing us, watching us. But after the increasing number of weird letters, and after that car followed Dec in the driveway so easily, I changed my mind.

As Graham interviewed bodyguards, we also had the security system at our house updated. It cost thirty grand. There were sixteen cameras in the house, a digital voice recorder, remote monitors, trip wires and heat sensors. There were dozens of eyes always watching us at home now. Wasn't it bad enough that we were studied every time we left the house? But whenever Berry bit her lip nervously and handed me another letter from Amy Rose, I was glad to have all the gadgets.

Two bodyguards were hired to work on a rotating basis, or if Declan went out of town, one would go with him while the other stayed with me. Declan's guy, a somber man named Adam, had actually trained with the Israeli secret service. Denny, the other guy, was a huge black man with a shaved head. He scared the hell out of most people. Just one look could send fans scurrying away. But when you got him one-on-one, he was smiley and goofy. He and I spent so much time together that he began to feel like one of our friends. Albeit a friend that we paid fifteen hundred dollars a week to hang out with us.

chapter 23

If walking the red carpet for the premiere of Dec's film with Lauren was something of a hoot, a thrill, and the premiere for *Normandy* was an exciting coming-out party, the Golden Globe Awards was something else all together. Declan was nominated for Best Actor, and it was a zoo. The minute we stepped out of the limo it started—the screaming, the furious shotgun staccato of cameras, the buzz of a million interviews being conducted ahead of us. During our previous red carpet experiences, we'd been on the fringe of the circus—a much, much smaller circus—but now Declan wasn't just one of the freak sideshows. He was under the big top, and he was one of the main attractions.

Before, we walked the red carpet by ourselves, we talked to a few people, we giggled a lot. Now there was a small team of publicists under the direction of Angela, who led the way, deciding who Declan should talk to. Adam and Denny trailed behind us, silent and menacing.

And the posing for pictures—how bizarre. This wasn't

the pack of ten or so photographers hanging outside our apartment, shooting us as we walked to our car. This was a literal wall of black-clad photographers and videographers.

"Stop blinking," one of the publicists whispered to me.

"What?" I was still staring at the monolithic structure of photographers, all standing on bleachers, so that the lot of them reached high into the air.

"You're blinking," she said. "They won't be able to use a shot if you have your eyes closed."

Hmm. Something to remember. Was it possible I could walk everywhere with my eyes closed, just so they could never use another picture of me?

I'd already been taught by the publicists how to stand with my posture perfectly straight, one foot in front of the other, my shoulders back, my arms slightly bent ("so you don't smoosh the top of your arms against your body," the publicist had said, shuddering. "Nothing will make you look fatter"). Despite that training, though, with all the photographers that day, I felt like a bird in a cage, there for people to feast their eyes on before they moved on to the snake house.

Because of the preposterous quantity of TV I'd been watching, I was able to greet nearly all the interviewers by name.

"Pat. Billy. How are you?" I said to the *Access Hollywood* crew.

I shook Melissa's hand and asked about Joan.

"Hello, Bob," I said, making my way to the *Entertainment Tonight* crowd. I glanced around, hoping for a glimpse of Ms. Hart.

Declan stared at me in wonder every time I did that. He thought I was making an effort on his behalf; others probably assumed I was a monumental ass-kisser. How to tell them that it was all a product of nocturnal boredom and loneliness?

"Kyra, is this one of your dresses?" I heard again and again. Now, *that* kind of attention I liked. I'd designed a sheath dress in a silver and white fabric with a black bateau neckline. The best part was that the circle-of-diamonds pin, placed in the middle of the bodice, was made of real diamonds, à la Harry Winston. I kept glancing down at it, covering it with my hand, needing to check that I hadn't lost twenty carats' worth of the highest-quality diamonds around.

The noise was so loud—the buzz and screams of the crowd, the chatter, the hum of TV cameras—that many times, Declan and I had to shout to answer questions. I tired of this quickly, but Declan loved it.

"This is crazy shit," he said, waving at the hollering crowds. He said it twice before *E! News Daily* had to turn off their cameras and ask him, smiling, if he wouldn't mind avoiding the "S" word. He apologized, the dimples on his face charming everyone. He always lapsed into his thicker brogue when he was nervous or excited, and the swear words would fly with more frequency.

"Oh, fucking Christ," he said a few times when we had a moment to ourselves. "Look, look." He pointed out Paul Newman, whom he'd always admired, and across the way, an actress he'd had a crush on a few years ago. He was enamored with all these people, with the stars. He didn't realize that he was one of them.

Before moving to L.A., I had never watched the award shows, save for the Oscars, which I saw every year during Emmie's Oscar party.

The Oscars being my only point of reference, I expected the Golden Globes to be the same. Mainly, I expected them to have the obscure, boring categories like "The Key Grip in a Motion Picture Featuring a Singing Dog." But no, the Golden Globes seemed to be the meat and potatoes—best actors and actresses, best drama, best comedy. It was entertaining, but as the time for the best dramatic actor award drew near, Declan and I got antsy. This was the first time he'd ever been nominated for any kind of an award.

"I think I'm going to be sick," he whispered in my ear.

I glanced at him. His face was slightly flushed. "Breathe," I said. "It's just like we've been talking about. It doesn't matter if you win. It really doesn't. I mean, hell, the fact that you were nominated alone means that you might get an Oscar nomination."

Declan shot me a look. "Don't say that." He was ultrasuperstitious. It was an Irish thing.

I leaned over and kissed him slowly on the cheek. As I did it, I saw a camera a few rows away swing around and catch us. Usually this made me instantly nervous, aware, once again, of the people watching, but this time it didn't matter. I saw Declan close his eyes in that moment and take a deep breath. When he opened them, he nodded at me. "Thanks, love," he said. "I'm all right."

Ten minutes later, Jennifer Aniston read the nominees for Best Dramatic Actor. Declan squeezed the blood from my hand, but his face remained calm.

"And the winner is," she said, slicing open the envelope with a graceful finger.

She opened the envelope. As she read it, a small smile drew over her face. Declan squeezed my hand harder. I held my breath.

"The winner," she said, "is Denzel Washington for *Stolen Lives.*"

My heart sank hard and fast, but Declan burst into fanatical clapping. He thought Denzel Washington was an amazing actor, and after meeting him at the Golden Globes luncheon, he was even more enamored with the guy. I clapped along with him, sneaking side glances at his face. He looked almost relieved.

★ ★ ★

After Declan's category was announced, I felt my cell phone vibrate in my purse. I took a quick peek at it—a text message. (I was such a tech whore by that time it sometimes frightened me.)

Meet me by the west bathrooms, the message said. It was signed, *B.*

"Bobby?" Declan whispered. Bobby and I were forever on the phone or text messaging each other. What I would have done in L.A. without him, particularly since *Normandy,* I couldn't imagine.

I nodded. "I'm going to the rest room."

"Tell him I said hi and congrats on Everett," Declan said. One of Bobby's clients, Everett Walden, had won a Best Supporting Actor award earlier.

I tried to stay low as I crept over Declan and into the aisle. Immediately, a woman with long blond hair appeared before me. A seat filler. She gave a low weird bow, almost as if we were in Japan, before she slipped into my seat.

The west lobby was nearly deserted, but I saw Bobby, gorgeous in a tuxedo, leaning against a far wall smoking a cigarette.

"You can't smoke here," I whispered to him.

"I can until someone makes me put it out. Actually, I'll put it out for you."

He crushed the cigarette on the heel of his shoe. "You are the most beautiful woman here."

"Thanks." I twirled around to show him my dress.

"One of your best."

"Well, it's probably the diamond pin. It's real this time."

"Harry?"

I nodded.

"Nice." He grinned. "Looks like you've made it. Hey, how's Declan? Is he okay?"

"He's absolutely fine. He loves Denzel." Inwardly, I thought how odd it was that I should be throwing around the single name *Denzel* as if I knew the guy. Odder still, my husband actually did. "Declan said to say congrats about Everett."

"God, it was great, wasn't it? He really deserved it." He pulled an airline-size bottle of vodka out of his breast pocket. "Want a hit?"

"Absolutely." I took a healthy gulp. It slid down my throat, warm and bitter. "How's your date tonight? What's her name, Playa?"

"Chaya. She's all right."

"Geez, when are you going to find someone to fall in love with?"

Bobby made a wry face. He looked at the empty hall-way. He shook his head. "It's definitely not Chaya. So how did the carpet treat you tonight? You handle it okay? I know you hate that shit."

"It wasn't bad. We had the PR people and Adam and Denny."

"You know it's only going to get worse with the Oscars coming up. Especially if Declan gets nominated."

"I know."

"I mean, it could get really crazy. When I was representing Julia, and this was a long time ago, it got off the fucking charts."

"I know, Bobby, I know," I said, a little irritated. "You tell me all the time."

"Hey, you said you wanted me to warn you about this stuff."

"I do, but I also know Declan is my husband and my best friend, all right? So I've just got to put up with this stuff."

He was silent.

"What?" I said.

"Nothing. More fun topic. What party are you going to afterward?"

"I think we've got ten of them."

"Well, shoot me a message, and I'll meet you guys somewhere."

"Deal."

He kissed me on the cheek, and I crept back into the auditorium to relieve my seat filler.

At our first bash of the night, I followed Sherry, Graham's wife, to the bathroom. This was a surprisingly difficult task with the throngs of people there. The feel in the air was like a keg party after high-school graduation—everyone relieved to be done and blowing off steam. As we made our way, I saw Al Pacino, looking haggard but somehow handsome, talking to Kirsten Dunst. Great dress she had on, vintage Balenciaga from what I could tell. By the bar, I spied Brad Pitt and George Clooney. Declan was in the VIP area congratulating Denzel. Unfortunately, no sign of Bobby, yet. Luckily, no sign of Lauren.

In the rest room, we had to wait in a short line. When I came out of the stall, Sherry was talking to a statuesque black woman. In fact, if I wasn't mistaken, she'd been one of the women who carried the Golden Globe statues onstage.

"Kyra," Sherry said, "this is Malory Nevlin. She used to be Graham's assistant."

"Hello," I said. I held my hand out to her, and I gave her hand a squeeze.

"Malory," Sherry said, "this is Kyra Felis."

"Hi, there." She had almost let go of my hand, but then she was pumping it again. I noticed that something glittered behind her eyes—an interest, a recognition, an excitement. This had been happening to me lately. People didn't used to have that glitter in their eyes when I met them at a bar in New York or at one of my old temp jobs or when I first moved to L.A. The glitter hovered there now because I was, apparently, *somebody.* I was Declan McKenna's wife; I was a fashion designer; I was someone who designed a dress for Kendall Gold. I had achieved a special status in the eyes of certain people, even though I didn't feel any different.

chapter 24

On the day of the Oscar nominations, Declan's alarm went off at 7:00 a.m. He knew the nominations would be read at five that morning, but he had turned off our bedroom phone, just as he always did, and set the alarm for one hour before he was due on the set of his new film, *Liquid Glass*. His costar in *Liquid* was Tania Murray, a girl of twenty-two who had just moved from the teen shows on the WB to grown-up roles. The fact that she would play Declan's love interest irked me. She was a decade younger than him. She looked *more* than a decade younger than him, with her tiny nose and shining blue eyes. But Graham and Max were convinced that Tania was the "It" girl of the next generation, and Declan had told me she seemed like a "lovely lass."

I'd asked Declan the night before if we shouldn't get up early and watch the nominations on TV.

"God, no, love," he had said. He'd looked horrified. "That would jinx it."

Clearly, though, he'd been awake for a long while, because

when the shrill beep of the alarm shot through our bedroom he bounded up and into a standing position at the foot of the bed.

"What should I do?" he said. He was naked, his brown hair shooting up at odd angles.

I pushed myself onto my elbows and blinked at him to clear the sleep from my eyes and my brain. "You should turn on the TV."

He started for the armoire, which held our new plasma screen, but then he stopped and swiveled around. "What if it's bad news? Shouldn't I hear that from someone I know?"

"Do you want to call Graham or Max?"

He twisted his hands together. "No, no. I don't want to talk to anybody."

"Then check the phone messages."

"Right, right."

He scooted his naked self back to the bed and sat on his side, grabbing the phone. He dialed our voice-mail number and held it to his ear. "Fuck," he said. "Thirty-three messages." He slammed the phone down and turned to me. He bit the corner of his lip, which made me want to kiss him. "Do you think that's good or bad?"

I smiled.

"What?" he said.

"You got it."

"What? Why would you say that?"

"Thirty-three messages? No one gets thirty-three messages before seven in the morning to say, 'Sorry you weren't nominated.' You got it. You got it!"

"God, don't say that, you're jinxing me."

"I can't jinx you when it's already happened! Check the damn messages."

He pulled me onto his lap and sat back against the headboard. With one hand, he dialed the phone. He bit his lip again as he put the phone to his ear.

"God, I feel sick," he said. And then five seconds later, "Oh shit, oh shit. Oh God."

"Dec?"

Still he listened, his face one of shock. He shook his head and clicked the off button on the phone.

"I got it," he said.

I screamed with joy. "Of course you did!"

"I got it," he said, disbelief riding his voice. "I got it. I got it," he repeated as if to make it real.

I squeezed him around the neck, squealing.

"I fucking got it!" he yelled, as if it had finally sunk in. He picked me up and, both of us naked, he twirled me around the room.

With Dec on the phone in the bedroom, and me on a cordless extension seated next to him, we called Graham ("I'm so proud of you, kid," he said, as if Declan were his child), Declan's actual parents in Dublin (his mother cried, his father said "bloody brilliant" at least fifty times), the twins (who kidded that he'd only gotten the nomination because they needed an Irishman), Emmie (who was at MacKenzie's house *again* and told Declan he deserved every accolade he got), Margaux (who yelled, "You rock!" into the phone), Bobby (who said, "I knew it, dude") and about fifty other people.

The producer called from the set of *Liquid Glass* and told Declan to take the day off. When Declan's publicist heard that news, she immediately asked if they could send over reporters from a number of TV shows who'd been begging for interviews.

"Why do they want to come here?" I asked Declan. We were by the pool at that point, eating pancakes (one of the few things I know how to cook) and drinking coffee. We were both moving at hyperspeed—shoving food into our mouths, smiling at each other quick before slurping coffee and picking up the phone again.

"They want an unscripted reaction with me in the place I heard the news."

"Our bedroom?"

"Well, at least our house."

"I don't know." I sat back away from the table and gazed at the Japanese waterfall. It made a soothing continual *shoosh* as the water hit the pool. "One of the reasons we moved to this place was to get away from the press. Now we're going to invite them in?"

"Look, love, it's not like we're going to invite those paparazzi eejits. This is just going to be a few reporters from the news shows."

"I don't like people being in our house."

"We have a mad amount of people here all the time."

He was right. Already, Trista was cleaning up my pancake mess in the kitchen, Uki was working in my office and Berry and Tracy in Dec's, and Liz Morgan was on her way over to man the phones. Alicia would be stopping by to go over numbers for my new collection. The bodyguards, Denny and Adam, had arrived for the day and were in the kitchen drinking soda and watching CNN on the little TV.

"You don't even have to see them, love," Declan said. "If you want to, just work in your office, and I'll tell you when they're gone."

I stared some more at the waterfall. I was thrilled for Declan, and I didn't want to rain on his very large, twenty-block-long parade. "All right," I said.

But it wasn't just a few reporters from one or two of the news shows. Declan's publicist saw an opening where there hadn't been one before, and she invited over people from the national morning shows, the local morning shows, the noon-news programs, the late-night shows, the entertainment-news shows and the talk shows.

I tried to stay in the office, as Dec suggested, but it was impossible to ignore the hum of people, the stomping footfalls. When I emerged, I found the main floor of our home covered under a tangle of wires and cords. People were everywhere, speaking on their cell phones, testing cameras and lights. Reporters discussed camera angles and possible questions with their producers; waiting cameramen slouched by their equipment, drinking coffee out of the daisy-yellow mugs I'd bought in Brentwood. Trista scurried through the crowd with a look of intense panic on her face. She wiped up a spill of coffee from the floor, threw a coaster under someone's mug.

In the middle of the chaos was Declan, seated on a tall stool that had been taken from our kitchen. A makeup person powdered his face, while Angela stood nearby with a clipboard, calling out the order of the next few interviews. Dec looked perfectly in his element. A content expression played over his features; his body was relaxed.

"Hi, Kyra!" Angela said, looking up to see me sneaking through the chaos. "Why don't we get you in one of the interviews."

"No, no," I said, surprised that she'd asked after the *Kate* magazine debacle. I dashed away before she could try to cajole me.

In the kitchen, Trista furiously scrubbed dishes. "You didn't hire me to handle parties," she said, her head still in the sink. It was one of the first sentences I'd heard her put together.

"It's not a party, but you're right, and I'm sorry. If you want to do the usual and leave the rest for me, I'll take care of it later."

She scoffed as if she seriously doubted my abilities. "Just give me notice next time. And you should try to keep people out of the bedrooms."

"What do you mean?" I said, but she hurried past me with a huge sponge, muttering something.

I pushed through the camera crews and reporters again and made my way to our bedroom. The scripts on Declan's nightstand were organized too perfectly, when usually he left them in a muddled stack and asked Trista not to touch them, and the design notebook that I kept by my nightstand was closed when I was sure I'd left it open that morning—another thing Trista usually left alone. My jewelry box was at a slightly odd angle on our dresser. In our bathroom, our medicine chest looked somehow altered, as if the birth control pills and Declan's allergy medications had each been lifted and set back down in a faintly different place.

I went back to the living room, negotiating the cords and light stands and waiting reporters with hurried, angry steps. Wasn't it enough that these people were all over house? Our lives? Was there nothing that was sacred?

"Angela," I said. She was wearing head-to-toe baby pink today, which, combined with her freakishly thin frame, made her look like an aging ballerina. "Someone has been in our bedroom."

"What are you talking about?"

"Trista saw people going into our bedroom, and it's clear that things have been moved around."

She started to laugh, then covered her mouth when she caught my furious look. "I'm sure no one would do that."

Without another word to her, I walked to the other side of the room, interrupting Declan's interview with a diminutive reporter who looked as if he was about to slide off his director's chair.

"Can I see you?" I said.

"What is it, love?" Dec said, not seeming in the least irritated by the disruption.

"Can I see you?" I repeated.

"A little break, eh?" Declan said to the reporter. He got off his chair and slid an arm around my shoulder.

"I want everyone out," I said, trying to keep my voice low.

"What?"

"People have been in our bedroom, going through our stuff."

"No, I'm sure—"

"I know this for a fact, Dec. I want these people out of the house."

"I can't bloody call off these interviews now." He blinked rapidly, as if he couldn't believe what I was saying, and I felt guilty for a moment. This was *his* big moment after all. But then I thought of our bedroom, the one room in the whole damn house that was solely ours.

"They've got to go."

"No…I mean, look love, I've committed to these people. I can't just cancel."

"You mean you won't."

"I…I mean…" He trailed off and shrugged, as if to say, *What do you want from me?*

I turned away. I went back to the bedroom again. But this time, I locked the door.

A few days later, after Declan had promised never again to hold an interview in our house, he and I finally found a free hour to go furniture shopping. We'd bought a few pieces when we moved in, but we still needed so much more. Our ice-rink living room, in particular, which had a few couches, a coffee table and a plant, was begging for a table and chairs in the corner, some reading lamps, rugs, art, you name it. I'd seen a butcher-block table with black Queen Anne legs in the window of a place on Melrose, so a few days after the Oscar nominations on a

Saturday morning, we headed there in Declan's Jag. I convinced him to leave Adam and Denny at home. It was only ten in the morning, I said. We shouldn't have any trouble. The truth was, I was desperate for a normal weekend morning with him, an average couple of hours that any husband and wife across the country might have shared.

We parked about two blocks away. Both of us wore baseball caps and sunglasses. I have always thought that no one should ever wear a cap outside a stadium, but they are truly one of the best ways to hide your face, and so I'd adjusted my fashion moral code and acquired three.

We walked the few blocks to the showroom without a problem. The salesman, a guy with dyed blond hair and a retro brocade vest, was on the phone. He waved at the floor, put his hand over the receiver and said, "Look around. I'll be right with you." He went back to a discussion about some club he'd been to the night before and the guy whose phone number he had gotten but somehow lost on the way home. By the time he hung up, Declan and I had already found the table I'd seen in the window, a few end tables we liked and a huge reading chair with ottoman.

The salesman sauntered up to us. "You have any questions?"

I pointed to the reading chair. "Can you get this in a gold linen kind of fabric?"

"Oh, we've got lots of fabrics. Let me grab the book."

He took his time making his way back to his desk and finding it. When he got back to us, he handed us the closed book in a lazy way. "There you go."

As Declan and I flipped through the book, talking quietly, I could feel the shift in the salesman's attitude as he recognized Declan. He had been leaning against a nearby bookshelf, chatting again on his cell phone, but soon he had slipped the phone into his pocket. Soon, he was standing straight, away from the shelf. In the next instant, he was at our side, fully at attention, pointing out fabrics, rattling off dollars per square foot.

"I loved *Normandy,*" he said at one point. He spoke this sentence in a hushed tone, slipping it between, "It usually takes six to eight weeks to special order the chair," and "I can throw in free delivery for you."

"Thanks, man," Declan said, heartfelt.

Within fifteen minutes, we'd picked out our fabric for the chair and bought it, along with eight more pieces. Delivery was arranged for the tables, and they'd call us about the chair. It was at this point I noticed the store had filled up with people, and yet no one was doing much shopping.

"I will personally call you and take care of everything," the sales guy said, now the picture of efficiency and attentiveness. "You will not have to worry about this. You have my promise." As he gave us this earnest speech, his eyes caught on something at the front of the store, and he squinted. "What the...?" he said almost under his breath.

Declan and I turned. Outside were hordes of people.

"For fuck's sake," Declan said. "Let's get out of here."

But we couldn't move two feet outside the door. Immediately, we were swarmed by photographers, guys with video cameras and people yelling for Declan's autograph. Declan tried signing one or two, but then others pushed themselves toward us, nearly pinning us to the side of the store.

Declan threw his arm around me and pulled me into his chest. "We don't want anyone to get hurt," Declan said. "Thanks for your support, but it's time for everyone to go home now."

"Please," I said. "Let us through." I could feel people pulling at my clothes. I could hear the fast *click, click, click, click* of cameras.

"Let them be! *Now!*" I heard behind us.

I turned to see our furniture salesman looking very red in the face and ready to hurt someone. "The police are on the way, so move!"

A few people scrambled at the word *police*, but the paparazzi didn't budge. They'd heard these threats before and knew they couldn't be arrested for taking a photo on the street. The video cameras kept rolling, the photographers kept shooting. "Declan, Kyra! Give us a break!" one of them yelled. "Just smile, for Christ's sake!"

I wished I could. I often wondered if I had given in easier, if I had forced myself to be a media whore, if I had always smiled for the cameras, maybe the whole thing would have died. They might have gotten tired of us. But at that moment, I felt irrationally panicked, as if this crowd of people might crush us, swallow us whole.

Soon, a few jaded cops shoved their way through the crowd. "All right, break it up. Let's go," one of them said.

The crowd parted reverently, and the cops led us away from the store. "You all right?" they asked us.

"Fine, fine," Declan said. "We appreciate your help."

"You should have your own security."

"We do, but we didn't think we'd need it today."

"This is just my opinion, sir," one of the cops said when we reached the car, "but I wouldn't leave home without them."

chapter 25

Ever since the *Kate* article, I had tried to avoid reading the press about Declan, about us. For one thing, there was simply too much of it. For another, most of it was fabrication. Yet I changed my mind one night, about a week after the nominations.

Dec and I went to dinner at a tiny, upscale Chinese restaurant. There were two photographers outside the restaurant. How they knew we were going to be there, I had no idea.

"Mr. McKenna!" one yelled, apparently trying the polite approach. "How about a picture with Kyra?"

Declan, ever obliging, stopped and told Adam and Denny it was okay. He put a hand on the small of my back. My body and smile were both stiff as the cameras flashed.

"No more," Adam said after a few seconds. He stepped in front of us and hustled us into the restaurant.

Even when we were seated at a secluded corner table it was hard to relax. Adam and Denny were already devising an enthusiastic plan to get us out the back door, but like sand in a beach house, the photographers tended to accumulate, and we knew we probably wouldn't escape without more attention. Within the restaurant, there was also the staring by other patrons, the ingratiatingly nice waiter with the screenplay in his bag if Dec wanted to see it, the overly deferential manager who was always watching from across the room.

We were halfway through our kung pao chicken when the manager came over and told us that Todd Wilmingham, the director, and his wife were in the restaurant and wondered if they could stop by to say hello. Declan beamed and nodded vigorously. He'd always wanted to work with Wilmingham.

Soon, they were leaning over our table, both extremely nice and extremely normal. I wondered how they'd managed it, when Declan and I had felt, as a couple, rather abnormal lately. Todd was a slightly overweight man with thick black hair and a chubby, cherubic face. His wife, Pamela, was a tiny woman with pencil-straight brown hair. She wore a small wedding ring on her left hand, the diamond rather dull, the setting an outdated bicolored affair. It was obvious that this had been her original ring. There was something so sweet about the fact that she wore it, rather than trading up for a multi-carat monstrosity.

As Todd and Dec talked about Todd's upcoming movie, Pamela touched my shoulder and murmured, "Hey, I wanted to tell you to ignore that piece the other day in the *Star*. It's complete bullshit. You look fantastic. Don't ever let that stuff bother you."

I blinked, felt inordinately stupid. "I'm sorry?"

She put a hand over her mouth for a second, then took it away. "Oh, God. No, I'm sorry. You didn't see it? Well, it doesn't matter. You should never read that junk anyway."

"What? What did it say?"

She shook her head. "Total junk." Soon, she and Todd were saying their goodbyes, leaving Dec and me alone, leaving me to interrogate him about the *Star* article.

"It was rubbish," he said. "Some crap about you gaining weight."

I laughed and felt relieved. "I never gain weight."

"Exactly."

But that night, I went into Dec's office and flipped through the stack of media clips that Graham was always sending over.

Finally, I found it. *Kyra in Depressed Funk over Declan's Infidelities,* it said. *Gains Thirty Pounds.*

I sat on his big leather office chair, the well-oiled wheels sliding backward. Declan's infidelities? This again? I couldn't help but read it.

There were some vague allegations about Declan "playing around on the set and off," but no names were mentioned. Accompanying the article was a horrible photo of me that must have been taken from below. In it, I'm glancing downward, accidentally compressing my chin, making my face a looming hot-air balloon. I look cranky, depressed and ready to eat my way through a large stuffed pizza. There was another picture there, too, one of Dec kissing Tania Murray. It had been taken on the set of their movie, but of course the caption didn't say that. I had to wonder—why did these articles about Dec and other women keep popping up?

"Is this anything I should be worried about?" I said to Declan, marching into the bedroom. I threw the paper on the bed.

He picked it up and glanced at it. "Of course not." I heard him fighting irritation.

"Are you sure?"

"Yeah, I'm sure. Are you sure you're not gaining weight?"

I tried to act pissed. I shot him a nasty look.

"C'mere, you nutter," Declan said.

I climbed into bed and onto his lap. "I wish they would stop saying things about us that aren't true," I said. "I don't like these people prying, and I can't stand having to share you with everyone."

He sighed, rubbed his hand over my thigh. "What can I do? I'll do anything."

I threw my hands up, which made me feel as if I was the actress. "You know I'm not one of those people who wants to be famous. It's obscene to me. It's surreal. I never wanted this."

"I did," he said softly. "It's different than what I thought, but I'll never pretend I didn't want it."

I pushed myself off his lap. "Is that true? Did you always want *this?*" I grabbed the paper and shook it.

"I won't be one of those people who works the first half of their life to be famous and then works the rest of the time not to be recognized."

"You wanted this?" I repeated.

He nodded.

I looked away, as if he'd caused it all.

Declan came home early from the set one day and ran to my office, where Liz and I were going over a list of calls I needed her to make. Uki worked silently in the corner, as usual.

Declan beamed in that way of his that said he had good news.

"What?" I said. "Is it the Oscars? Did you find something out?"

"No, no. Well, it is about the Oscars, but not like that. The Oscars are like a bloody state secret. No, I've got a little Oscar surprise for you, love."

"Ooh," Liz said. "I love surprises!" She put down the sheet

of paper she was holding and turned to face Declan as if he was the first act in a play she'd come to see.

"What is it?" I said.

"Well…" Declan paused dramatically. "I've been asked to ask you if you'll make an Oscar dress for someone."

"Oh my God!" I jumped off my chair. "Who? Who? Not Kendall?"

He made a pleased little smile. "No."

"Well, who? I mean, who would ask you instead of me?" I tapped my pen on my hand. And then it hit me. In Declan's new film, Meryl Streep had a cameo. "Oh Jesus, is it Meryl Streep?"

"No. It's not that big a deal." Declan laughed. "It's Lauren."

I sat down and stared at him. "What did you say?"

"Lauren. You know. She called me on the set today and said she didn't have our home number, and she wanted to ask if you'd make her something for the Academy Awards."

I was silent for what seemed like a full minute. "Lauren," I said finally. "Lauren Stapleton."

"Yes. Look, love, I know she's not one of your, er, favorites, per se, but hey, it's a great opportunity, right?"

"I am not making a goddamn dress for Lauren!"

Dec looked shocked that I'd raised my voice, and his eyes shot to Uki, then Liz.

"Could we have a second alone, you guys?" I asked them.

Uki bustled from the room. Liz said, "Oh, sure. No problem," and followed.

The minute the door closed, I spoke to Declan. "What makes you think I'd make a dress for that bitch?"

He sighed a little and sat on the arm of the couch. "For fuck's sake, Kyr, I thought you'd be happy."

"Happy? You thought I'd be happy to make a dress for someone who's been nothing but rude to me?"

"What's she actually done, then?"

"She called my dress *homemade* for one thing. And she treats me like shit. *And* she clearly has a thing for you."

Dec scoffed. "She does not. You know that 'dating' thing of ours was just for the media exposure."

"Maybe for you."

"No, for both of us. Trust me, Lauren does not have feelings for me. And whether you like her or not, I think this is a great break. You're always saying that gowns are your favorite pieces to design. If you get Lauren wearing your dress, you'll get a lot of exposure."

I slumped back in my desk chair. He had a point.

"Why don't you at least call her and see what she's looking for."

"*I'm* not calling *her.*" I sounded like Queen Elizabeth asserting proper protocol.

"Then let me have her call you. You can make up your mind after you talk about it. I really don't think you should pass up this chance."

I sat silently. "Fine," I said at last. "Have her call me."

Liz came back in my office a few minutes later. "What are you going to do?"

"I either take the moral high ground and say no because I can't stand her, or I look at it as a business opportunity and ignore the rest."

Liz sank onto the small couch I'd put under the window. "You have to go with your business, at least while you're still trying to make it. You've got to do anything you can."

"I suppose." Absently, I picked up a pencil and drew a few lines of a sketch.

I didn't know if I would work with Lauren, but the concept had given me an idea.

That same day, I called Kendall Gold. I had spoken to her a few times since I delivered the dress to her, mostly thanking her for talking me up around town. She always took my calls, was always wonderful to me. True to form, she got on the phone immediately that afternoon.

"Kyra!" she said. "How are you? And how's Declan? Tell him congrats for me."

"I will. He's getting nervous but he's thrilled." I was in my office and for once I was alone. I got up and kicked the door closed.

"The Oscars are a crazy time," Kendall said. "It's taken me this whole year to fully accept that I won. Now I'm just glad to be attending and partying—nothing else."

"Have you thought about what you're wearing?"

"Have I thought about it? Of course I've thought about it. I've obsessed about it."

"Any decisions?"

"I never make a decision until a day or two before. Basically, my stylist and I get a few dresses from designers we like, and then, on the day before, we try them all and pick."

I took a deep breath. "Want to add another designer to your list?"

She gasped. "Would you make something for me?"

"That's why I'm calling."

"Oh, Kyra! You made my day! I wanted to ask you, but I figured with Declan getting nominated and you probably making your own dress you'd be too crazed."

"No, I would love to do it. Actually, I've been asked to make one for Lauren Stapleton."

"Eh," Kendall said, sounding distinctly unimpressed.

"My sentiments exactly, but I'd like to design for other people, too. If anyone is interested, that is."

"Well, you know I am. And honey, you're hot property now. Not only are you a designer in your own right, but you're married to an Oscar nominee. Do you know what that means in this town? There are a million women who'd die for you to design for them."

I felt a swoop of nausea. "I only want to design for people who really like my stuff. Not because of Declan."

"Oh, don't get all pissy. You're dazzling in your own right."

I laughed. Kendall had a way of simplifying everything and making you feel wonderful at the same time.

"Now, I know for a fact that Hannah Briscoe and CeCe Springfield are both looking," Kendall said.

"Really?" I stood up and paced the office. Hannah Briscoe was a film actress, who looked like a very thin version of Marilyn Monroe and always dressed like a lady. No jeans and T-shirts for her. She would be perfect for my designs. CeCe Springfield, who had starred in one of the Best Picture–nominated films, was young and trendy, but I could go that way, too. Couldn't I? For a moment, I doubted myself, my abilities. I was really only talking to Kendall, after all, because I was married to Declan.

"I've got both of their numbers," Kendall said. "Let me call them first, and if it's okay, I'll pass them along to you."

"Oh, Kendall, you're a godsend."

"No problem. Just make sure you design my dress first."

I stopped my pacing. "Deal."

By the end of that day, I not only had numbers for Hannah and CeCe, I'd talked to their stylists. I told myself again and again that it didn't matter whether I was getting this attention because of Declan or not, because I, Kyra Felis, was designing three more dresses for the Academy Awards.

The remaining few weeks before the Oscars were a blur of frantically scribbled designs, constant meetings about fabric and patterns, phone calls with stylists and the ever-increasing media attention.

Dec was the man of the hour, and he loved it. He barely

slept during those weeks, but he didn't seem to miss it. He went to the set nearly every day, and the cast and crew stayed late to allow him time to be interviewed by every conceivable show, paper and magazine. The cast and crew loved him, as most people did, but most of all they loved that they were working with an Oscar-nominated actor. It was something they could talk about for the rest of their careers.

I hardly saw him during those weeks, except to have him fall into bed next to me at the end of the day, and awake to find him reading his lines.

"You asleep?" I'd say.

"Nah." He would kiss me. "How are the dresses coming?"

"Slowly."

I would tell him about the fabric for Lauren's dress, which I'd had to change four times in order to find one that appeared light enough but would support the beadwork. Then there was the seam on Kendall's, which kept buckling over the hips no matter how many times I had the factory redo it. I didn't tell him that I wasn't sleeping much either, because when I did, I dreamed about a tiny version of me riding on Declan's wide, flapping coattails. Instead, Dec would kiss me again, then jump in the shower, and I'd make my way through the house to my office, and we would start it all over again.

It was as if the Academy Awards were a mountain that we were both waiting to climb. We were at base camp, preparing for the push to the summit, and neither of us could think of anything else.

Leaving the house was an unbelievable pain in the ass. No longer was it possible to simply trot out to my car and make a coffee run. Photographers had learned where we lived, and they parked at a turnaround a mile away, waiting for Declan or me, or hopefully both of us, to come speeding around a corner. The few times we tried to have dinner together recently, they seemed to know where we'd be, forever awaiting our arrival with their cameras and their shouts of "Declan! Kyra! Look over your left shoulder! This way!"

I talked to Bobby about this, and he advised me to "roll with it." "It's not going to stop," he said, "so just take it in stride."

Kendall Gold, meanwhile, said it was sure to get less intense eventually. The watchers couldn't be everywhere, and although every celebrity had paparazzi problems, it wasn't normal for them to always be around, to be able to divine where we were going. Graham had told us the same thing.

I began to wonder if someone was deliberately leaking our plans. There were so many people in our household, in our employ, many of whom might know where we were at any given time—Trista, Uki, Berry, Tracy, Alicia, Angela, Liz, Graham, Max, Adam and Denny. Declan said I was being paranoid. I thought maybe he was right, because I was starting to feel a little crazy. Whenever I left the house, even for something minor, I had to notify Denny, then fight with him about which of us would drive, and whether I should go in a back door or walk in the front like an ordinary person (albeit an ordinary person who is followed by a couple of paparazzi).

I might have been okay with all of this. I might have been able to handle it, except that on top of it all the letters from Amy Rose had started again. For some reason, Declan hadn't heard from her for a while, or maybe he and Graham and Max had kept her letters hidden. But then she started sending them to me.

Dear Kyra,
I just had to write you, the first one said. *I tried to ignore you for so long, because I know you're only interested in*

*Declan because of his fame. I know I must be patient. But it
seems that now you won't go away. Please step back and let
us be happy. Please, just let us live the life we were destined
to have.*
Sincerely, Amy Rose

The letter frightened me, and yet it strangely touched me.
It was something I might have written to a paparazzo, or
Amy Rose herself, if I'd thought it would do any good.

chapter 26

"What are you wearing?" Margaux asked me. "I mean, my God, it's the fucking Academy Awards!"

We had finally gotten on the phone at the same time. Between my newly hectic schedule and Margaux's juggling of her lawyerly duties and the infertility treatments she'd decided to try, we usually only had time to leave each other messages.

"I think I've got my dress taken care of." I told her about the copper dress I'd designed myself.

"Where's the pin?"

"At the shoulder."

"Perfect. So how are the other dresses coming along?"

I groaned. "I'm freaking out. Sometimes I look at them and think they're great. Other times, they look like complete shit, and I know I'm a fraud."

"You're not a fraud! You deserve this."

"Well, it's been one setback after another. I've only slept maybe four hours a night for the last week, but I think they're finally ready. The fittings are today."

"So how is *Lauren?*" Margaux said this as if she was asking about a particularly deadly airborne virus.

"A pain in my ass."

"Jesus, talk about pressure. The Oscars are only days away."

"Don't remind me."

Forty-five minutes later, I was at Lauren's place in Santa Monica. It was a large beach house, the ocean a blazing blue outside the French doors of her living room. I was surprised to find the house tasteful—Stickley furniture, light-colored Oriental rugs, long, comfortable chenille sofas, flowing ivory curtains that puffed and billowed with the breeze. Interior designer, I thought. Definitely. I refused to think that Lauren, on her own, might have decorated the place.

She kept me waiting for thirty minutes.

"She should be right here," the stylist said, who also sat on a Stickley chair, awaiting Her Highness's arrival. "She's usually not this late."

Finally, Lauren floated into the room wearing a short black wrap dress that was probably D&G. Sunglasses pushed back her mane of oatmeal hair and sat high on her head, as if any minute she might jump into a convertible and drive down the coast.

"Sorry," she said in an amused tone. "I was on a call with Marty."

"Scorcese?" the stylist said, impressed.

"Yes, you know how chatty he can be. Anyway, Kyra! Hello!" She swooped down on me and air kissed me on both cheeks. "What have you got for me today?"

In one sentence she made me feel like a soap salesman who had stopped by the farmhouse.

I ignored the question. "If you're ready to try on your dress, I can make whatever adjustments you like and have it ready for you tomorrow." I didn't mention that after this visit, I had to see Kendall, Hannah and CeCe, and that I would probably be up most of the night hand sewing the alterations to their dresses as well. That is, if anyone liked them.

"Great!" Lauren said breezily. "Let's see it."

I moved as confidently as possible to the mauve velvet garment bag I'd laid over a couch. I unzipped it and took out her dress. It was a butter-yellow, formfitting, chiffon gown with a beaded bodice and a hem that had a deep triangular cut so Lauren's famously long legs would show with every step. I was inordinately proud of this dress, despite the woman I had made it for, because after all the fabric searches and changes, after all the anxiety and self-loathing, it had come out exactly how I had seen it in my mind—ephemeral and glamorous. I had even hand sewn the beading myself.

"Ah," Lauren said. She cocked her head to one side and then another, studying it. Meanwhile, I held the dress aloft. I was so much shorter than she, I had to hold it high, and my arms began to quiver as she circled me, assessing the gown.

"It's stunning," the stylist said finally, although she looked at Lauren for confirmation.

"Mmm," Lauren said. "I might as well try it on."

She stripped slowly, her eyes still on the gown, first untying the cloth belt that held her dress together, then letting the dress slide off her shoulders and fall to the floor. Under the wrap, she wore matching bra and panties I had seen at La Perla. The bra was sheer, clearly showing her high breasts and large nipples. The panties had tiny satin strings that held together two sheer triangles, one which barely covered her ass, and the other which broadcasted the fact that Lauren Stapleton waxed off all her pubic hair.

I immediately averted my gaze, laid the dress back on the couch and began searching for the tape measure and pins in my bag. But I couldn't help wondering—had Declan slept with her while they were "dating"? Had he gotten an up-close and personal view of Lauren's ultra-Brazilian? The thought made me sick. And then angry. By the time I turned around, holding a pair of large scissors and a mouthful of pins, I must have looked deranged.

"My!" Lauren said. "Ready for action, aren't we?"

I grunted and gestured for her to try on the dress.

She slid it over her head, and once it had settled on her hips and she had stepped into a pair of shimmery ivory sandals, the stylist gasped. "I love it," the stylist said.

Lauren stepped up to a full-length mirror that had been moved into the room for the occasion. "It's nice," she said, "but it hangs funky around the waist, don't you think?"

I took the pins out of my mouth and pushed them back into their cushion, because the truth was, I didn't think any tailoring was needed. The dress was flawless. The yellow of the gown made Lauren's hair seem golden and angelic, the beads accentuated her breasts, and the hem gave flashes of her tanned, smooth legs every time she moved.

"I think the fabric hangs perfectly on your waist," I said. There was no puckering of the fabric there; the seam was imperceptible.

"I don't know." She posed in the mirror, her eyes never leaving her lithe, Amazonian body.

"I think this is the dress," the stylist said. "It screams glamour, and it's so much better than the others we have."

Lauren sent the stylist what seemed like a warning look. "I'm not sure. I mean, the hem has to be changed for sure. This slit thing in the middle needs to come higher."

"If it comes any higher, you'll be showing off your nifty wax job," I said.

I regretted it immediately, because Lauren turned to me with a triumphant little smile. "Well, make it so it's higher but not *that* high." She giggled, a false laugh that seemed to trill through the living room and out the French doors to the sea. "Just make the changes," she said, speaking now in a tone I was sure she used with her cook when ordering her soy smoothie in the morning. "I'll let you know if I'm going to wear it or not."

Hannah's fitting was next. After leaving Lauren, I felt anxious again, unsure. *What* did I think I was doing designing dresses for the Academy Awards when I hadn't held a steady design job in years, hadn't sold a line in over two until just recently? The answer nagged at me. I was in this position because of Declan. It was that simple. I wouldn't have been designing gowns for the stars were it not for my husband.

Some confident part of my psyche tried to rally, arguing that while Declan had provided the opportunity, I was here because I was a damn good designer. I tried to stay with this mind frame as I unzipped the garment bag housing Hannah's dress. We were in her stylist's office. Hannah was perched on the edge of a desk, wearing white pedal-pusher pants and a white blouse. With her white-blond Marilyn Monroe hair, she looked old-world and timeless, but it was that image I had decided that I wanted her to eschew, at least for a night.

"Now, here's what I'm thinking," I said as I slowly drew down the zipper. "It's black, first off."

"Hannah doesn't wear black," the stylist snapped. "I thought we told you that." She stood to the side, a short, fit woman with spiky brown hair and a sleeveless T-shirt.

"Hear me out," I said. "I know the image you usually go for is something classic and elegant, but I think you should shake it up a bit."

"Shake it up?" the stylist said snidely.

Hannah held out her hand. "Go ahead."

"I'm not suggesting you go goth or anything like that, but instead of your gentle, feminine look, I think you should be feline and powerful. Instead of your pinks and pale yellows, I think you should be in streamlined, daring black. And instead of ruffles and fishtail pleats, I think you should show a little skin."

With that, I shook the dress out of the bag with a flourish. It was a sheer black gown with a nude lining. The deep V in front cut all the way to the navel, where a very large circle of Harry Winston diamonds rested. The skirt was flowing and fluid but with a thigh-high side slit.

"It's fantastic," Hannah said. She took the dress behind a screen and minutes later, she emerged. She had put on the black stiletto heels I'd brought with me in her size. She threw her shoulders back, stuck out a long, pale leg and put her hand on her hip. "What do you think?"

"Damn," the stylist said. "It works."

I beamed. It did work. Hannah had been transformed.

Surprisingly, the fittings for CeCe and Kendall went just as well. For CeCe, I'd designed a flirty, floral-print, Moschinoesque gown, a sure departure from the cargo pants and funky tops she usual wore. For Kendall, I went with a pink satin dress with a halter neck and the circle pin at the base of a very low back.

Lastly, I had to put the finishing touches on my own dress, a burnished-copper gown with tiny silver ribbons sewn through it for a shimmering effect. The bodice was corseted and the skirt had a tiny hoop under it so that my waist appeared minuscule. I thought the copper would complement Declan's eyes, and when he first saw the dress, two days before the Oscars, he looked as if he might cry for a second.

"God, you're beautiful," he said.

We were in my office and I stood before the window, the sunlight resting on my bare shoulders.

"You're just emotional because you're tired," I said.

"No, love," he said. "It's you."

The next day I heard from the stylists of Kendall, Hannah and CeCe. They would all be wearing my dresses.

Liz Morgan and I whooped and hollered and slapped high fives, practically dancing around my office. Uki clapped politely and watched us with wide eyes. Maybe I *was* good enough.

"Now you've just got to hear from Lauren," Liz said.

But the hours went by with no word from her or her stylist. Liz called a few times, but she only got voice mail.

"I've left two messages," Liz said. "Should I call again before I go home?" It was already four-thirty.

"No," I said. "And you can go home to Jamey if you want. You've been working way too much."

"I'll wait with you." She picked up a stack of orders that we had been neglecting.

I crossed the room and hugged her. "Thank you," I said. "You're a good friend."

I turned to Uki. "What about you? Do you want to leave early today?"

She shook her head no. "Too much to do."

I putzed around my office then, working on one task, then another, unable to concentrate on anything for long. Between my nervousness for Declan and my anxiety over the dresses, I was a jittery mess.

At six o'clock, the phone rang. Liz held up crossed fingers and snatched it up. "Kyra Felis's office. Yes, how are you, Kathy?" she said, nodding at me. Lauren's stylist. "Uh-huh. Sure. I understand. Okay, okay. Well, I'll let her know. Thanks." She hung up.

"And?" I said.

"And," Liz said, standing from the desk. She had a pinched

expression on her face, but suddenly it broke into a smile. "She's wearing it!"

This time, even Uki screamed.

chapter 27

Oscar night, it turns out, is really Oscar day. Declan and I were both up by six.

"Sleep?" I said to Dec, expecting to hear the now usual, "Nah."

But he blinked at me and smiled. "It was brilliant. I didn't wake up once."

We both worked out in our new gym—Declan on the StairMaster, me on the treadmill. I missed the mornings when I would run around the Venice canals and down the beach to watch the surfers. There was something pointless about a treadmill, something inherently frustrating, but I needed to feel my best today, so I trudged through the half hour.

At eight, Graham stopped by to wish Declan luck. "If you lose, just smile and clap," he said, "but you should know I think you deserve the statue."

The two men hugged. For the briefest of moments, Declan turned his head to the side and rested it on Graham's shoulder. It seemed as though Graham had become the father Declan always wanted—someone who was around, someone who was unconditionally supportive. Once or twice I had thought to point out to Dec that he paid Graham to act that way, but it seemed cruel, and I really did believe that Graham adored Declan just as much.

Graham left to do his own Oscar preparations, and within an hour after that, a team of aestheticians were at the house to give us calming facials, manicures, makeup jobs and a pedicure for me. Declan's stylist arrived next. I'd selected Declan's clothes for the evening—a black Armani suit with sharp lapels, along with a shirt and tie the color of heavy cream. The stylist, however, would make sure the tie was straight, the shoes buffed. She would help him decide about a handkerchief or maybe Declan's pocket watch from his grandfather.

While Declan conferred with his stylist, I was having a princess moment. A representative of Harry Winston had set up shop in our living room and was displaying millions of dollars' worth of diamonds. I could choose any of these baubles to wear for the evening. I would have to return them, of course, but that didn't make the decision any easier. Should I, for example, select the three-tiered choker or maybe the serpentlike bracelet that snaked up the arm? A tiara seemed too much, but I couldn't help trying it on. Finally, I chose teardrop diamond earrings and a platinum rope bracelet with inset diamonds. I resisted the necklaces, not wanting anything to compete with the circle-of-diamonds pin (also by Harry), which would sit at the shoulder.

At last it was time to get dressed and into the limo. "Ready?" I said to Declan, kissing him on the nose. We were in the foyer, and we were too dressed up and made up for any real contact.

"Yeah," he said. "I think I'm okay. You look gorgeous, love."

"You, too." He was, quite simply, dashing in the dark suit, the ivory shirt, his golden eyes gleaming and expectant.

There were two stretch limos outside the house. We got in the first one. A few of the publicists, who would maneuver us through the red carpet and the many interviews, rode in the second limo. The other publicists were already at the Kodak Theatre.

Declan and I held hands, squeezing them every so often. "I can't believe I'm going to the Academy Awards," I said.

"I can't believe I'm nominated," he said.

The ride swept along at a fast pace. In no time, we turned onto Highland Avenue, only a few miles from the Kodak.

"Almost there," Declan said. "Shit." He started bouncing one of his legs, then biting his lip. He squeezed my hand again and again.

But then the limo ground to a halt. The divider slid down. Adam, sitting in the front with the driver, said, "Get comfortable. It's going to be a while."

"Why?" Declan said.

"Traffic. Everyone's lined up to get to the entrance."

"Well, how long?"

Adam conferred with the driver. "Could be an hour, maybe more."

"An hour?" Declan sounded anguished. "Let's just walk."

"You're not walking," Adam said, sounding very much like a parent. "We can't cover you if you're walking. It's too crazy."

Dec got on the phone and called the publicists in the other limo, who, in turn, called the publicists who were already at the theater, all of whom were adamant that he not get out of the car. They had to time his arrival exactly right so he didn't compete with the other big stars.

"Shit," he said. "What are we supposed to do for an hour?"

"Call your parents," I said. "We were supposed to do that anyway before we left."

We spent fifteen minutes talking to Declan's parents and sister, but that still left lots of time.

"Let's call someone else," he said, looking at his watch.

I tried Emmie's number. A man's voice answered. "MacKenzie?" I said.

"Hello, Kyra!"

"Hi. Is Emmie having people over?"

"No, just the two of us."

"Oh." I'd never known Emmie to have single men to her place. It was as if Britton was the only man who could fill that role, and if he wouldn't, then no one else would be invited. But apparently, MacKenzie was different.

Emmie got on the phone, thrilled to hear from us, flattered that we'd called. She talked to Declan mostly, and I'm not sure what she said, but he seemed calmer when he hung up. The phone rang again. It was the publicists who were already at the theater. Wait a little longer, they said. It was too early.

"Too early for what?" Declan said.

Believe us, the publicists said, you don't want to be early. Just trust us. So we sat there. By the time they gave us the okay to get out of the car, I was already exhausted.

Pandemonium reigned when we opened the door, making most of our previous red-carpet encounters seem like church socials. This red carpet was huge and glutted with beautiful people, shouting reporters and looming video cameras. Above us, balconies had been built to hold the reporters from the entertainment-news shows. Strangely, some of the reporters on the carpet had little stations where they had to stand, their names written on a card at their feet. It was as if these people were museum pieces. I liked that they couldn't move away from their card, couldn't rush Declan, but the yelling flustered me, and they were *all* yelling. "Declan! Kyra! Just one question! Please!" It didn't matter what they screamed, though, because Declan and I had little input in who we spoke to. That was the job of the publicists, who decided precisely who we would have a discussion with and for exactly how long.

Like the Golden Globes, there was a wall of photographers here, but this one somewhat resembled the Berlin Wall before it fell—formidable and imposing. The photographers shouted our names; they shouted questions—*How do you feel tonight? Can you believe you're here? Who are you wearing?*

Between the overwhelming amount of people and lights, not to mention the heat and the fact that I hadn't used the bathroom in over two hours, I started to feel light-headed. It was all too much. But I kept that smile taped to my face; I remembered not to smush my arms against my body; I remembered to put one foot in front of the other and follow Declan down the carpet.

We were being interviewed by *Entertainment Weekly,* and photographed by a certain section of the wall of photographers, when the reporter suddenly went wide-eyed. I turned to find Kendall Gold.

"Kyra!" she yelled. She pulled me into a tight hug. "What do you think?" She twirled around in her pink dress. The low back was achingly sexy and the halter neck showed off her tanned, toned shoulders. Her hair was twisted up in an elaborate updo.

"You look gorgeous," I said.

"Dress by Kyra Felis!" she announced to the crowd, striking a pose with her arms outstretched.

The cameras flashed crazily. "Let's get you two together!" the photographers yelled. We posed, and I felt inordinately proud. My own fashion publicist must have seized the moment, because within minutes, she was at our side looking sweaty and harried, but with CeCe Springfield, Hannah Briscoe and Lauren Stapleton (along with all *their* publicists) in tow. "All these dresses were designed by Kyra Felis," my publicist announced.

The photographers responded, hungrily shooting film, but I couldn't smile, couldn't even respond, because Lauren *wasn't* wearing my dress. Instead, she had on a skin-toned gown with an ugly asymmetrical wing on the front, which, I supposed, was intended to be postmodern.

Before I could say anything, Lauren had beaten me there. "Oh, I'm not wearing Kyra's dress," she said mischievously.

The reporters and photographers near us seemed to sense something good on the horizon, and they all went silent.

"No, I'm wearing Mehta Vamp," Lauren said, naming a new designer who had been written up recently in *Bazaar.* "I had to go with a true professional for the Oscars."

I blinked. I licked my lips. Had she just said that? She had not only insulted me, but she'd insulted Kendall, Hannah and CeCe, who had worn my dresses. The photographers began snapping their cameras again, the reporters began shouting, most asking if there was a "feud" between Lauren and me. I glanced around for Dec, but he was standing four feet away with a reporter from *People.*

Kendall Gold stepped in front of Lauren, elbowing her out of the way. "The only feud going on today," she said, "is the war between good fashion and bad. Here's a sample of the good, boys." She pulled CeCe, Hannah and me close to her. "Smile big," she whispered to me. "I mean really flash those teeth."

So I did. And the cameras went wild for the four of us pushed together and beaming. By the time I turned around, Lauren was being hurried away by her PR people.

After that encounter, I was ready to get inside the theater and maybe hide in a bathroom stall for a few hours, but instead, Declan and I gave what seemed like a thousand more interviews, posed for a million more pictures.

At one point, we were close to the huge glut of screaming fans that was held back by black barricades. "Declan! Declan!" they yelled. They held out his photograph and felt-tipped pens. They clicked their disposable cameras. I noticed a couple of women crying.

"C'mere, Kyr," Declan said. He took my hand and rushed us through a line of security men toward the fans. I glanced behind and saw Denny and Adam running after us, speaking into their radios, looking concerned and pissed off.

"Are you sure?" I said. I wanted nothing more than a vodka tonic and my seat in the theater, and the truth was, the intensity of these people scared me. Why did they love Declan so much when they didn't know him?

"Just for a second, love," Declan said. "It only seems fair."

I nodded. It was only fair that I do what Declan wanted at that moment. It was his night.

The fans went wild when we reached them. They shoved their photos and pieces of paper into Declan's hands, begging him to sign. More cried. They surged forward toward him as if one body. They yelled, "I love you! I love you!" Declan autographed anything they put in his hands. He was used to it by now; he could sign his name in a second and move on to the next. I stood by his side, smiling as kindly as I could, trying not to be freaked out by the whole spectacle.

"Kyra!" I heard from my left. "Will you sign this?" I could see a pair of arms outstretched over the barricade, and I could see in those hands a copy of the article that had been written about me in *Kate* magazine. Not my favorite, but what the hell, I thought.

I moved from Declan's side, and took the article from the woman. She wore a purple floppy hat pulled low over her forehead. "There you go," I said after I'd signed it.

She pushed the hat back, and instead of taking the magazine, she grabbed my wrist. Tight. I realized then that this woman was familiar. It was her dark, dark eyes and the frosty pink lipstick.

"You're…" I said.

"Amy Rose," she replied, giving me an eerie smile that only barely lifted the corners of her mouth. I suppose the woman's heart-shaped face would have been pleasing to some. She had a small chin, wide cheekbones and those large, dark eyes. But to me, she looked devilish, evil.

I tried to pull my hand away. "Excuse me."

She held firm to my wrist. I felt the sharp, jagged edges of her nails pinching my skin. "I've got to tell you something," she said. "It's time for you to go."

"What—"

"That's right," I heard an authoritative voice say from behind me. It was Denny, thank God. "It's time for her to go." He grabbed me by the shoulders and wrenched me away. I glanced to my right and saw Adam urging Declan away from the crowd.

"That was Amy Rose," I whispered to Declan when he reached me, but he was already on to another interview.

By the time we got to the doors of the Kodak, I was a mess.

"What? What is it?" Declan said, finally catching on to my stricken expression.

"That was Amy Rose back there!"

"Jesus," he said. He hugged me tight. "I'm sorry I wasn't there."

We congregated in a corner of the lobby with Adam and Denny, who were well acquainted with Amy Rose's letters. I wanted them to call the police, to have her removed from the property.

"They won't do it," Adam said. "She didn't threaten you."

"Yes, she did! She said it was time for me to go!"

"That might have meant it was time for you to go in the theater."

"That's not what she meant. I want the police notified, at least."

Declan's main publicist, Angela, pushed herself into our tiny circle. "We're not calling the police, guys," she said. "If we do, it will cause the biggest media story."

"So what?" I said, appalled. "Don't you care about our safety?"

"Of course. But it doesn't sound like anything truly threatening, and she won't be admitted in the building. Plus, if we get the cops here, the show could be held up. It will be in all the papers, it will be all that everyone is talking about."

"Who bloody well cares?" Declan said. "If Kyra wants to call them, I think we should."

Angela placed a hand on my arm. The gesture reminded me of Amy Rose and I fought not to pull away. "Look, Kyra," she said. "I want this night to be about Declan, about his nomination. Don't you?"

"Of course," I said softly.

"If we get the police here, the night will be about a nutty fan. She'll get the attention she wants, and Declan won't. Do you see what I'm saying?"

"Do whatever you want, love," Declan said.

I sighed. By now, I felt a little silly. She was outside, not next to us, and what had she really said anyway?

"Okay," I said. "Let's just forget it." I kissed Declan's cheek. "Let's go have some fun."

But the ceremony was interminable. I tried to muster interest for the Best Short Foreign Film category, and Best Special Effects, yet it was impossible. I couldn't help waiting, wanting, the Best Actor category. It was toward the end of the show—Murphy's Law—by which time I was famished and weary. I was particularly tired of putting on a happy face and clapping serenely every time the camera swung its inquisitive head toward Declan and me, which was often.

Bobby, who was at an Oscars party, rather than the actual ceremony, told me to keep my phone on, even though it wasn't allowed, and he kept torturing me with text messages.

I'm on my fifth vodka martini. I'm drinking for you, too, the first one said.

A few minutes later, he messaged, *Smile more, you look miserable. Also, you have something on your teeth.*

I surreptitiously scrubbed at my front tooth with an index finger.

Got you, the next message said.

Then later, *You could out-bling J. Lo with those earrings.*

Declan, I think, was in more pain than I was. He had on a big fat grin, and he clapped like crazy, especially when *Normandy* won in other categories, but I could feel the tension coming off him in waves.

"I just want this to be over," he whispered to me.

Finally—finally!—two hours and fifty-eight minutes into the show, it was time for Best Actor. In a stroke of fortuitousness, Hannah Briscoe was announcing the award, along with her current costar. They made some forced, witty banter about leading men, but I couldn't focus on their words.

They began to read the names of the nominees, followed by a montage of clips from the actors' movies. The other nominees were tough competition—Jack Nicholson for *The Taming,* Denzel Washington for *Stolen Lives,* George Clooney for *Cheaters,* and another relative unknown named

Harvey Carpetta for *Theory of Beauty*. Declan's name was read last. Was that good? I wondered frantically. Or did that mean that he wouldn't win? Maybe being read last meant you were runner-up?

Declan put a hand on my knee. I could feel the heat of his skin. I grasped his upper arm.

"And the winner is…" Hannah said sweetly. She began to open the envelope, but it got stuck somehow. "Oops," she said, causing the audience to titter. She tried again.

That moment lasted days. In a time warp of excruciating slowness, she finally opened the envelope, she put her dainty fingers inside, she withdrew the heavy card, she opened *that* card, she read it, she showed it to her costar, they both smiled, Hannah leaned into the microphone, she cocked her head a little as if to say, "Wow," she smiled again, she opened her mouth, and said, "And the Oscar goes to…"

Years seemed to go by before I heard, "Declan McKenna."

I burst into immediate tears so powerful there was nothing I could do to stop them. Declan pulled me to my feet and embraced me.

"I'm so proud of you," I said, bawling. "I love you."

"Christ," he said. "I love you, too."

He managed to break away from me and make his way to the stage. In a flash, he was there, hugging Hannah and shaking the hands of her costar. He thanked Kaz Lameric for his vision and for taking a chance. He thanked the screenwriters for a brilliant script. He gushed about the producers and all the work they'd done. He thanked the editors, who had made a cohesive and gripping drama out of thousands of hours of film. He was grateful for his costars, who made him look good. He thanked Max and Graham.

The lilting background music started to play, the music

that signaled he had only seconds left before they escorted him offstage.

"Oh God, no," Declan said, laughing. "I want to thank my parents and my family and friends in Ireland."

The music played louder.

"And most of all," Declan said, the music growing ever stronger, "I want to thank my wife, Kyra Felis. I made this film before we met, but without her..." He shook his head, he looked on the verge of tears. He held his Oscar up with a triumphant arm. "Without her," he yelled as the music reached a crescendo, "this wouldn't mean anything. Kyra, you are my angel!"

chapter 28

Oscar Winner's Night on the Town
(Minus the Missus)

Academy Award winner Declan McKenna partied until the wee hours of the morning after receiving his Oscar statuette. The film star was seen at nearly ten soirees that evening but spent most of his time at the *Vanity Fair* party, which boasted such other elite attendees as Drew Barrymore, Harrison Ford, George Clooney and Meryl Streep. The one person who was noticeably absent was McKenna's wife, fashion designer Kyra Felis...

Honestly, I don't know where the reporters get this stuff. There's often a hint of truth in these articles—here the truth was that Declan did attend the *Vanity Fair* party—but they often get so much of it wrong. I was there, although I don't know why I should get so defensive about it. The truth is,

I simply wasn't at Declan's side most of the night. I spent nearly half an hour talking to Graydon Carter (charming, great hair, to-die-for clothes), and another forty-five minutes or so at the bar with Bobby, railing about Lauren. Kendall dragged me around for a while, introducing me to everyone, telling them they were idiots if they didn't start wearing my clothes soon.

Face-Slapping Fit for Declan's Wife

Oscar winner Declan McKenna was once quoted as saying, "I don't get angry very often. It's something to do with my Irish heritage. We're much more passive." Well, it turns out, Declan's wife, fashion designer Kyra Felis, must be handling the anger for him.

Felis reportedly slapped actress Lauren Stapleton during the Miramax after-Oscars party following a skirmish about a dress Felis had designed. Stapleton had purportedly promised to wear the gown, but instead showed up in a daring dress by Mehta Vamp. When Stapleton tried to explain her fashion reasoning to Felis in the ladies' room, Felis apparently went into a rage and slapped Stapleton, forcing other partygoers to break up the two…

Now this one I kind of liked. Mostly, I enjoyed the concept of bitch-slapping Lauren, and the tough-girl image the article gave me. Alas, the reality is that although I desperately wanted to maim her, I held myself back. I killed her with a certain catty kindness.

I did, in fact, run into her in the bathroom at the Miramax party. I heard her before I saw her. She was in a stall with a friend, complaining in a loud whisper that Harvey

Weinstein wouldn't give her the time of day. When she came out, I was there, fake beaming at her. I had consumed somewhere between five and twenty vodkas; between the alcohol, Declan's win and my four dresses at the awards, I was flushed with victory.

"Kyra!" Lauren said, as fake friendly as me. "How long have you been there?"

"Oh, here, there, I'm everywhere," I said inanely.

She blinked at that. "Look, sweetie, I hope there are no hard feelings about the dress." She moved to me and patted my shoulder, the way one might a child who'd taken honorable mention at the science fair.

"No hard feelings at all," I said. "I think it worked out for the best."

"Is that right?"

"Sure. I mean, you needed a true professional to design your dress, and I needed true actresses to wear mine. It all comes out in the wash, doesn't it?"

I checked my lipstick in the mirror, and left.

As someone who is, for better or worse, famous, you get to do many things that other people don't, and yet there are so few people who understand those things.

When I was a normal woman, I could call Margaux or one of my other girlfriends in New York. I could tell them a story about some guy not calling me back. I could share a tale about getting fired from a temp job. I could always find someone who understood implicitly.

But when you're having dinner with Kaz Lameric or meeting Brad Pitt, these are events most people don't have in their mental roster, and you're bragging if you talk too much about them.

Even if you're lucky enough to have a few people who understand you, or pretend to understand you, odds are that they want something eventually. You can't entirely trust them.

So you keep your mouth closed. And you get lonelier.

Except for Bobby. Bobby was still my saving grace in L.A., the one person who automatically understood what Dec and I were going through, the one person who wasn't particularly impressed with celebrity, who didn't need or want anything from us (especially since Declan had told him officially that he wouldn't be leaving Max for Bobby's team at William Morris). It was with Bobby that I could let my guard down and talk about how cool it was that we had met David Bowie, how ridiculous the ass-kissing was when Declan went on *The Tonight Show.*

The enormous amount of press that Declan and I garnered after the Oscars made day-to-day living so much worse. We were now a confirmed media product, one they wanted to place on the shelves as often as possible.

When Declan left for the set, they followed him. When I had a meeting in the fashion district with Rosita or Victor, they followed me. When Declan and I were able to do something together, they swarmed. The paparazzi weren't just at the usual spots—the premieres or the party for Kaz Lameric's sixtieth birthday, for example. Instead, they knew *all* our spots. It was as if they had a sixth sense about the restaurants we'd frequent, the resort in Palm Springs where we'd try to escape for a weekend, the Tiffany's store where we'd shopped for a birthday gift for Dec's mom.

Bobby, as usual, counseled me on the laid-back approach and told me to get used to it. Liz told me to enjoy it. This was what every actor dreamed of, she said, while I said softly that I wasn't an actor. Kendall said much the same thing as Bobby but expressed doubt that the paparazzi could really know where we were all the time. I agreed with her in some way—I mean, how could they *always* know? It was uncanny. Or was it?

I began to seriously consider whether someone close to us was tipping off the press and the paparazzi. Was it Trista? I wondered. Could the cleaning whiz with the bad attitude who rarely spoke be gabbing into a cell phone in the garage, calling photographers? Or was it Berry, Dec's assistant, who was always asking Declan for a raise? Maybe this was her way of making some side cash. It could be Uki, too, I thought. She was in my office all the time. She heard my phone calls, had access to my date planner. Of course, there were the bodyguards, Denny and Adam, but I doubted that these two had anything to do with it, since the paparazzi only made their job more difficult, and they had already put in a request to add two people to our "security staff." Then there was Max, Dec's agent, and Graham, his manager. They professed to feel sorry for us when we were followed, but in some way, weren't they a little happy? Didn't the constant press increase Declan's exposure and therefore eventually make them more money? There were the publicists, too, who knew our every step. There was Tracy, Dec's second assistant.

The wondering made me paranoid. I can see it for what it was, now that I'm not so close to it. Everyone became a suspect, people who wanted things, people who were watching. And, as nice a guy as Denny was, it was tiring to always have him at my side. Sometimes I felt as if I'd married him not Declan.

One day when I was thoroughly sick of studying everyone out of the corner of my eye and tired of constantly having people around, I shook off Denny by pointing out something at a stoplight. When he shifted himself in the driver's seat and looked in the direction I'd pointed, I clutched my bag, jumped out of the car and dodged into Fred Segal, the one in Santa Monica.

I slipped into the Italian-eatery side, and headed into the women's bathroom, where I sat in the last stall and tried to guess what the women looked like by gazing at their shoes under the wall. After forty minutes or so, when I was sure that Denny had passed through the store and was looking elsewhere by now, I dodged out of the rest room, with my baseball cap low over my eyes. I wandered the boutiques, fingering cashmere sweaters, running my hand over the smooth leather of a bag, all the while pretending that it was one year ago, that I was in the Saks on Madison Avenue, that I was alone again, that no one was ever looking or staring, that I could take the subway back to my old apartment anytime I wanted. It lulled me, these thoughts, so that I began to wander almost dreamily. The problem with these fantasies was that Declan wasn't in them. It felt as if I was missing a limb. I tried to ignore that aspect of the fantasy as I strolled to a makeup counter in one of the boutiques.

"Here," the saleswoman said. "Give me your hand. You absolutely *must* try our new hydrating thera-lotion. It's stunning, really. You don't have dry skin, I can tell, but we all age, you know how it goes. Seriously, try this." She wielded a pot of white cream and a Q-Tip.

I could tell by her spiel that she didn't know who I was. In fact, I was sure I was the ninety-fourth person who'd heard this spiel today. I was just like everyone else.

I held out my hand and watched as she applied the cream in a little circle over my wrist. I feigned interest in the "silky texture." I'd never known what to do with these women. What, exactly, was I supposed to feel, to say? Certainly, the skin on my hand wouldn't test the same as that on my face. Was I the only one who knew this? I murmured something under my breath like, "Nice, very nice," caught between whether I should leave politely or buy two hundred dollars' worth of product to make her feel better, to make me feel ordinary.

"All the celebs are wearing this," she said when I mentioned that I wasn't sure if I needed any moisturizer. "Like Courtney Cox? She uses this all over her body. And that Kyra, you know she's married to Declan McKenna, she came in last week and bought from me."

"Really?" I glanced around, wondering if I was being filmed for one of those reality shows where they play jokes on celebrities.

"Oh, she always buys from us."

"Is that right?"

I had become a sales technique.

Hypothetically, fame should have made me confident, even if I hadn't wanted that fame. After all, there I was, regularly selling my designs for the first time, married to a movie star, having no worries about paying bills. I should have, hypothetically again, been walking taller, smiling gracefully at everyone I passed, feeling serene and self-assured. Alas, this wasn't how it worked, at least not for me. Instead, I became more unsure of myself than I ever had been before. I lost the thread that kept me connected to the me I'd always known.

So much of my life was viewed at a distance. Not just by the reporters and the tabloids and the public, but by me, too. One night, for example, Declan and I attended a premiere for Paul Carlyle, Declan's old acting coach, who had the starring role. Flashbulbs flamed as we got out of our town car. A reporter from *Access Hollywood* dumped the interview she was conducting and ran to us before any of the other reporters.

"How are you tonight, Declan?" she said. "And Kyra, this must be one of yours." She gestured with her phallic microphone at my navy blue shawl-collar dress.

I nodded and greeted her by name. Dec started chattering away about Paul, how he couldn't wait to see the film. He was so good at this, unlike me, while I noticed that I left my body in a way. I could see the other reporters huddling around us, shoving their microphones near us. I could see the evil red glare of the power lights. I floated higher and higher, watching it from above, watching the way I nodded at one reporter, laughed with another. I watched the way I stood, one foot in front of the other, my arms slightly away from my body, the way I'd been taught. And yet, gazing at it all, I had a hard time feeling it. I was unable to unite this life with my old, this me with the one I used to know.

chapter 29

On a Wednesday morning, about six weeks after the Oscars, I got up early before anyone was at the house. I threw on some running pants and a T-shirt and made my way to our workout room. Declan was in San Francisco for a few days, shooting on location for his new movie. I missed him, but finally it felt right to be alone in the house. And God did I need it. I would take a run on the treadmill, I decided, then get a little work done before the troops descended, and I would feel even better. I would feel more like your typical woman, your typical wife, your typical working gal.

To let in some air, I opened the doors that led from the workout room onto the pool patio. The waterfall made soothing splashing noises at the other end. I stretched, got on the treadmill and ran hard for ten minutes, letting the pounding of my feet beat away everything—the feeling of being under constant surveillance, the paranoia that someone close to us was leaking our plans, the perpetual bolstering of my confidence so that I could ignore the rumors about Declan, the odd out-of-body feeling my life so often had now.

It was an overcast morning, but all at once it started to rain. A gust of wind burst inside, sending my newspaper skittering across the floor, knocking over the near-empty water bottle. I closed the door and got back on the treadmill. I turned on the TV that hung from an arm near the ceiling and flipped through the shows that Declan had TiVo'd—History Channel specials on World War II, a sitcom that his friend Brandon had a small part on, some HBO specials. And of course there were the entertainment-news shows, which Declan had arranged to be TiVo'd automatically in order to check the coverage. I watched them occasionally so I could at least know what people were saying about us, about me. Were they, for example, claiming that I was an alcoholic? Or had Declan's alleged infidelities forced me to gain fifty pounds? I felt better when I knew what I was up against.

I clicked on *Access Hollywood* and selected the show from last night. The trick to these things, I had learned, was to watch the first three minutes where they ran the teasers. If there was nothing about Declan or me there, the show was deleted.

Nancy O'Dell's voice came on, highlighting their "top stories"—a Julia Roberts movie premiere, a benefit where Kendall Gold had spoken, and the death of a seventies radio star. Probably nothing on Declan, I thought, since they usually stuck him at the beginning. I raised the remote and was about to delete the show, when I heard, "And news about Declan and Kyra. Are they on the rocks? Is he in love with Lauren Stapleton again?" Across the screen flashed a picture of Declan and me with a cartoonish jagged line drawn between us, then video footage of Lauren and Declan at some premiere, probably taken before I ever met him.

I hit the emergency pause button on the treadmill and stood there panting while I fast-forwarded through the show. My heart beat hard against my ribs. *It's not true,* I thought. *You know it's not true.* But why did I feel so panicked? So fearful?

Finally, I found the segment. Pat O'Brien, looking rather pleased about this "big story" said, "Well, there's word tonight that Oscar winner Declan McKenna and his wife, Kyra Felis, may be on the outs, and Declan might be reunited with Lauren Stapleton."

I screamed and threw the remote against the mirrored wall. I watched as they showed a clip of Lauren at that first premiere I'd been to, saying, "I suppose we'll always be an item" and stroking Declan's hair. Then recent footage of Declan and me in front of a restaurant, me blinking madly into the intrusive light of the video camera while Declan smiled easily. Another shot of Lauren answering questions on a red carpet somewhere.

Over the clips, Pat O'Brien's voice explained about Lauren and Declan's past "relationship" and our "quickie marriage." "Even people in Declan's own camp tell us that trouble is brewing," he said.

The next clip floored me, literally made me sit on the treadmill as if a crushing weight had fallen over my body. There, on the screen, was Liz Morgan with the words "Actress/Friend" below her face. Her frosty hair was blown straight, and she'd clearly had her makeup done professionally. She looked beautiful, despite the chagrined expression, as she said, "Kyra and Declan have fought about Lauren. I've seen them at it. It's definitely a source of tension between them."

Her face faded and was replaced by a shot of Pat saying something inane about how *Access Hollywood* would continue to follow the story, as if our fictional marital problems were something that needed to be covered like the war in Iraq.

Two hours later, Liz buzzed the gate of our house. She was scheduled to work for me that day, but I couldn't believe she had the audacity to show. I went to the foyer, where Denny stood by the front door.

"You sure?" he said. He was a man of few words, but he had made it clear that he knew about her little interview. He didn't hit women, he'd told me, but he would be happy to toss her in the trunk of his car and drive around for a few hours.

"It's fine," I said, although nothing was fine.

Declan had called from San Francisco shortly after I'd seen the show. It was crap, he had said, "complete fecking crap." I believed him, but I was so upset about Liz, so betrayed by someone I thought was a friend, that I felt wary about Declan, too. I told him how sick I was of all the coverage, how tired I was of having to always wonder whether I was being followed, whether Declan was doing something that would make it look as if he was cheating on me. He had to get off the phone then because of his morning call, and I was left feeling confused and raw.

Liz rapped on the door, which Denny immediately opened. He stood there a moment, staring down at her, probably fighting his desire to hog-tie her and drag her through the city by a rope. Finally, he grunted and moved aside to let her pass.

"Hi," she said when she saw me. Her eyes were bright, wide. "Not working yet?"

"Just waiting for you."

"Oh great, well. Mmm. What…ah…what are we doing today?"

"Are you kidding me?"

"Kyr." She took a few steps toward me.

"Don't," I said. She froze. I crossed my arms over my chest. "You've got to be fucking kidding me that you came here today."

Tears filled her blue eyes. "Kyra, I'm sorry. You won't believe how it happened, and I didn't say anything that wasn't true, I just said—"

"You said Declan and I fight about Lauren!" I uncrossed my arms, shouting my words.

"Well, you do. That one time—"

"That one time we were talking about whether I wanted to design a dress for her. We weren't fighting about her and Declan being together!"

"Right, and I didn't say that," Liz said softly.

"You made it sound *just* like that, and you know it."

She wiped a tear away from her eye with a hot-pink fingernail. "If you listen to what happened, I'll know you'll understand. See, I met this guy who's an associate producer on *Access Hollywood.* We got to talking, and he also used to be a producer on *Manny & Me,* you know that show on Fox?"

I didn't answer.

"Well, anyway, he said that if I would give him a quote about you guys, he would talk to the *Manny* casting director about me."

"You sold me out so you could get an audition? My God!" I covered my mouth with my hand; a churning nausea filled my stomach.

"I didn't sell you out, I just said something that was true."

"Get the hell out of here."

"I'm sorry, sweetie." She rushed to me and wrapped her arms around my shoulders.

I stood woodenly, refusing to return the embrace.

"I'm so, so sorry," she said, "but you don't know how hard it is to break into this business. I just needed an in. I need a start somewhere. It's been so easy for Declan. You don't get how hard it really is, and I didn't mean to hurt you, I just wanted—"

"Oh my God," I said, a thought dawning on me like a frying pan to the face. "Are you the one who's been telling the paparazzi where we're going?"

"What? No!"

"Have you been selling me out all this time? Giving info to the press about what restaurants we'll be at, what parties? Is that how you've been making money?" The nausea churned harder in my stomach, causing me to want to double over. Instead, I pressed my hands into my belly.

"I did not do that!" Liz yelled. "I swear, Kyra. You have to believe me!"

"Go," I said, quiet now.

"No, honey, listen for a sec."

I shoved her away. "I listened. Now get out."

Liz shook her head, as if it was me who failed to understand the situation. And in some ways, I guess she was right. I understood so little anymore.

I called Bobby late that night. I'd thrown myself into work all day, letting the deadlines and phone calls and all the people around me wash away thoughts of Liz. But now, finally, with the house silent, I sat huddled against the headboard, lonely and miserable.

"She's a conniving bitch," Bobby said about Liz. "Forget her."

"How can I forget?" Sometimes, having a guy for a good friend just wasn't the same as talking to another woman who understood the obsessive workings of the female mind.

"She's out of your life now, hallelujah."

I was silent. I couldn't be celebratory about losing a friend.

"And don't worry about that Lauren rumor," Bobby said. "That's just wacked."

"I know."

"And you'll probably hear some stuff tomorrow about Declan and Tania. Also crap."

"Wait, what are you talking about? Why would I hear something tomorrow?"

Bobby represented Martie Schafer, who was playing the role of Declan's mom in the new movie. I'd always imagined Martie as a serene older woman, but it seemed she was as gossipy as a thirteen-year-old, because she was always calling Bobby with catty stories from the set.

"I guess Tania and Declan went out to dinner tonight," he said, "and people have been talking for a while, but it's bogus."

"What do you mean people have been talking for a while?"

"It's just the PR machine cranking up, trying to generate some publicity, saying Declan's having an affair with her, the usual bullshit."

I knew it was bullshit. I knew this as a logical, educated woman, but still I mumbled an excuse, hung up quickly with Bobby and dialed Declan's cell phone. It went right to voice mail. Eleven o'clock. Could he be asleep already? Or was it possible he was with Tania?

I dialed his number again, and again. I was compulsive, crazy. I wouldn't stop. Over and over, I hit number one, my speed dial for his phone, and listened to his voice—*Hey, it's Declan. Leave a message. Hey, it's Declan. Leave a message.*

I got up from the bed and began pacing the bedroom. Why would his cell phone be off? Was he avoiding me? Did he have something to hide? Something I'd been too willing to blame on the press?

I tried watching TV but couldn't concentrate. I thought about calling Margaux, but it was two in the morning in New York. Taking the phone, still dialing obsessively, I went to the kitchen and began eating random bits of food from the fridge. I went to the workout room and walked slowly on the treadmill, all the while hitting that speed dial with relentless precision. *Hey, it's Declan. Leave a message.*

When he called an hour and a half later, I was back in bed, nearly through a bottle of merlot. "Why the hell has your phone been off?"

A pause. "What?"

I knew he had heard me. He couldn't have not heard me, because I practically screamed my words. So I stayed silent.

"I had it off on set," he said, "and we went right from there to dinner. I just forgot."

"You forgot," I said accusingly. What, exactly, I was accusing him of, I wasn't sure. I only knew that my suspicions had simmered and boiled and turned into a churning rage.

"Yeah, I forgot." He sounded slightly pissed off now. "I'm tired. What's this about?"

"You know what it's about!"

"Christ, Kyra, just tell me. I really don't need this."

"And I do? I need to be stuck here in L.A., reading rumors about Lauren and hearing about you having dinner with Tania?"

"Who did you hear that from?"

"Bobby," I said, getting up.

"Jesus, Bobby again."

"Yeah, Bobby again. He's the only friend I've got here. Who do you expect me to talk to?"

I heard him breathing. "Of course you're friends with

Bobby. I'm glad for that. I truly am. It's just that this is all such shite."

"What is?"

"Whatever you're accusing me of!" Now it was his voice that rose. "I'm not having an affair, Kyra! Not with anyone. I love you. You know that! I went out to dinner with Tania to talk about the scene tomorrow."

"And what will the papers say about that?"

"Who the fuck cares what the papers say?" he bellowed.

We went on like that for half an hour. I had finally pushed him enough that Declan, who was never a fighter, who always told me I was right and left it at that, was screaming right back at me. We'd finally become the couple they had painted us to be in the papers.

Two days later, I went home to New York for the funeral of one of Emmie's best friends, Ruby. Ruby had been a gorgeous old woman—tall and willowy even as her face creased and crumpled. She was a decade older than Emmie and had been her mentor at the first literary agency where she'd worked.

Because of his filming schedule, Dec wasn't able to go with me and so there were only two photographers at LAX, and when I got to LaGuardia at midnight, there was no one. No photographers, no reporters, no personal assistants, no bodyguards. I loved it.

I went straight to Emmie's. There was a note on the kitchen counter in my side of the apartment.

Welcome, darling. I wanted to wait, but I'm too sad about Ruby to stay awake. In the morning…

In my old room, my double bed was still there (Emmie didn't "believe" in twin beds), and it was still covered by the crazy pink-and-purple quilt I'd made during college. I'd washed it so many times that it was thin and soft as silk. I stripped off my clothes and crawled under it. The hum of the city lulled me like a mother's song. I fell into the hardest sleep I'd had in months.

In the morning, I woke early to find the city impossibly quiet. I peered out the window and saw that there had been a freak April snowstorm, the city now buried under a blanket of fresh snow. People always run for the cover of their homes when there's a big snow in Manhattan. They use umbrellas to keep the snow away, then they get to their apartments and stay there, letting the restaurants and shops go quiet. But I immediately found a pair of my old boots in Emmie's closet and went out to Central Park. My boots skidded through the wet, unshoveled snow. Tree limbs hung heavy with white; icicles clung to the bottom of park benches.

When I got back, Emmie was sitting in her living room, surrounded by her books, but for once, she was still—no entertaining, reading, laughing on the phone or making notes. She wore a pink flannel nightgown, which made her look oddly like a little girl.

"Kyra," she said when she saw me, but her voice lacked its usual verve.

I crossed the room and sank onto the couch, hugging her tight. "How are you?"

"Devastated." She sat back and crossed her legs daintily as if wearing a cocktail dress at the Ritz. "It's just more of the same. You would think I would be used to this at my age, but I'm simply not. I will never get used to this."

"Of course not." I rubbed her hand. I had always felt enormously ineffectual at comforting her. "Where's Mac-Kenzie?"

At that, she smiled. If I'm not mistaken, she may have even batted her eyelashes at the thought of him. "He'll be here to pick us up in two hours." She kissed me on the cheek. "I think I'll sleep until then if it's okay with you."

"Sure," I said.

She began to push herself up with her arms, but then she sat down again. "How are you, dear? I didn't even ask."

"I'm fine."

She cupped my cheek, peered into my eyes. "Is that right?"

"Sure, things are good. You know Dec has four new projects lined up since the Oscars and my designs are selling well, and the house is great. Well, it's fine, and—"

"No, how are *you,* dear?"

I took a breath. "It's tough right now. But I'm glad to be here."

Emmie simply nodded.

I met Margaux for coffee later that morning. I was already at a table with two lattes for us when she walked into the shop. Her hair looked fluffy and beautiful, lying on the collar of her brown shearling coat. Her cheeks were pink, her eyes clear.

"So sorry about Emmie's friend," she said. She hung her coat around the chair and sat down.

"Thanks," I said. "Emmie is really down this time."

"Still with MacKenzie?"

"Oh, yes. That seems to be what's getting her through it."

"That's how it should be."

Something in her voice, some wry tone, caught me. "What's going on with Peter and you? Any news?"

She laughed. "Yes. I've got news."

"You're…" I gestured toward her stomach.

"No," she said decisively. "I am not knocked up."

"What then?"

"Well...let's see." She scratched her head distractedly. "I'm going to be splitting my time between here and Colorado."

I shook my own head. "Excuse me?"

"Denver."

"Do you even know where Denver is?"

She laughed again. "Of course. The firm is opening an office there, and they asked me to head it up."

"You accepted?"

She nodded.

"You gave me hell for moving to Los Angeles, and now you're moving to *Denver?*" I said.

"I'm not moving. I'll just be there a few days a week."

"Why?"

"Ah, hell, Kyr. It's not working with Peter and me. It hasn't been for a long time, and this baby thing was crazy. Thank God I didn't get pregnant." She took a sip of her latte. "We're separated. It's official as of two days ago."

"Oh, no." I reached over and squeezed her shoulder.

"Thanks, but it's okay. It really is. We're not meant to be together, not like you and Declan. So it's over. But I can't stay here in New York, at least not all the time. I need a major change. And then perfect timing—this job came up in Denver, so I'm doing it!"

"Hey, you'll be closer to me."

"Exactly. I can help keep an eye on you guys. On Declan, if you need it. Any truth about him and these women?"

"No." I felt definitive saying that. Now that I was away from it all, I could see it more clearly, and I knew Declan wasn't cheating on me. If only the papers would stop saying that he was.

At two o'clock, MacKenzie Bresner buzzed Emmie's apartment and, without waiting for a response, let himself in with his own key.

I was standing in the living room, wearing a black dress, waiting for Emmie to get ready.

"Hi," I said, surprised. As far as I knew, I was the only person who'd ever been granted a key to Emmie's place.

"Kyra," he said with affection, crossing the room to shake my hand, then hug me.

I hadn't seen MacKenzie in over a decade, but he was still a bear of a man, tall and big-chested. He had meaty paws for hands, which made it impossible to imagine him typing the subtle, heartfelt prose he was known for.

"How is she?" he asked simply.

"Hanging in there." In truth, Emmie had looked pale and weak. I'd even suggested that she skip the funeral, but she adamantly refused.

Yet now, Emmie came into the living room, leaning hard on her cane, wearing a stylish, black St. John knit suit and a smile for MacKenzie that lightened her whole face.

"Dear," she said to him. He pulled her into an embrace so tender I felt it was only right that I turn away.

I went into the bedroom and found a voice mail from Dec on my cell phone. "I miss you, baby," he said, his voice low, clearly talking on the set. "Tell Emmie I'm sorry and come home soon."

At the funeral, Ruby's husband, Gene, sat slumped in the first pew, his suit pooled around him as if he'd just lost twenty pounds in the last minute. When I spoke to him afterward, he said, "This is worse than the war. It's worse than everything I saw there." The blue of his eyes were the only youthful thing about him. He was hollow, carved out by his wife's death, and it terrified me.

This is what we have to look forward to, I thought. Either Dec or I will have to go through this. Unless we're lucky enough (*lucky?*) to both die in the same car accident or plane crash, the way my parents had, one of us will lose the other. One of us will be torn apart.

Suddenly, I had to get back to L.A. It didn't matter that I detested the reporters or the bodyguards or the driving. It didn't matter about the cameras and the constant people. I needed to be with Declan above all else.

As soon as I could escape, I kissed Emmie and MacKenzie, got my bags from her apartment and went straight to the airport.

chapter 30

I had called Denny from LaGuardia, and he was there to pick me up when I got to LAX. It was seven at night, the city starting to buzz for the evening. I was walking toward the car, when I saw the back door open. And there was Declan. I left the baggage on the sidewalk and ran to him.

If possible, the paparazzi were worse when I returned to L.A. The rumors about Declan's infidelities and our marital problems had only made the media more hungry for photos and video clips. They were there at every turn in the road, every trip to the fashion district, every restaurant we went to, every store we stopped in.

The feeling of being hunted goes something like this: it starts with a prickling along the back of your scalp, particularly behind the ears. You haven't seen them yet, haven't even heard any strange noises, but your body knows they are there. All your organs tighten. Your skin feels hot, electric. You swivel your head ever so slightly, but you see nothing.

You tell yourself to calm down, but your body ignores you, and your pulse starts flicking its fingers against your neck. Why did you tell Denny you could handle this one alone? You reach into your bag. Car keys. Fumble with the main key, trying to ready it in your hand. *Where is the car? Where is it?* You swivel your head again, this time with wider arcs, and then you see him. Behind a tree, shooting already. You check for wounds. You're okay. But you see the others. Not as discreet or sneaky as the one in the tree. The one in the tree was a scout, the runt of the pack. The others—the bullies, the ones who've done this longer—they charge now. Calling your name, then screaming it. *Where is the car?* Hurry, hurry. They move with you, in front of you, behind you, until you are surrounded. You try to smile at first, but you know you look like a grimacing, nervous girl. You let the grin drop from your face. *Where is the fucking car?* You make a mistake and ask them, *Haven't you got enough?* They keep shooting, calling your name. They are hunting you now for the sake of sport, not to feed their families, as they would have you think. They shoot you again, they brush close to you, they press their weapons in your face. *Isn't that enough?* you say again. But they won't stop. They want you to lose it. They want to shoot you dying. You've been told this. You've been instructed not to react. But it's so hard to hold on when you're bleeding. The car. There it is. You will live. You fumble with the key again, nearly dropping it before you finally slip it in the slot and escape inside.

"Do you believe me now?" I whispered to Declan one evening, as we drove away from L'Orangerie, where we had tried, once again unsuccessfully, to have a quiet dinner. I couldn't wait to get home. The house, although huge and filled with people, was a safe haven now. Unlike the restaurant. Despite Adam's prearrival sweep, five paparazzi materialized outside when we got there. There were fifteen when we finally left. We had only decided on the restaurant that afternoon, and so it had to be true. Someone we knew was leaking our plans to the press.

Declan heaved a great sigh, the tires squealing as he tried to keep Adam and Denny, who were in the car behind us, in his sight and yet outrun a photographer who was following us in a blue Honda. "Fuck, love. I guess so. It's rather hard to believe. Who could it be?"

"Anybody! There are a million people who know what we're doing at any time. I mean, I thought it was Liz, but it can't have been her. She's been gone for a while." I swallowed hard, trying not to let the disappointment about Liz creep in again. "But there's still Berry, Uki, Trista, your publicist, my publicist, then there's Tracy, the new security guys, Denny and Adam, Max, Graham, there's—"

"Whoa. Hold on, Kyr. Graham and Max would never."

"And you say Berry would never, and Denny and Adam would never, but *somebody* is leaking this stuff. I can't live like this, always wondering who the hell it is."

"All right, love," he said. He stopped at a light and took his hand off the stick for a moment to stroke my hair. "It's all right. We'll pull them in and start asking some questions."

The next day, Declan and I formed our good cop/bad cop team (I was the bad) and called in the members of our staff one by one. The house was quieter than usual, probably because word had gotten out that something was amiss.

Trista was first. "I don't know what you're fuckin' talkin' about," she said in her charming way. "I come in, I clean this fuckin' place—for a lot less than my sister makes down the road—and I go home. I don't give a shit about you two."

"Well," Declan said when she'd left the room, "I appreciate her honesty."

I had to agree.

Berry was next. She burst into tears when we told her why she was there. *Got her!* I thought.

But then she raised her head, wiping her eyes. "I can't believe you would think that of me!" she wailed. "Declan, I've worked harder for you than anyone I've ever been with. There's a code of confidentiality for personal assistants, you know." I thought about telling her such a code was only for doctors or attorneys, but she continued, "I would never, never do something like that!"

Adam was next. Then Denny. They were both insulted, but they understood. They swore they'd always been close-mouthed when it came to our whereabouts. Ditto for the new security guys and Declan's second assistant.

Angela, Dec's publicist, came by the house, too. She seemed rather excited to be in on something so cloak-and-dagger, but no, it wasn't her, she promised. She would question her team, but she was sure none of the other publicists would do that.

My publicist said the same thing. So did my rep, Alicia, and Uki, who, in her soft way, swore she wouldn't do something so dishonorable.

Declan promised to ask Max and Graham about the matter, and when the day was done, we were no closer to figuring out who was the Judas. Declan trusted everyone's assurances. I trusted no one.

The staff began to resent me around the house. It was as if everyone sensed that Declan believed in them, while I simply believed that they were rooting through my underwear drawer when I turned my back. Trista was more hostile than usual. Berry gave me the very cold shoulder. Uki, whom I'd always had a warm relationship with, was downright frosty. Adam and Denny stopped telling me stories and kidding me about my high heels and simply became the silent security men we paid them to be.

"Fuck 'em," Bobby said when we talked on the phone. "You're their boss. Of course they're going to hate you."

But I knew it was more than that, and it began to wear on me. I left the house as little as possible—it simply wasn't worth the strain of being followed—and yet the house was now wrought with tension and too many disdainful eyes.

A few days later, Declan left to shoot a few insert scenes in San Francisco. Now I had no buffer, just undisguised contempt.

Finally, I'd had enough of it. I told everyone to leave at four o'clock one day. I wanted to be alone—for once. Denny, still formal with me, said that he was getting paid to be here, and he would just stand outside the front door.

"Thanks, Den," I said, using the nickname I'd called him for months, hoping it would remind him I wasn't the enemy, "but I need to really be *by myself.* Can you understand that?"

He considered me for a moment, then grunted in assent. "You'll set the alarm before you go to bed?"

"Of course."

"You've got my cell phone?"

"Yes."

"And my home phone?"

"Definitely."

"And—"

"Den, please. I'm safe here." And the truth was, I felt safe. Our house was the one place I knew that for sure.

He patted me awkwardly on the arm, then left. Berry, Uki and Trista followed shortly after. Declan's second assistant was with him in San Fran. The publicists and my rep were working elsewhere. And suddenly, I was blessedly alone.

I had new patterns to look over in my office, but instead

I took a stack of books out to the pool. It was a beautiful, early-May day—all sun and blue skies and seventy degrees— the way L.A. is supposed to be. I sat near the waterfall and let the sounds block out the noise in my head. I read an advanced copy of MacKenzie's new novel, which he'd given me when I was in Manhattan. It was a story of grief, told through the eyes of a man very much like MacKenzie, who lived in upstate New York and who had lost his wife after years of marriage. I became engrossed in it. I wanted desperately for the character to find love again at the end, and yet I wondered if such an ending would be believable. Doesn't a grand love come only once?

When the light started to wane, I finally closed the book and went inside to make myself a salad. I sat at the island, eating in the pristine silence of the kitchen. I began to feel lighter, more relaxed.

I poured myself a glass of merlot and brought the bottle and the phone into the sunroom. I put on a Lena Horne CD. We'd finally gotten some couches for this room—tan linen and plump with down. I sank onto one of them, took a sip of my wine and dialed Margaux's number.

"How are you?" she said, answering on the third ring. "I hope better than me because I'm up to my ears in boxes." Margaux was moving out of the apartment she'd shared with Peter.

"I'm great," I said.

"Really?" She sounded skeptical. Anytime I talked to Margaux lately, I'd been miserable about the hounding press, the potentially treacherous employees.

"I'm decompressing," I told her.

"Does this involve a bottle of red?"

"Good guess. But mostly, I sat on my ass by the pool, I made a salad, and now I'm calling my best girlfriend."

"Well, aren't you the everyday Jane."

I laughed. It was precisely what I felt. "How's the packing going?"

"I am in the depths of hell."

Margaux talked about the horrible task of dividing up her stuff from Peter's, and the fights over ownership of CDs and photographs. Silently, I prayed I would never have to do such a thing. If I could get a day like this to myself, even just once in a while, that would be enough to maintain my sanity, my marriage.

It was nearly black in the room when Margaux and I began to wrap up our conversation twenty minutes later, but the lights of the canyon shone prettily through plate windows.

"I miss you," I said to Margaux. "I can't wait until you're on the west side of the country. It's the best side."

"You don't really believe that, do you?"

"No, but it will be better when you're closer to me." I smiled and lifted the bottle to pour myself another glass.

But then I heard a rustle from across the room. I froze. "Is someone there?"

"What's going on?" Margaux said.

A click of something small being dropped on the wood floor, then stillness. Too still.

"Who's there?" I said, my voice coming out hollow in the large room.

"Are you talking to me?" Margaux said.

I couldn't answer. Fear gripped me. I thought of the useless alarm system which I'd forgotten to arm when I came in from the pool.

I sat on the edge of the couch, peering through the darkness. The lights of the canyon now seemed pitiful illumination. I put the wine bottle on the floor and reached for the light on the end table. When I turned it on, the room burst into sudden brightness.

And there she was. The pool door, I thought. Had I locked it? But it didn't matter now.

"Amy Rose?" I said.

"I've come for Declan."

She wore baggy khaki pants with mud stains on the front (probably from scaling our cliff) and a black cotton jacket. "Hi," she said nervously. "Sorry to bother you."

"Uh…" Had she just apologized for breaking in to my house? How did one respond to such a thing? "What are you doing here?" My hands were shaky, my legs twitchy. I wanted to bolt from the room, but she was blocking my way around our couches.

"Well, Declan wasn't returning my letters, and you weren't really listening to me, so I thought I'd just pop by."

Right. *Pop by,* as if you're a neighbor seeking a cup of sugar. I tried to act as queerly nonchalant as she, but my body had gone cold with fear; my hands had begun to tremble.

"Declan isn't here right now," I said. "So maybe we could schedule a time for you to meet him later." *Yeah, later, when I've got you in a straitjacket.*

She chuckled sadly, she raised a hand and smoothed her brown hair. "You won't tell him I stopped by."

"Oh, believe me, I'll tell him."

"No. I know you."

"Do you?"

She took a step toward me, her hands moving inside her jacket pockets. I slid back on the couch.

"Look, this isn't really your fault," she said.

Yeah, you think so?

"I'm seriously sorry about this." Amy Rose bit her lip and gave me an apologetic look. She moved a little closer. "It's just that I know you're the one keeping him away from me. I know that when you get out of his life I'll be the one living here with him. You see what I mean?"

You fucking freak is what I wanted to say. Instead, I said, "Sure. Well, why don't I leave now and you can just wait for him."

She chuckled again. "Do you think I'm stupid?"

No, just deranged. Or, as Dec would say, "unhinged." "Of course not."

She took a deep breath, her hands moving again in her pockets. "I'm sorry to do this." She took a step forward, then halted. "I'm *really* sorry."

She charged at me then. Her hands came out of the pockets, and I saw a shiny silver blade. Incongruously, I thought, *She doesn't have a gun?* I was relieved for a half second before I saw her arm jutting toward me with the knife. I rolled over on the couch and jumped to a standing position. Her arm was buried deep in the couch, but she dug the knife out.

"Please don't make this so hard," she said like a doctor trying to give a six-year-old a tetanus shot.

I took a step back, ready to run for the kitchen or the front door, but I had backed into another one of our new end tables. She was only two feet from me. She shifted her hand position on the knife and held it tightly in her raised fist. She charged again. In that instant, I caught a glimmer of the wine bottle at my feet. I ducked to pick it up, making her crash into the end table and miss me again. Before she could turn around, I grabbed the bottle, raised it high and brought it down hard on her head.

chapter 31

Margaux had heard enough through the phone to call the LAPD. They were at the house, along with the ambulance, within minutes. Amy Rose woke up when the paramedics leaned over her to check her pulse. She blinked when she saw the commotion in the room.

"Ma'am," one of the paramedics said, "do you know where you are?"

She turned her head until she saw me. Then she began to sob.

It took hours to sort everything out. The paramedics treated Amy Rose for a possible concussion, then took her to the hospital for observation, the scream of their siren echoing down Mulholland Drive. The police questioned me and collected evidence, and by that time, Declan had arrived home via a chartered private plane.

"Kyra," he said, running into the living room where I sat on a chair next to a policeman. His eyes were anguished and red. He pulled me to my feet and hugged me tight. "Are you all right?"

I nodded. "I'm fine."

But when everyone left thirty minutes later, I told him, "I can't do this anymore."

We were still in the living room, and I sat curled in Declan's arms. It was the only place I wanted to be, and yet I knew this was also where so many others wanted to be. And those others would always intrude on our lives one way or another.

"We'll beef up the security system," Declan said.

"We already have a state-of-the-art system and it was my fault I didn't set it."

"We'll have overnight guards."

"Dec. Listen. I want fewer people in our lives, not more." I burrowed my face deep into his chest, breathing in the scent of him. It brought tears to my eyes.

"Well, we'll do something else."

"What?"

There was an awful silence.

"Are you going to quit being an actor?" I asked.

"What? No, but—"

"And I wouldn't want you to. It's just that… It's just that I don't want to live like this anymore."

"And I'm saying we'll make some changes."

"Will it change how many people are constantly in our house? Will it stop the paparazzi from hounding us? Will it really change anything?"

Another painful quiet.

"It won't matter, hon," I said. "It won't stop people from always wanting something from you, always being all over us." I squeezed my eyes shut before I could say my next words. "I think we need to be apart, at least for a while."

His body froze. "Don't say that."

"I think we need it. I think *I* need it." I thought of how I'd been able to live with ease for that day in New York.

"Look here." He held me slightly away from him and stared intently in my eyes. "We're not giving up on this. I won't let you."

"I just want to be away from this for a while."

The anguish in his eyes flared. "You can't just move out."

"I don't want to, but I have to. I love you, baby. You know that, but I'm so tired of this."

"Then go with me somewhere, someplace we can talk. We'll have a holiday together, some space. You owe that to me, love. My God, you can't leave me."

"Where would we go? There are always people around."

"Hong Kong, Tibet, Peru, I don't care. Shit, love, I'll go to Minneapolis. You pick. We won't tell anyone. And we'll try to sort this out. Just give me a week, all right?"

I stared at his brown tousled hair and the gold of his eyes, thinking that only one year ago, I had met him in that casino. Only one year.

"Okay," I said.

I chose Quogue, an odd-sounding place on Long Island, technically part of the much talked about Hamptons. But the village of Quogue was tiny and unassuming. It had no Armani or Prada stores, like East Hampton; it had no main drag filled with cutesy shops and cafés like West Hampton. Quogue had an inn, a liquor store, an overpriced grocery store and the beach.

I had been to Quogue when I was in my early twenties when I rented a share there. At the time, I was gravely disappointed with the place—we were so far from any of the happening restaurants or bars; there was nothing to do— but now, that was exactly what I wanted. Since it was the end of May, before Memorial Day when the annual pilgrimage to the Hamptons really began, I was able to find a rental on the beach that was an old Coast Guard station converted into a house. From the pictures and details on the Internet, I could tell it had three bedrooms, a wraparound porch, a dune deck and, blessedly, its own private beach on the Atlantic. I booked the house over the Internet using the name Kyra Franklin (Emmie's last name).

We told no one of our plans. We simply said we were leaving for a week, that we wouldn't be available by phone or fax or pager or e-mail. This news was received with much shock, as if we'd confessed to enslaving small children in our basement. Wouldn't we call in once a day? they asked. No, Declan said. He wouldn't be around, wouldn't be reachable. Luckily, the film could spare him for seven days while they shot the scenes that concerned Tania Murray and her onscreen family. Alicia, my rep, was understanding—I think she'd sensed that I was near my cracking point—but she said I had patterns that needed to be approved for copies of the Oscar gowns, which at least ten department stores planned on carrying. I told her I trusted her to do it, zipped up my bag and shut off my cell phone.

We booked a private plane right into Westhampton Beach. We had the charter company arrange for a rental car, which was waiting for us on the small landing strip. We thanked the crew, got in the car and drove away toward our little house in Quogue, where no one knew us.

When we got there, the house was just as I'd imagined. Sparsely but cleanly furnished with wood floors, antique furniture and white walls. The focus of every room was the beach. We called the local store and had our groceries delivered. I paid for them at the front door, wearing a big, straw hat, just in case, but it seemed that we had finally gotten away with it. We'd finally scored a cache of time just for ourselves.

We slept in late in the mornings. Our master bedroom had its own porch with two chaise longues, and we read our books there every morning until we were hungry. I ate pickles and peanuts. Declan made Irish oatmeal as thick as cement. We began cocktail hour promptly at three, then made late lunches. I sipped a crisp sauvignon blanc and Declan had a beer. We brought our meal out to the dune deck, suspended above the crash of the ocean. We played cards, we talked about little things we'd missed from each other's lives lately. We napped before dinner, a little drunk from our happy hour. Sometimes the nap included sleep, other times not. We made late dinners, we walked the beach barefoot, we laughed together for the first time in months.

Dec and I did not talk about the separation I'd suggested. I think he was hoping it would float away on a salty ocean breeze. I must have been pining for the same thing, because little by little the rest of the world receded. I felt normal again. I felt as if I was in an average, happy marriage. Maybe weeks like this were what we needed.

The only person I called that week was Bobby. I used my cell phone from the deck one day while Declan took a walk. Bobby was supposed to have a big meeting at William Morris—something *huge* he had said, something that could get him promoted—and I wanted to wish him luck. He wasn't there, but I left him a message about Quogue, about the house, about how happy I was.

On our last full day, it was hot and gorgeous. Declan started happy hour a little early and promptly fell deep asleep on a chaise longue. I decided to get more sun before I went back to L.A., where, strangely, I spent most of my time indoors. I took two magazines and went over the dune to the beach. I lay down a towel and flopped onto my stomach, just another girl in a bikini and straw hat. I untied my bikini to get some sun on my back. The gown I planned on wearing to an upcoming premiere was backless. I paged through *Vogue* and *Vanity Fair*. When the print began to make me drowsy, I took my hat off and rested my head on my arms. The heat sank into my body, into my mind. It filled all the empty spaces. I sighed and closed my eyes.

Soon, I heard the sound of a helicopter, one of the many that shuttled people to and from their beach homes.

But then the *thwack, thwack, thwack* of the blades became undeniably closer, until it sounded as if it was almost on top of me. The sand started to whip. I got up and turned around to figure out what was happening, and my untied bikini top slid off with the movement.

I held a hand up to protect myself from the sand that was now stinging my skin. There, hovering above me, was not one helicopter but two. Men with telephoto lenses hung out of each, snapping pictures of my now topless body. I grabbed at one of the flapping magazines. It tore off in my hand, leaving me with only a flimsy page. I tried to cover my breasts with it. I reached for my towel, but it flew away in the fierce winds of the helicopters blades.

"Declan!" I screamed, but I didn't know if he could hear me over the ferocious rumble of the engines. I ran toward the stairs that would lead me to the house, but the helicopters got lower. The sand swirled furiously around me until I couldn't see where I was going. I was disoriented and panicked, screaming for help, lost in a sea of sand, and yet somewhere a realization dawned.

Bobby. It had been Bobby all along.

It was Bobby who'd done this, who was leaking our comings and goings to the press. He was the only one who knew where we were. The only one who I'd never suspected. He was my friend.

Crying now, I kept running in the cloud of sand. Where were the stairs? My feet slipped out from under me, and I went down, face-first, in the sand. I felt an arm lift me up. I fought against it. Was it one of the photographers somehow? But when I stood up, I saw it was Declan.

"Let's go!" he yelled. He pulled me until we found the stairs. We ran up them, and then Declan began sprinting toward the house. "C'mon," he yelled when I didn't chase after him.

The helicopters had an even better view of us now that the sandstorm had died down and we were on the deck. They hovered above us, shooting, shooting.

"Kyra, c'mon!" Declan screamed.

But I only walked calmly, still covering my chest with a now lifeless magazine page.

Part Five

chapter 32

Hitting the Brakes

One of Hollywood's hottest duos, Declan McKenna and fashion designer wife Kyra Felis, are in the news again. They made headlines last week after topless photos of Kyra were published in Britain's *Hello!* magazine, and now the two have announced that they're pulling the emergency brake on their fast-speeding relationship.

Officially, the couple says they aren't planning to file for divorce, but insiders say that Kyra has moved back to her native Manhattan while Declan remains at the couple's Mulholland Drive home.

Friends say that the couple has been fighting ever since their San Diego wedding last fall. One such friend, and an ex-neighbor of the two, reports that Felis screamed and even threw household items one night after Declan strolled in at 7:00 a.m. Other insiders report that McKenna may not have liked his wife's notoriety. "As an Irishman," one source says, "he wants a more traditional woman and a more traditional relationship."

The relationship may also have been strained by persistent rumors of McKenna's infidelity, as well as a break-in at the couple's home by a crazed fan, Amy Rose Peterson, now in custody at a mental health facility in Los Angeles.

Declan fought against my decision. He suggested counseling, but I reminded him that there were no therapists who specialized in celebrity acclimation. He offered to move to another house in L.A., somewhere more secluded, but we both knew they'd find us eventually. Declan said things would improve now that we knew it was Bobby who had been telling the paparazzi where we'd be, but I knew if it wasn't Bobby, it would be someone else, and after a while Dec stopped arguing against that fact.

We both knew that Declan was on the upswing of a very long career, one he wanted desperately, one filled with an absurd amount of fame and acclaim. It was a life filled with an extraordinary amount of people. There was always a potential that one of them would be another Bobby, and even if every staff member and family member and friend was perfectly trustworthy for the rest of our lives, the hounding by the press wouldn't stop. It might lessen without the leaks, but it would never cease. And I simply didn't want that life any more.

"It won't ever get better," I said. We were in our bed, and I was curled up in a ball, facing him. My eyes felt heavy and grit-filled. My throat hurt from talking, from crying. "No matter how much I love you, I can't do this every day."

"Don't," he said, not bothering to wipe his own tears that

tracked from his golden eyes down his cheeks and into the corners of his mouth. But I noticed that he had run out of answers.

For most people, I imagine that moving back into the room where you spent your childhood would be either mortifying or comforting. For me, it was neither. I moved my clothes and my design work into Emmie's place. I found a new rep in Manhattan (Alicia would continue to represent me in L.A.), and I hired a new assistant. I was glad to have a place to go, relieved to be back in New York and thrilled to be alone. But something was off. Emmie, for example, was often in upstate New York with MacKenzie. She tried to spend more time in Manhattan after I moved back, but I didn't want to disrupt her new life, and I was lousy company. Margaux was always back and forth from Denver to New York with her new job.

But it wasn't that I missed Emmie or Margaux so much; I missed Declan. He was home for me—not L.A., not even Manhattan anymore—and I'd lost my home.

I think Bobby finally figured out that I knew. His text messages had gone from *Where the hell are you? Miss you,* to *Kyr, call me,* to simply *We have to talk.*

I sent him just one—*Fuck you.*

Then about a month and a half after I'd moved back to Manhattan, he left a message on my cell phone.

"Kyr," he said, "it's me." His voice sounded heavy, old. I wondered for a moment if someone had died. "I'm in town visiting a client. I know you're probably here in the city, so just meet me, will you? I'll be at the lobby bar of the Royalton at six. I'll wait for an hour. Come talk to me, okay?"

I considered waiting until 6:55 just as a means of torture, but I was ready to confront him. There was no sense waiting. At 6:05 I walked up the steps of the Royalton Hotel and into the darkened, modern lobby. Along the left side were groupings of funky tables and chairs. Blue light shone from discs in the floor. And there, seated on a white cloth chair was Bobby. He wore a white shirt, the cuffs rolled up, and black pants. His legs were crossed so that one leg rested on his knee. He had a drink in front of him that looked untouched. He glanced at his watch, then around the lobby. His eyes reached the door, and he stood abruptly when he saw me.

I walked toward him, watching how he put his hands in his pockets, then pulled them out again. He shifted back and forth on his feet. He was nervous—a confirmation.

I noticed a few glances from other patrons in the bar, a murmur of "Isn't that…?" but I didn't care the way I normally would. I stayed focused on Bobby's face.

"Hey there!" he said, trying a cheery tone. He moved forward to hug me. When my arms remained at my sides, he took a step back. "Want a drink?"

I shook my head no.

"Well, sit down."

I considered him for a moment, then sat on the edge of one of the white chairs.

He took his seat. "Kyr, listen, I—"

"Why?" I said quietly.

His eyes roamed my face. "Uh…"

"Why did you do that to me?"

"What… What do you mean?"

"Jesus, Bobby, don't play dumb. At least give me the courtesy of admitting it."

"Okay, well in my defense, I—"

"Is there a defense to this?" I said incredulously. "You know how much I hate the press and the photographers.

You listen to me tell you how it makes me crazy, you listen to all my plans, and then you go and sell that information to the paparazzi? What is *wrong* with you?"

"I didn't mean to—"

"Are you taking drugs or something? Did you need the money for that?"

"It wasn't the money," Bobby said, shaking his head.

"What then? How can you possibly explain—"

"I'm in love with you," he said. He stared at his drink, as if he'd like to dive into it.

We sat. Seconds ticked by. People at the next table began to sing "Happy Birthday." Bobby continued to gaze at his cocktail.

"When?" I said softly. "I mean, how long?"

"In some ways, I think it's always been like that, but I didn't recognize it until you married Declan. He's a great guy, don't get me wrong, but I couldn't stand seeing you with him. It was making me insane. And then when you told me at the Globes that he was your best friend. God…" He trailed off. He looked up and finally met my eyes. "That killed me."

I sat back in the chair and put my head in my hands. Finally, I looked at him again. "You thought if I saw how nuts Declan's life would always be, I'd leave him?"

A small nod. "I knew you already hated the fame, so I reconciled what I was doing by telling myself I was helping you. I was showing you what you were in for over the next thirty years."

I laughed, a harsh sound. "Well, it worked, didn't it?"

"I can't stand what I did. I don't know how it happened. I mean, at first, I leaked a few things. Then you were hanging tough, so I did it again. The more I saw you with Declan, the more it was making me nuts. I felt like I'd never had my chance with you, and if I could just get that chance.

If you could just see that it was never going to change with Declan. I kept slipping things to the press—I didn't want to hurt you, I only wanted you to understand what your life was going to be like. And I guess, well…it just got away from me."

"That's one way to put it."

"God, Kyr, can you forgive me?" He reached over to touch my hand, but I pulled it away.

I stood up. "I don't know, Bobby. I don't know about anything anymore."

I've heard people say that after you've suffered a loss, night is the worst time. For me, it was the mornings. Mornings used to be a time of promise, a clean slate. But now, the mornings were when I remembered. For the past seven or so hours I would have lost myself in sleep, in dreams, where Declan was still by my side, and Bobby was still one of my dearest friends. And yet when I awoke, the reality hit like a sharp, hard stab to my chest. I would sit, stunned, on the side of my bed, willing myself to start breathing again, forcing the tears away.

I often called Declan when I woke like that. It was early in L.A. but he picked up the phone because he knew it was me.

"Come back, love," he'd say, his voice sleepy, sad.

"I can't."

"Bobby won't muck things up for us anymore."

"It's not just Bobby, you know that."

Silence. He couldn't argue with me about that. Bobby had made things worse, but he hadn't created the situation, and it was one that wouldn't go away. Although I was photographed occasionally now, it was nothing compared to being with Declan. The combination of the two of us, constantly at premieres and dinners with other actors, constantly in the scene, would always draw attention, and it was that ever-present attention I couldn't bear.

"I just miss you," I said.

We would sit on the phone quietly then. I squeezed my eyes closed and pretended he was next to me. I conjured up his golden eyes and his strong arms with the freckles that danced across them. I imagined those arms around me.

People told me time would heal, that my separation from Declan would get better as the days and months went by. But it seemed that getting better would mean I would always know—even in sleep—that Declan was no longer at my side, and I thought that sounded worse.

chapter 33

Declan McKenna on Lauren: We're Just "Mates"

Hurray for friendship—that's what Declan McKenna has to say in the new issue of *GQ* magazine. The Irish heartthrob, who separated from wife, Kyra Felis, three months ago, calls former flame, Lauren Stapleton, a good buddy whom he can turn to in times of trouble. "Lauren understands the pressure I'm under with my new films and my new fame," McKenna says. "We used to date a long time ago, but now we're just mates. I think men and women can be great mates. It doesn't have to mean anything more than that." McKenna also addresses his problems with Felis. "We're in different places right now," he says.

PAGE 6
SIGHTINGS

Declan McKenna at Spago in L.A. dining with actress and ex Lauren Stapleton, along with entertainment law-

yer Tony Fields and his wife, Alexa Kennedy...
McKenna's estranged wife, Kyra Felis, dining solo at 92
in Manhattan.

Declan & Lauren Produce Pandemonium

Declan McKenna and Lauren Stapleton induced a
crowd frenzy when they appeared for a screening of
McKenna's new film *Liquid Glass*. The couple, who had
been denying rumors that they had reunited in the
wake of McKenna's split from wife, fashion designer
Kyra Felis, were hand in hand. The statuesque Stapleton
wore a revealing gown by designer Mehta Vamp.
McKenna, who kept glancing at his date's décolletage,
wore a very large smile.

"I can't believe you," I said when Declan picked up the
phone.

As usual, it was early, and he groaned. "What are you on
about?"

I got up from the rumpled sheets of my bed. When was
the last time I'd washed them? I kicked the door of the bedroom closed. Emmie was in the city for once, and I didn't
want her to hear this. "Is she there?" I said.

"Who?"

"Don't give me that crap. You know who."

He grunted, then breathed out long and slow. I could
imagine him throwing back the Zen-green sheets, walking
to the windows, opening the blinds and gazing out at the canyon. "Kyra, *you* told me to move on. You said we were over."

"And you can just forget me after a few months?"

"I haven't forgotten you, and you know it." His voice was
quiet now, sad.

"But *Lauren?*" I said. "My God!"

"She's got a good side."

"I must have missed that side."

"Look, it's mostly business," he said.

"Is it?"

"People love it," he said without answering my question.

"What people?"

"I don't know, Kyra. I just do what I'm told. Angela and Graham tell me where to show up and who to take with me. I do my job."

"You never used to do things like that for PR."

"I did before I met you." He coughed. It made him sound like an old man. "When you and I got together, I didn't have to do stuff like this. I wouldn't. Now that you're gone, I'll do whatever they want, and now that you've broken us, I can be with whoever I want."

We were both silent for a moment.

"I don't care anymore," he said. His voice had become hard.

I did not know it, but before all this—before I found and lost Declan—there was a certain levity to my heart. An innocent weightlessness. I hadn't known it because it was difficult to feel my heart when it was like that. Oh, I suppose I felt it when it soared—like when I said "I do" on that lawn in La Jolla—and I thought I knew sadness. But it turns out I was wrong. Even the loss of my parents didn't sink my heart when I was a child. I didn't know enough then to truly realize what I'd lost. But I recognized it on the phone with Declan that day. I knew what I had lost, and my heart was as heavy as stone.

Emmie took me to dinner. MacKenzie was on a book tour, but even without him by her side, Emmie glowed. Her red hair, which she'd just had touched up, was shiny and cut to perfection. She had on a creamy ivory blouse, with a chunky silver necklace from Tiffany's. Her limp seemed less evident.

"Let's start with champagne, shall we?" She signaled the waiter before I could respond and ordered a bottle of Veuve Clicquot.

I sat back against the red leather booth and listened half-heartedly to Emmie's critique of MacKenzie's book reviews.

"It's true," she said. "Ageism exists in the literary world, too. If Mac had written this book when he was forty, they would call it brave and subtle, but now they call it sentimental. It's *such* twaddle."

I nodded once in a while. I murmured vague sounds of outrage.

"My dear," she said when our champagne was poured, "I have a toast."

"To the success of MacKenzie's book," I said, raising my glass.

She touched the rim of her flute to mine. "Yes, yes, of course, that. But no, I have a different toast. Here's to you making it work."

"What do you mean?"

"Toast, toast," she said, waving her flute toward me.

I clinked glasses with her. "Okay, I give. Tell me."

"My dear, you and Declan. You just need to make it work."

I set my glass on the table. "God, Emmie. If you only knew how I tried. It's not something you can shape like a lump of clay."

"Why not?"

"Because Declan's life is what it is. I know lots of people might love the celebrity life, but I just don't. I need my privacy. I need not to be followed all the time. I need to make mistakes that don't get broadcast around the country.

I won't ask Declan to change who he is or the way he's living his life. I have to either take it or leave it. And I can't take it—I really can't. So I had to leave."

Emmie made a *pshh* sound of disgust. "You're being much too tragic."

I laughed despite myself. "I've lost the love of my life, and you're telling me I'm being too tragic."

"Well, it's true. You're rather catastrophic about this. It's not so black and white."

"Of course it is. I either live in L.A. with Dec and put up with all the crap that goes with it, or I don't. I choose not to."

"There are other options."

"Like what?" I took a sip of my champagne. The bubbles tickled my nose. It seemed too whimsical a drink for my mood. I put the glass back on the table and pushed it away.

"I don't know, Kyra. That is for *you* to figure out. Just make it work."

"Right. Okay."

Emmie topped off my champagne glass. "There's no need to be patronizing. I think I know what I'm talking about."

"Really? Did you make it work with Britton?" It was a low blow, but I was desperate to get off the topic.

Emmie gave me an intense look with her teal eyes. "He had a family. He had children. I could not make that work, because there were people who would have been gravely hurt. You, on the other hand, are hurting no one but yourself."

I shook my head and glanced around the restaurant. It was early in the evening, and the place wasn't full, yet.

"Have you spoken to darling Bobby?" Emmie said. Despite what he'd done, she still had a soft spot for him. ("I always knew he was in love with you," she'd said.)

"A few times."

Bobby and I had talked twice since the Royalton Hotel.

He cried, he apologized, he explained, he said that the only thing he wanted in the world now was my friendship. He also said that he'd taken a leave of absence from work and was seeing a shrink three times a week. After forty-five minutes on the phone one night, Bobby near tears again, I forgave him. I had been feeling such a desperate loss of all things well and good in my life that I wasn't quite ready to chalk up Bobby as one of those losses, even if he had contributed to the overall picture. Plus, it's surprisingly hard to hate someone who says they love you.

"Well, there you go," Emmie said. "You're making it work with Bobby."

"Not quite. I forgave him, but Bobby and I will never be the same."

"Perhaps not, but my point is that you're making an effort. You're looking for ways to remedy the situation. That's what you need to do with Declan."

"Sure," I said with very little life in my voice.

"Kyra." Emmie pushed her glass aside and took my hand. "I haven't asked much of you over the years, isn't that true?" Something about her voice sounded grave.

"Is something wrong?" I said.

"Answer the question."

"Well, no. You've never pushed me to do anything."

"And I'm not pushing now." She squeezed my hand tighter. Her skin felt papery and cool. "I'm asking you to try. That's all. Take out what you have with Declan and gaze at it. Look at it from different angles. Do you see?"

"I don't know. I guess. I—"

"Kyra." She smiled a little. She looked at me in the way she had when I was little, right after my parents died—with compassion, with sadness, with love. "Make it work."

chapter 34

Not so long ago, right before I met Declan, I wanted a witness to my everyday life. I got what I asked for. Millions of people witnessed my life for a time. You were probably one of them. Oh, I know you don't buy those tabloid magazines, but you glance at them in the checkout line, just like I used to.

Today, when I went out for coffee, I looked at one of those magazines. I couldn't help it, because there was a picture of Dec and me, along with a bunch of other famous couples who've split up—Tom and Nicole, Meg and Dennis, Demi and Bruce.

What Is Wrong with Celebrity Marriages? the headline read.

I glanced over my shoulder. I scanned the parked cars for the jut of a telephoto lens. I studied the open apartment windows across the street. Old habits die hard. Finally, I turned back to the paper and flipped it open.

The bit about Declan and me was in a section called "One-Minute Celeb Marriages," where it discussed marriages that had happened and disintegrated "faster than you can boil water." Declan and I were held up as the prime recent example of such a marriage. I began to feel shaky as I read the piece, almost faint. I couldn't blame anyone for seeing us like that. It's true that our marriage hadn't even lasted a year. Yet it was appalling just the same. I knew in my heart that ours wasn't simply a blip on the Hollywood marriage scene. It is—*was,* I should say—so much more than that.

If we'd been a regular couple—maybe if he was a teacher and I a boutique owner—would we still be together? My initial reaction is to say yes. If it weren't for those photographers, those reporters, those fans, if it weren't for Amy Rose, if it weren't for Bobby, then we would be happy. But that's putting too much blame on other people. I was there; Declan, too. We aren't blameless. If anything, maybe fame was a test of our marriage and, so far, we had failed.

After I saw that article, I went to the public library at Bryant Park. It's where I used to study and sketch. It was Bobby who introduced me to the genealogy room. Long, carved wood tables with low reading lamps; huge arched windows that overlook the street; a golden glow imbuing the whole room with warmth. I used to love to sit there, letting myself be lulled by the soft *tap tap tap* of footsteps on the marble floor, the murmured voices at the desk. The place drew me into a space where my designs flowed, my mind flowered—shade that bodice, pull the sleeves a little longer, drop the hem. It all came so easily when I was there in the past, so I went back today, thinking the same thing would happen to my writing. I needed help. I have become blocked in the telling of this story as I get to the end of what I know to be true. As I get to the present.

It's been a catharsis to write this, to chart the past that I've lived for the last year or so, but as I get to the end of that past, to now, I find myself stalling. Because it seems as if I should decide. I should be able to take that history and apply it to a decision about the present. And yet I wonder if I am too late. Declan doesn't call as often as when I first moved back to New York, and when he does he sounds resigned and distant. I fear he is taking me at my word and leaving me alone.

The genealogy room isn't helping today. Cell phones ring from inside bags. A bum to my left snores so loudly, it's hard to ignore. Likewise, it's impossible to ignore thoughts of Declan. Even when he is no longer leaving messages for me, I hear him calling. Now that my story has lost some of its steam and I'm a bit flattened by the telling of it, I don't know if I can ignore that call. I don't know that I want to.

What do you do when the person you love leads a life you hate? Do you make them give up that life just to make you happy? No, I couldn't do that, because it wouldn't make me happy—if he's miserable, so am I. It's all a terrible conundrum, a cluster fuck of an emotional riddle.

I get up from the table and wander the bookshelves. I find a book listing Irish passenger arrivals into the Port of New York from 1820–1829. I look to see if there are any McKennas there, maybe one of Declan's ancestors, and sure enough I find a listing for a thirty-year-old woman named Mary McKenna, a "spinster" it says, who came over from Ireland in 1828.

I trace Mary McKenna's name with my finger for a moment, then I close the book and leave.

Kendall's assistant tells me that she's "on set" and won't be returning calls for six weeks. My cell phone rings forty-five minutes later. "Where the hell have you been?" she says.

"Taking a break, but I'm on my way to the airport now."

I tuck the phone under my chin and throw my bags into the trunk of a cab.

"Where are you running off to?"

"Back to L.A." I slide into the cab seat and tell the driver, "LaGuardia."

"Good girl," Kendall says. "Does Declan know?"

"Not yet, and I need a favor so I can make a very splashy entrance."

"My favorite kind." I hear someone talking to her in the background. She yells, "Give me five minutes!"

"Sorry to bother you," I say.

"Oh gosh, don't be. I need a time-out. So what's up?"

"Well, actually, I just need some advice. Do you remember the first time we met, you told me to manage the paparazzi?"

She laughs. "It's how I stay sane."

"Well, that's what I need advice about. I need to control the paparazzi to my advantage."

"Kyra," Kendall says. "You've come to the right person."

It's 7:00 p.m. when I arrive at LAX—I'm on schedule, but just barely. Since no one but Kendall knows I'm flying in, there are no photographers when I arrive. I get in a cab and take it to Shutters. I'm told there are no rooms available, but then the hotel manager spots me, pulls away his front-desk clerk and produces a key to a suite.

"We're happy to have you, Ms. Felis," he says. I remember that there are benefits to fame.

The room is monstrous and yet tasteful with Frette linens on the bed and a balcony looking onto the Pacific. I stand out there remembering how awed I used to be by this view when I first moved to L.A. I have been awed by so little lately. Except Declan, and how much I need him.

As planned, I call Kendall's cell phone. "I'm at Shutters, and I'll be heading out in thirty minutes," I say.

She reminds me about the plan. She gives me a rousing, "You can do this."

I change into one of my Kendall dresses, this one with a yellow and pink print. Perfectly splashy. I step into pink kid-leather sandals with a flower on the toe. I pull my hair up in a high ponytail and swipe some pink gloss on my lips. My pulse starts to pick up when I lift my purse off the bed. Ready to go. As ready as I'll ever be. If this fails, if I've misread the situation, or bungle what happens tonight, I will be publicly humiliated like no one has ever been.

"Can we get you a car?" the manager says when I step out of the elevator into the lobby.

"No, thank you. I'm just going around the corner to Capo. I think I'll walk."

"Oh, I wouldn't do that, Ms. Felis. Word of your arrival has gotten out, and there are already a number of media-type persons outside."

"Good," I say. I try to look confident, but I have to fight my usual desire to run. *They are here because you want them here,* I remind myself.

I thank the manager and walk slowly to the door. I review Kendall's instructions in my head. I pray that the information I was able to pry out of Denny proves correct.

When I step outside, it's dusk, and the sky has a beautiful navy blue sheen to it. But within a second, it is eclipsed by flashes and the glaring lights of video cameras.

"Ms. Felis! Kyra!" they yell. "Give us a smile!"

I battle the urge to hold up a hand and hide myself. Instead, I throw back my shoulders and think, *Declan, Declan, Declan.* This puts a legitimate smile on my face. The photographers go crazy. There are at least fifteen.

"Any chance of a reconciliation with Declan?" one of them yells.

"Why don't you come with me and find out." I begin walking up the street.

The photographers and videographers move with me. Some run ahead, shooting footage of my face. Others trail behind, documenting the whole scene. A white van pulls up, and two others jump out. Another few run down the street toward us. I am the Pied Piper of the paparazzi.

I am so nervous I have to concentrate on each step. *Do not trip,* I say to myself. *Keep smiling. They are here because you want them here.* I'm trying to use something that's made me unhappy—in this case, the paparazzi—as a tool for happiness.

By the time I reach the entrance of Capo, there are at least twenty-five people trailing me. I stand for a moment looking at the restaurant that Declan and I so often came to. And according to Denny, he's here now, with *her.*

I think of Kendall's directions—*Don't hesitate outside the restaurant or the manager will shoo the photographers away.*

"Um…hello. Hi," I say, turning to the photographers, standing on my tiptoes and waving my purse. "I'd like you to come inside with me," I say when they have quieted down. "There's something you should witness."

"We can't go in there," one of them calls out. "They'll have us arrested."

Kendall told me this would happen. She told me what to say. "If you come with me, you will get a money shot. One of the biggest of all time, and it will pay your legal bills plus so much more."

"I'm in," says a videographer.

"Me, too," others call out.

I take a huge breath. I tuck my purse under my arm. "Let's go, gentlemen."

When I step inside the restaurant, nearly everyone turns. The room grows silent. For a second, I don't see Declan, and I panic. Did Denny give me bad information to throw me off? God, no. Please, no. But then I spot Dec and Lauren in a little alcove near the front windows. Lauren sees me first. Her mouth opens, and she scoffs, an annoyed expression on her face. But then she sees the gaggle of photographers and videographers behind me, and she puts on a practiced, pleasant look. This is what Kendall and I were counting on—Lauren being such a media slut that she wouldn't put up a public fight. My goal is twofold: disgrace Lauren and get my husband back, all at the same time.

But if my plan fails, if Declan makes the wrong decision, it will be me who is disgraced.

A manager in a black suit with slicked-back hair hurries up to me. "Ma'am, please. What are you doing?" To the photographers, he says in a low, threatening tone, "Out. *Now.* The police are on the way."

I pat him on the arm. "This should only take a minute." I glance over my shoulder at the wolf pack. "Follow me."

Declan has seen me now, and as I walk toward them, he watches me, clearly confused. He stands, one hand still on the table. It's that hand, too close to Lauren, that terrifies me. I nearly falter. I want to run back to my Frette linens and hide. But I've come this far, and there are dozens of paparazzi blocking my path back to the door, so I keep putting one foot in front of another, until, at last, I'm standing at their table.

"Kyra?" Declan says, not *Kyr* or *love.* "What's going on?" He's wearing a black sport coat with flecks of gold in it. His brown hair curls over the collar, and I want to run my fingers through that hair. I want to throw my arms around him.

Lauren stands, towering over me. "Well, well, well," she

says. "Hi, boys!" she trills to the men behind me, waving. Their cameras go *click, click, click.*

"Declan," I say. "I've got something to ask you."

"Better make it fast," one of the photographers says. "The fuzz is pulling up."

I glance out the front windows and see a police car speeding down the street, a swirling blue light on its roof. I look back at Declan, then Lauren, who now has her arms crossed and is looking at me, like, *This should be good.* Her confident posture frightens me. The rest of the patrons have stopped eating and watch us expectantly. Now or never.

I cough to clear my throat. "Declan," I say again. "I've come to take you home. Not to Mulholland Drive or Manhattan, but someplace that is truly home. I need you to trust me on this. Can you do that?"

"Kyra," he says. His eyes are puzzled. He glances from me to Lauren. "What are you talking about?"

"Good question," Lauren mutters. But she smiles again because the press is near.

"I want to be your wife again." Saying the word *wife* makes me glow. I miss that word. "I want to be your wife forever. And I've made a decision. I can't tell you what that means right now because there's no time." I look out the front windows and see two cops leaping from their car.

"I need you to trust me," I say. I hold out my hand. "Declan McKenna, will you come home with me?"

"Ha!" Lauren says.

Declan blinks rapidly. He looks like a bewildered little boy.

"Get the hell out of here," Lauren says in a voice that's nearly a whisper. Just as I'd thought. She won't let things get too ugly with the media around.

"Declan?" I say, ignoring her. I hold my hand higher, my fingers outstretched.

Declan opens his mouth but nothing comes out. The room is hushed, heavy with anticipation.

"Dec?" I say. I want to drop my hand. I want to run from this room.

Still Declan is silent. He shakes his head as if he can't believe what's happening. Have I lost him for good?

He opens his mouth. He closes it again. He coughs. His eyes search mine.

My arm threatens to shake, but still I hold my hand out to him.

Finally, finally, he says, "Love, I'll go anywhere with you."

He takes my hand. He pulls me into his chest, and a torrent of flashes fills the room.

chapter 35

Declan & Kyra Make Dublin Home

Ever since the now-famous episode at Capo restaurant in Los Angeles, when Kyra Felis stormed in with a horde of paparazzi and declared that she was there to take Declan McKenna "home," rumors have been swirling about where that home might be. A publicist for the two now tells *Us Weekly* that the duo have purchased a Georgian house near St. Stephens Green in Dublin, Ireland, McKenna's *home*town. "They're extremely happy," the rep says. "Kyra will run her design business from Ireland, and Declan will travel when he needs to be on set or attend a premiere. They're making it work."

Book Club Questions
for *The Year of Living Famously*

1. Would you like to be famous? Do you think you could truly handle the rigors of fame?

2. Why is our culture so fascinated with celebrities today? What is it that makes many of us seek celebrity for celebrity's sake?

3. What would you do if you found yourself in Kyra's situation and you were married to someone you loved, but "that someone" led a life you hated?

4. What did you think about the development of the stalker in the story? Why do you think people develop fantasies about famous people? Are there certain celebrities that you feel you can relate to?

5. The price of fame is often the opening of one's private affairs for public viewing. What do you think the public has a right to know about various types of celebrities? If an actor is famous for his work, versus his public persona, how much of his or her life should he or she get to protect?

6. In the book, fame affected Kyra and Declan differently. What types of personalities survive the transition most easily? How did Declan's fame affect the people in his life in ways he might not have anticipated?

Also available from Laura Caldwell

Burning the Map

Get ready for a journey
of life-changing proportions.

Casey Evers was on a path. Career, love—she
had it all locked up. Problem was, did Casey
truly want to go where she was heading?

Sometimes the only way to figure out where you
are and where you want to be is to stop
following directions. Join Casey as she burns
the map and finds her own way.

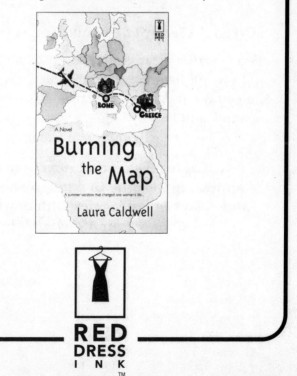

Also available from Laura Caldwell

A Clean Slate

Given *A Clean Slate* would you start over?

Faced with a clean slate and no memory of the past awful five months, Kelly McGraw realizes she can do anything she wants, go anywhere she wants and be anything she wants. But what exactly does she want?

"...Caldwell's second novel puts an appealing heroine in a tough situation and relays her struggles with empathy."
—*Booklist* on *A Clean Slate*

RED DRESS INK™